How to be both

ali smith
How to be both

HAMISH HAMILTON
an imprint of
PENGUIN BOOKS

HAMISH HAMILTON

Published by the Penguin Group
Penguin Books Ltd, 80 Strand, London WC2R 0RL, England
Penguin Group (USA) Inc., 375 Hudson Street, New York, New York 10014, USA
Penguin Group (Canada), 90 Eglinton Avenue East, Suite 700, Toronto, Ontario, Canada M4P 2Y3
(a division of Pearson Penguin Canada Inc.)
Penguin Ireland, 25 St Stephen's Green, Dublin 2, Ireland (a division of Penguin Books Ltd)
Penguin Group (Australia), 707 Collins Street, Melbourne, Victoria 3008, Australia
(a division of Pearson Australia Group Pty Ltd)
Penguin Books India Pvt Ltd, 11 Community Centre, Panchsheel Park, New Delhi – 110 017, India
Penguin Group (NZ), 67 Apollo Drive, Rosedale, Auckland 0632, New Zealand
(a division of Pearson New Zealand Ltd)
Penguin Books (South Africa) (Pty) Ltd, Block D, Rosebank Office Park,
181 Jan Smuts Avenue, Parktown North, Gauteng 2193, South Africa

Penguin Books Ltd, Registered Offices: 80 Strand, London WC2R 0RL, England

www.penguin.com

First published 2014
001

Copyright © Ali Smith, 2014
The permissions that appear on p. vi constitute an extension of this copyright page

The moral right of the author has been asserted

Set in 15.73/13.224 pt Sabon MT Std
Typeset by Jouve (UK), Milton Keynes
Printed in Great Britain by Clays Ltd, St Ives plc

A CIP catalogue record for this book is available from the British Library

HARDBACK ISBN: 978-0-241-14521-0
TRADE PAPERBACK ISBN: 978-0-241-14682-8

www.greenpenguin.co.uk

acknowledgements and thanks

The eye and camera icons are designed by Francesco del Cossa and Sarah Wood

Thank you, Daniel Chatto, Polly Dunn, Robert Gleeson, Jamie McKendrick, Cathy Moore, Sarah Pickstone, Matthew Reynolds, Kadya Wittenberg and Libbi Wittenberg

A huge and special thank-you to Kate Thomson

Thank you, Andrew and Tracy and everyone at Wylie's

Thank you, Simon, and thank you, Anna

Thank you, Xandra

Thank you, Mary

Thank you, Emma

Thank you, Sarah

permissions

For Frances Arthur
and everyone who made her,

to keep in mind
Sheila Hamilton,
walking work of art,

and for Sarah Wood,
artist.

Et ricordare suplicando a quella che io sonto francescho
del cossa il quale a sollo fatto quili tri canpi verso
lanticamara :
Francesco del Cossa

green spirit seeking life
where only drought and desolation sting;
spark that says that everything begins
when everything seems charcoal
Eugenio Montale / Jonathan Galassi

J'ai rêvé que sur un grand mur blanc
je lisais mon testament
Sylvie Vartan

Although the living is subject to the ruin of the time, the
process of decay is at the same time a process of
crystallization, that in the depth of the sea, into which sinks
and is dissolved what once was alive, some things 'suffer a
sea-change' and survive in new crystallized forms and shapes
that remain immune to the elements, as though they waited
only for the pearl diver who one day will come down to them
and bring them up into the world of the living –
Hannah Arendt

Just like a character in a novel, he disappeared suddenly,
without leaving the slightest trace behind.
Giorgio Bassani / Jamie McKendrick

one

Ho this is a mighty twisting thing fast as a
      fish being pulled by its mouth on a hook
           if a fish could be fished through a
                  6 foot thick wall made of bricks or an
          arrow if an arrow could fly in a leisurely
      curl like the coil of a snail or a
star with a tail if the star was shot
          upwards past maggots and worms and
               the bones and the rockwork as fast
                coming up as the fast coming down
           of the horses in the story of
       the chariot of the sun when the
bold boy drove them though
          his father told him not to and
             he did anyway and couldn't hold them
        he was too small too weak they nosedived

crashed to the ground killed the crowds
of folk and a fieldful of sheep beneath
and now me falling upward at the
rate of 40 horses dear God old
Fathermother please spread extempore
wherever I'm meant to be hitting
whatever your target (begging your
pardon) (urgent) a flock of the nice
soft fleecy just to cushion (ow) what the
just caught my (what)
on a (ouch)
dodged a (whew) (biff)
(bash) (ow)
(mercy)
wait though
look is that

sun

blue sky the white drift
the blue through it
rising to darker blue
start with green-blue underpaint
add indigo under lazzurrite mix in
lead white or ashes glaze with lapis
same old sky? earth? again?
home again home again
jiggety down through the up
like a seed off a tree with a wing
cause when the
roots on their way to the surface

4

break the surface they turn into stems
and the stems push up over themselves into stalks
and up at the ends of the stalks
there are flowers that open for
all the world like

eyes :

hello :

what's this?

A boy in front of a painting.

Good : I like a good back : the best thing about a
turned back is the face you can't see stays a secret :
hey : you : can't hear me? Can't hear? No? My chin
on your shoulder right next to your ear and you still
can't hear, ha well, old argument about eye or ear
being mightier all goes to show it's neither here nor
there when you're neither here nor there so call me
Cosmo call me Lorenzo call me Ercole call me
unknown painter of the school of whatever you like
I forgive you I don't care – don't have to care –
good – somebody else can care, cause listen, once
an old man slept for winters tucked in a bed with
my Marsyas (early work, gone for ever, linen, canvas,
rot) stiff with colours on top of his bedclothes, he
hadn't many bedclothes but my Marsyas kept him
warm, nice heavy extra skin kept him alive I think :
I mean he died, yes, but not till later and not of the
cold, see?

No one remembering that old man.

Except, *I* just did, there

though very faint, the colours now

can hardly remember my own name, can hardly
rememb anyth

though I do like, I did like

a fine piece of cloth

and the way the fall of a ribboned bit off a shirt
or sleeve will twist as it falls

and how the faintest lightest nearly not-there
charcoal line can conjure a sprig that splits open
a rock

and I like a nice bold curve in a line, his back has
a curve at the shoulder : a sadness?

Or just the eternal age-old sorrow of the
initiate

(put beautifully though I say so myself)

but oh God dear Christ and all the saints – that
picture he's – it's – mine, I did it,

who's it again?

not St Paolo though St Paolo's always bald cause
bald's how you're supposed to do St Paolo –

wait, I – yes I, think I – the face, the –

cause where are the others? Cause it wasn't just
it, it was a piece belonged with others : someone's
put it in a frame

very nice frame

and the stonework in it, uh huh, the cloakwork
good, no, *very* good the black of it to show the
power, see how the cloak opens to more fabric

where you'd expect flesh to be, that's clever,
revealing nothing and ah, small forest of baby
conifers tucked on the top of the broken column
behind his head –
    but what about that old Christ at the top of it?
    Old?
    Christ?
    like He made it after all all the way to old man
when everyone knows Christ's never to be anything
other than *unwrinkled eyes shining hair the colour
of ripe nut from the hazel tree and parted neatly in
the middle like the Nazarenes straight on top
falling curlier from the ears down countenance
more liable to weep than laugh forehead wide
smooth serene no older than 33 and still a most
beautiful child of men* old man Christ, why would I
paint an old (blaspheming)?
    Wait cause think I remember : something :
yes, I put some hands, 2 hands below his (I mean
His) feet : something you'd only see if you really
looked, hands that belong to the angels but all the
same look like they don't belong to anyone : like
they're corroded with gold, gold all over them like
sores turned into gold, a velvet soup of gold lentils,
gold mould as if blisters of the body can become
precious metal
    but why on earth did I?
    (Can't remem)

7

Look at all the angels round Him pretty with
their whips and scourges, I was good

no, no, step back take a look at a proper distance
at the whole thing

and other pictures in this room : stop looking at
your own : look at others for edification.

Think I recog

oh Christ – that's a –

Cosmo, isn't it?

A Cosmo.

St Gerolamo –?

but ha ha oh dear God look at it piece of oh ho
ho ho ridiculous nonsense

(from whom my saint averts his eyes with proper
restraint and dignity)

showy Cosmo's showy saint, mad, laughable, his
hand in the air holding the rock up high about to
stone himself so the patrons get their money's
worth : look at the tree all gesture-bent unnatural
behind him and the blood all adrippy on his chest :
dear God dear Motherfather did I come the hard
way back through the wall of the earth the
stratifications the rocks and the soil the worms and
the crusts the stars and the gods the vicissitudes
and the histories the broke bits of forgettings and
rememberings all the long road from gone to here –
for *Cosmo* to be almost the first thing as soon as I
open my

Cosmo bloody Cosmo with his father a cobbler,

no higher than mine, lower even : Cosmo high on
nothing but court frippery vain as vain can : veering
as ever in all his finery towards the gnarled and the
unbeautiful : the fawning troupe of assistants
attending to each mark he made like his every
gesture was a ducal procession.

Though that picture over there, also a Cosmo, is
truthfully, yes I admit, quite good

(but then the hanging baubles above her head *I
myself* showed him how to make better when we
worked in the, wasn't it, palace of beautiful
flowers? the time Cosmo feigned not knowing me
though he knew exactly who I)

and that over there, that's him, isn't it? Never
seen it before but it's him : yes : ah : it's a beauty :
and that one there's him too, is it?

That makes 4. In this 1 room.

4 Cosmos to my 1 saint.

Please God dear God send me right now back to
oblivion : Jesus and the Virgin and all the saints and
angels and archangels obscurate me fast as possible
please cause I am not worthy &c and if Cosmo's
here, if the world's all Cosmo same as it ever was –

but then again

from Cosmo I learned how to use the white lead
to mark details in the underwash

(*I forgive*)

and from Cosmo I learned how to make the
incision marks in the paint for the extra perspective

9

(*I forgive*).

And anyway, look.

Up against Cosmo's Gerolamo whose is really the real saint here?

Just saying.

And, just saying, but whose saint is it anyway that that boy with his back to me's spending all his time

torch bearer, Ferara, seen from the back, he was a boy who ran past me in the street : it was when they were calling for painters for painting the palace of not being bored and I was up for the job, I'd worked on the panels of the muses at the palace of beautiful flowers with Cosmo and the rest and was now well known in Ferara and even more well known in Bologna, I didn't need the court, no one in Bologna gave a toss about the court (anyway the court didn't need me, the court had *Cosmo*) no, wait, start at the

cause it truly began with the man they called the Falcon cause of his first name being Pellegrin : he was Borse's adviser, a professor and scholar, he'd known Greek and Latin since he was a boy and he'd found some magic books in eastern languages that no one else even knew about : he knew the stars and the gods and the poems : he knew the legends and stories that the Ests all loved about the kings on their horses and their sons and half-sons

10

and cousins and their magicians in caves and their
joustings and maidens and rivals and who was in
love with whom and whose horse was the best and
the cleverest and fastest and most of all their
neverending triumphant outwittings of the infidels
and crushings of the moorish kings : the Falcon'd
been appointed in charge of the new design of the
walls of the big room in the palace of not being
bored and he was looking for painters other than
Cosmo (*terribly in demand*, going around town
bejewelled like a Marquis and though it was said
that Cosmo'd be *playing a major part* in the wall
design for the palace of not being bored in reality
Cosmo'd glide in and out like a swan, I myself saw
him a total of twice doing the minimum of sinop,
for which, being so *in demand* he was mightily well
paid, I heard) anyway he (not Cosmo, the Falcon)
summoned me to his house.

The Falcon lived behind the building works for
the castle : he came to the door when the door girl
called him and first he looked my horse behind me
up and down cause he was a wise enough man to
know you can tell much about the person by the
horse, and the coat on mine was glossy even after
the road from Bologna, waiting for me with his
head right down, his nose an inch above the ground
and his nostrils connoisseuring the destination,
never needing tethered or watched, cause let

11

anybody but me try mounting Mattone they'd fly
without wings through the air and hit the
brickwork.

So when I saw him look to my horse I liked him
the better for it : then he turned to me, had a look
at me, and I had a look back : he wasn't old and
wise, he was roughly the same years as me, thin for
a scholar who're usually heavy and inadequate
from all the nothing but books : his nose was
imperial Roman (the Marquis'd like that, they were
mad for old Romans, the Ests, almost as mad as
they were for the stories of routing the infidel and
conquering Afric) and his eye was fast : he looked
me up and down : his eye stopped at the front of
my breeches : he stared there as he spoke : he'd
heard I was good, he said.

Then he looked back up at my eyes and waited to
see what I'd say and right then – my luck – the boy
ran past us in the street, a beauty of a boy moving
so fast that I felt the air shift (still feel it now when I
remember) cause the boy was himself all air and
fire, a lit torch in his hand, in the other a banner,
was it? a long bit of tunic? he ran up the steps
holding it up so that it caught the wind in the loops
of it, he was off to the court : that's where the jobs
were, at the court, and the rumour was that the
pictures they wanted in the palace this time were
court pictures, pleasure pictures, not sacred things
but pictures of the Marquis himself, of a year of his

12

life in the town and him doing the different things
he did in the months of his year with real everyday
things running through them exactly like that boy
running past : I thought to myself *if I can catch*
that running boy I'll show this Falcon whose eye
(my own eye saw) was taken by the back of the boy
how good and how fast and how well I'd
 then they'd know how exemplary
 and imburse me accordingly
 so I said as the boy disappeared *Mr de Prisciano,*
a pen and a paper and somewhere to lean and I'll
catch you that rabbit faster than any falcon he
raised an eyebrow at the cheek of me but I was
being comical, he saw (still not unsweet on me
himself at this time) and called for the door girl to
fetch the things I wanted while I kept in my head
the speed and the shape of the boy, the way he'd
held up the silk and caught the air as he went, a
breathing thing in itself, that's what I wanted, cause
I'm good at the real and the true and the beautiful
and can do with some skill and with or without
flattery the place where all 3 meet : the maid
brought the things and a board for bread (a wink to
her without him seeing, she reddened a little under
her cap, I reddened back, bianco sangiovanni,
cinabrese, verde-terra, rossetta, also the cap, pretty
thing, its edge all silk fray, I'd use it later on the
thread-cutter's head in the working women round
the loom in the corner of the month of March

13

cause though the Falcon specified he wanted Fates painted into March – like he wanted Graces painted into April – I wanted them real women and real working too).

I wiped the crumbs off the board in the doorway (the Falcon watched them fall on his threshold, narrowed his eyes) and on the paper though the boy had vanished I mapped his constellation there, there, there the back of his head, base of his spine, place of this foot, the other, this arm, the other, and sketch in a head (well the head barely mattered, it wasn't what mattered) but I spent most time on his back foot, the place with the curve of the sole on the rise : get it right, how it sprung the whole body, just that single detail and it'll lift the whole picture like the foot lifted him : get it right and the picture itself will lift (cause the way he'd gone up the stone steps had made even the stone of them unheavy) : he was off to a ceremony maybe, the boy? He had the torch lit though it was daylight, ergo I added the suggestion of a door so he'd need a lit torch, doubled a line into a lintel above his head for somewhere to go and I shaded in front of and round him so the torch in his hand had more purpose (made the flame on it like long hair flowing, but upward instead of downward, beauty of impossibility) then round him on the ground a scatter of small rocks, twig here, 4 or 5 by the wall, then right at the front 3 stones and a brickslice very like a slice of cheese all arranged round grassblades in a curtsey for the Falcon as if even grass will bow respectfully at such a man.

(After which, a final touch, there at the end of a grassblade, 2 or 3 points, a slip of the pen? a butterfly? for my pleasure alone cause no one else'd notice.)

Long gone, the picture, I expect.

Long gone the life I, the boy and the man I, the sleek good sweet-eyed horse Mattone I, the blushing girl I.

Long gone, torch bearer Ferara seen from the back, ink on paper folded torn eaten, wasp nest shredded into air burnt away to ash to air to nothing.

Ow.

I feel the loss, dull the ache of it

cause I *had* it, the place where his legs met his body, the muscular dark where his tunic flared up in the breeze as he went, I had it like telling the oldest story in the world cause there's a very pure pleasure in a curve like the curve of a buttock : the only other thing as good to draw is the curve of a horse and like a horse a curved line is a warm thing, good-natured, will serve you well if not mistreated, and the curves of his sleeves concertina-ing down and back from his shoulders, blanket stitch then scallop-bite edge, round his waist a double yarnstrand to hold him well.

I like a twist of yarn, 2 strands twisted together
for strength : I like a length of rope : the rope after
a hanging they sold, I remember, in the market, was
cut into pieces you'd buy for luck so you'd never
yourself be.

Hanged, I mean.

What, – – was, was I? –

surely not – never, was I, hanged? – oh.

Oh.

Was I?

No.

Pretty sure : I wasn't.

But how did I, then? End?

I can't recall an end at all, any end I ever, can't,
any, demise, no –

cause maybe –

maybe I . . . never ended?

Hey!

I did that picture : hey!

Can't hear me.

Sunlight hitting the yellowing leaves, I was a
child, small, on a stone slab warm from the sun,
almost too small to walk I think and something
was twisting itself down through the air and landed
in the middle of the pool of horse piss, the foam
and the bubbles nearly all off it but the smell of it
still fine in the dip in the stone between the old path
and the new path that he'd made in the yard for the
carts for the stones, my father.

The thing that fell caused a circle to happen, a ring to appear in the piss : the ring widened and widened until it got to the edges and vanished.

It was a small black ball like the head of an infidel : it had a single wing, a hard and feathery-looking thing stuck straight out of it.

The ring that it made in the pool when it fell, though, was gone.

Where'd it go?

I shouted the words, but she was trampling cloth in the big half-barrel : she was making the cloth turn white with the soap, she was singing, didn't hear me, my mother.

I called again.

Where'd it go?

She still didn't hear me : I picked up a stone : I aimed at the side of the barrel, I missed, hit a chicken in its sidefeathers instead : the chicken made a chicken noise, jumped and nearly flew : it ran about in a dance that made me laugh, it panicked all the geese and the ducks and the other chickens : but my mother had seen the stone hit the chicken and she leapt out of the barrel and ran towards me with her hand in the air cause she was a despiser of cruel things.

I wasn't, I said. I didn't. I was calling you. But you were preoccupied so I threw it to get your attention. I didn't mean to hit the chicken. The chicken got in the way.

She dropped her hand to her side.

Where did you learn that word? she said.

Which word? I said.

Preoccupied, she said. Attention.

From you, I said.

Oh, she said.

She stood in the dust with her wet feet : her ankles were beaded with light.

Where'd it go? I said.

Where'd what go? she said.

The ring, I said.

What ring? she said.

She got straight down and looked in the pool : she saw the winged thing.

That's not a ring, she said. That's a seed.

I told her what happened : she laughed.

Oh, she said. *That* sort of ring. I thought you meant a ring for a finger, like a wedding ring or a gold ring.

My eyes filled with tears and she saw.

Why are you crying? she said. Don't cry. Your sort of ring is much better than those.

It went, I said. It's gone.

Ah, she said. Is that why you're crying? But it hasn't gone at all. And that's why it's better than gold. It hasn't gone, it's just that we can't see it any more. In fact, it's still going, still growing. It'll never stop going, or growing wider and wider, the ring you saw. You were lucky to see it at all. Cause

when it got to the edge of the puddle it left the
puddle and entered the air instead, it went invisible.
A marvel. Didn't you feel it go through you? No?
But it did, you're inside it now. I am too. We both
are. And the yard. And the brickpiles. And the
sandpiles. And the firing shed. And the houses. And
the horses, and your father, your uncle, and your
brothers, and the workmen, and the street. And the
other houses. And the walls, and the gardens and
houses, the churches, the palace tower, the top of
the cathedral, the river, the fields behind us, the
fields way over there, see? See how far your eye can
go. See the tower and the houses in the distance? It's
passing through them and nothing and nobody will
feel a thing but there it is doing it nonetheless. And
imagine it circling the fields and the farms we can't
see from here. And the towns beyond those fields
and farms all the way to the sea. And across the
sea. The ring you saw in the water'll never stop
travelling till the edge of the world and then when it
reaches the edge it'll go beyond that too. Nothing
can stop it.

She looked down into the horse piss.

And all from the fall of a seed, she said. You see
that seed there? You know where it came from?

She pointed above us to the trees behind our
house.

If we put that seed in the ground, she said, and
we cover it with earth and it gets the chance,

enough sun, enough water, with a bit of luck and justice it'll make another tree.

The trees were much bigger than even the brickpiles : the trees went way beyond the roof of the house made by my father's father's father : we were a family of wallmakers and brickmen : it was what the men of our family did when they left boyhood : my family helped build the Est palaces, the Ests had rooms at all cause of us : we were historic, as anonymous wallmakers go.

I fished the seed out of the piss : it was a thing that has to fall to rise : it looked like a shrunken head like the heads that got put on the walls after uprisings but with a wing coming out the back of it : it smelt fine of horse : it had 1 wing not 2 like birds : perhaps that was why it fell : and cause it had, something would rise.

I dropped it back in : it fell again : 1 day right here cause of it a tree would be shooting upwards, with a bit of luck and justice.

A new ring formed, disappeared, went through me invisible and off out into the world.

My mother was back at the barrel climbing over the side : she started singing again : every time she tramped down rings like the seed-rings I'd seen appear and disappear came off her legs in the water in the barrel : the rings widened, came out round her round the barrel then they went through me and round me too (a marvel) and off into the rest of the world in a huge sort of holding that happened when something came into or passed through another thing : the sun was already shrinking the piss : a new ring formed where the piss had been and gone : in its going it changed the stone of the path to a lighter different colour.

Then it was another time : there were yellow flowers dropping off the trees : they landed with a sound : who knew flowers had a voice? I was much better at throwing now : now when I threw I could always hit the barrel – and not just hit it, I could choose where to hit it, on the metal buckle or the top or bottom rim or whichever stave I aimed at.

I could throw now too so that I never hit a chicken unless I wanted to : it was cruel, though, to want to, and tempting, so I'd become an expert at almost : since if I threw it so it almost hit (but missed) a chicken would still do the funny dance to the music of the general bird outrage : there were no chickens or geese to almost hit today though, cause every time I came out into the yard now all the chickens and geese and ducks ran away shouting to the front of the house, and every time I came round the front after them they ran away to the back.

Ferara was the best place for brickmaking cause of the kind of clay from the river : you burnt the seaweed and stirred in the ashes and seasalt and baked the bricks : you could do anything with brickwork, all the colours, all the designs : then there was stone with all its many names and costs : my father held, sometimes, if he was in a good mood about money, a little piece of something up and we shouted what it was and the winner won the shoulderback round the yard with him the horse : perlato : paonazzo : cipollino with its coloured veins, my mother making me laugh pretending a stone held near the eyes could make her cry : arabescato, just the fineness of the word near made *me* cry : breccia, made up of broken things : and the sort I can't remember the name of that's 2 or more stones crushed together to make a whole new kind of stone.

But here in Ferara there was brick and we were a place you got bricks from.

I took aim halfway up the pile and I hit that exact right brick : a plume of brickdust flew up.

I scrabbled about at the edge of the pile for more broken bits, bunched my vest up and carried the pile of bits of brick in it back to the step : I sat down on the threshold ready to throw : it was even harder to keep your aim when you were sitting down : good.

Stop throwing bricks at my bricks!

That was my father : he'd heard the throwing and seen the dust flying : he marched the yard : he kicked away at the bits I'd collected : I ducked, knowing he'd slap me.

Instead he picked a broken piece of brick up, turned it over in his hand.

He sat down heavy on the step close beside me : he held up the bit of brick.

Watch this, he said.

He pulled at his trowel, got it out of his tool belt past his stomach then held the edge of it above the broken brick : he let the edge of the trowel hover for a moment at the brick's edge : he touched with gentleness with the trowel's edge a particular place on the brick : then he raised the trowel and brought it down very hard at exactly the place he'd touched : a bit of brick broke clean off and fell among the fallen flowers.

The piece of brick left in his hand was neat and square, he showed me.

Now we can use it to build with, he said. Now nothing's wasted.

I picked up the fallen piece.

What about this bit? I said.

My father scowled.

My mother overheard me say it and she laughed : she came over, she was wearing her work dress the colour of sky, clay marks all over it like smudges of cloud : she sat on the other side of me : she had a brick in her hand too, she'd picked it off the pile as she passed : it was a nice thin brick, good colour, a doorway or window brick, from the ones made with the best clay : she winked at me.

Watch this.

She held out her other hand over my head for my father to pass her the trowel.

No, he said. You'll ruin the brick. You'll ruin the side of my trowel.

Sweet Cristoforo, she said. Please.

No, he said. Between you both I'll have nothing left.

Well, when you've nothing –, my mother said.

It was what she always said : *when you've nothing at least you have all of it* : but this time when she got to the end of the word *nothing* she lunged out of nowhere for the trowel and he wasn't expecting it, jerked his hand up and away too late, she leaned herself round me quick as a snake (warm and sweet the smell and her linen and skin) and she'd got it, she jumped up, twisted free, ran to the trestle.

She held the brick out in front of her, tapped at it hard 3 times and she scraped

(my trowel! my father said)

and she put the handle of the trowel on top of it and hit the brick and the trowel with the little stone mallet – once, then again : bits of brick flaked off : she tapped the brick with her finger : a large piece fell out of it : she stopped and wiped the dust off her nose : she held the trowel out to him : in her other hand she held up what was left of the brick she'd been breaking.

A horse ! I said.

She gave it to me : I turned it over in both my hands : it had ears : it had scrapes : the scrapes were what made the tail.

My father was pouting down at his trowel : he rubbed the dust on its point with his thumb and examined the handle, not laughing : but my mother kissed him : she made him.

Another time : hot, and the cicadas : my mother was drawing a line in the ground with a stick.

I saw what it was before it became it : it's the neck of a duck!

Then she moved to a new piece of ground and drew a line and then another then joined them to 2 other lines and a curve : it's the place where the leg of a horse meets its body!

She finished the horse, started again, drew a line, then another, made a scuff in the dust and drew lines in the scuff : it's a house! It's our house!

I found a stick of my own in the tall grass and broke it near the base so it had a thick end and a thin end : I came back to the pictures : with the thin end I added 3 curves to the roof of the house she'd drawn.

Why have you put a tree on the roof? she said.

I pointed up at the roof of our house behind us, at the place where a twig that had taken root in the ridge on the top stuck up in the air.

Ah, she said. You're right.

25

I coloured with pleasure at the being right : with the thicker end of the stick I drew a slope, a circle, some straight lines then a curve : we both looked over at my father's back : he was at the far end of the yard loading the cart.

My mother nodded.

That's good, she said. It's very good. Well seen. Now. Do me something you can't see with your eyes.

I added a straight line to the forehead of her horse.

Very witty, she said, oh, you're a very witty cheat.

I said I wasn't, cause it was true, I had never with my eyes truly seen a unicorn.

You know what I meant, she said. Do as I asked.

She went to collect the eggs : I closed my eyes, I opened them : I turned the stick upside down, used the thin end of it.

That one's him angry, I said when she came back. That one's him kind.

Air came out of her mouth (by which I knew that what I'd done was good) : she nearly dropped the eggs (by which I learned that the making of images is a powerful thing and may if care's not taken lead to breakage) : she checked the eggs were safe in her dress, all unbroken, before she called him over to see his faces.

When he saw the angry one he hit me over the head with the inside of his hand (by which I learned that people do not always want to know how they are seen by others).

He and my mother stood and looked for a time at his faces in the dust.

Not long after this, he began to teach me my letters.

Then, when my mother was gone into the ground, and me still small enough to, one day I climbed into her clothes trunk in her bedroom and pulled the lid down : it was all broadcloth and linens and hemp and wool, belts and laces, the chemise, the work gowns, the overgown, the kirtle and sleeves and everything empty of her still smelling of her.

Over time the smell of her faded, or my knowing of it lessened.

But in the dark in the trunk I was expert and could tell almost as well as if I was seeing which was which, which dress, which usage, by the feel of it between finger and thumb: kitchen use, Sunday use, work use : I went deep in the smell and became myself nothing but fabric that'd once been next to her skin : in the dark between the layers I shoved down or up with a fist and felt for a tapering strip, a ribbon or tie or lace coming off the edge of one of the sleeves or collars, a tassel, a strand of whatever, and was awake till I'd twisted and wound something of her round a thumb or a finger : at which point I was able to sleep : when I woke I'd

27

have freed myself up unawares in my sleep from the tether I'd made : but there'd still be a curlicue shape in the strand of stuff afterwards which held for a time, before it went back to the shape of its own randomness.

One day when I woke and opened the lid and came back to the daylight the cloth I'd been asleep in dragged out after me, blue, still warm from me : I sat beside it on the floor : I put my head and my arms into it then my whole self inside it : it sat on my shoulders and spread out away from me, it so big and me so small it was as if I'd dressed in a field of sky.

I put my head through the slit in the sleeve as if it was the neck opening : I dragged the dress through the house, me in it.

I wore nothing but her clothes from then on : I dragged them in the housedust for weeks, my father too weary to say no, until the day he picked me up in his arms (I was wearing the white one, big, filthy now, ripped a bit where I'd tripped on the stones one day and where it'd caught on the doorframe another, today I was all sweat and heat in it, my face a colour I could feel) so that the trail of the heavy materials left the floor and hung behind us both over his forearm like a great empty fishtail as he carried me through to her room.

I thought he would beat me, but no : he sat me

down still in her overgown on the shut trunk of clothes : he himself sat down on the floor in front of me.

I'm going to ask you kindly to stop wearing these clothes, he said.

No, I said.

(I said it from behind the stiff shield of the front of the dress.)

I can't bear it, he said. It is like your mother has become a dwarf and as if her dwarf self is always twinkling away in all the corners of the house and the yard, always in the corner of my eye.

I shrugged.

(But cause the shoulders were so high over my own deep in the dress, no one but me knew I'd shrugged.)

So I would like to make a suggestion, he said. If you agree to put these clothes away, I mean stop wearing them.

I shook my head slow from side to side.

And if you were to put, say, breeches on, or these leggings I've here, instead –, he said.

He put his hand in his smock pocket and pulled out boys' clothes, light and thin in the heat : he dangled them enticing like you do with a mouthful of green a mule that won't be moved.

– then I can get you a job and a schooling, he said. For the job, you can come and work with me at the cathedral. It would be a help to me. I need help. I need an apprentice, about your age. *You* could be that help.

I lowered myself down inside the dress : the shoulders came up above my ears.

You already have my brothers, I said.

You could be like your brothers, he said.

I eyed him through the lace-up of the neck and the chest : I spoke through the holes in the dress.

You know I am not like my brothers, I said.

Yes, but listen, he said. Cause maybe. Maybe. If you were to stop wearing these too-big clothes and were to wear, let's say, these boys' clothes instead. And maybe if we allow ourself a bit of imagining. And maybe if we have a bit of discretion. You know what discretion is?

I rolled my eyes in behind the chestlace for even as a child I already knew, or so I believed, more than he ever would, what discretion is : worse, I knew he was pandering to me with his making of suggestions, more my mother's style than his, when it would've been much more usual for him simply to hit me and forbid me : I despised him a bit for this pandering and for using what he considered big words as if these might be the key to me agreeing to do as he wanted.

But the words he used next were the biggest of all, the biggest words anyone could've.

If you were, he said. Then we might find

someone to train you up in the making and using of colours on wood and on walls, you being so good with your pictures.

Colours.

Pictures.

I stuck my head so fast out the top of the dress that the weight of the dress shifted and nearly knocked me off the box : I saw him stifle and have to disguise, cause he wanted to keep the moment serious, the first smile I'd seen on his face since the going of my mother.

But you'll have to wear your brothers' clothes, he said. And you might, if I find you a training, best be, or become, one of them. Your brothers.

He looked to see my response.

I nodded : I was listening.

We can probably get you Latin without it, and mathematics, he said. But schooling will be easier with it. We are not rich though we've more than enough and schooling in itself is not the problem. But unless you enter a nunnery, which is the one sure way you can spend your days making colours or filling the pages of holy saint books with your pictures, a training in colours and pictures – I mean out here in the world, with a life lived as a part of it, a life beyond walls – is another thing altogether. Do you agree?

He looked me in the eye.

It is a sure thing always, he said. You would

31

always have work. But nobody will take you for such a training wearing the clothes of a woman. You can't even be an apprentice to me, wearing the clothes of a woman. I think we could start you working with me next week on the bell tower. By which I don't mean you'll work on the bell or the tower, I mean I will let you draw it and furnish you with the materials to, and in this way you'll be seen to be working with me and your brothers, and then, when you are established, when it is clearly established in others' eyes as to who you have *become* –

He raised an eyebrow.

– we will get you into a painters' workshop or find you a master of panels and frescoes and so on, and we will show him what you can do and we will see if he'll take you on.

I looked down at the front of my mother's gown then looked back up at my father.

Such a master might let us pay in eggs, or birds, he said, or the fruit off our trees, or even in bricks. I am hopeful. But most of all I'm hopeful that if such a man sees what you can already do he might teach you for less, for the sake of doing justice to your abilities, and show you how to correct your natural mistakes, how to shape the head of a man like they do with their squares and geometries, and bodies too, and the measurements it takes, how to make those measurements, the ones which show where to put the eyes and the nose and so on in a face and where to place things on the tiles of a floor or across a landscape to show some things closer and some much further away.

So things far away and close could be held together, in the same picture?

So there were ways to learn to do such a thing?

I reached for the lace ties at my chin. I held them in my hand.

All these things you will need to know, he said. And if we can't find someone I'll give you what training I can. I know a great deal about buildings and walls and the workings, the rules and the necessities of construction. The construction of pictures, well. It's bound to have something in common.

I pulled on the ties and I loosened the gown front : I stood up and the whole gown slipped off the clothes trunk then slipped down away from me like the peeled back petals of a lily and me at its centre standing straight like the stamen : I stepped out naked over its folds : I held out my hand for the leggings.

He went through to my brothers' things and came back with a clean shirt.

You'll need a name, he said as I pulled the shirt on over my head.

My mother's name began with an f : Ff : I tried it on my tongue to see where it'd lead : my father misheard me : Vv.

Vincenzo? he said.

He flushed up with excitement.

He meant Vincenzo Ferreri, the Spanish priest dead long long ago, 20 whole years or so and everybody saying for all those years he should've been made saint : the travelling sellers were already selling him like a saint in the pamphlet writ by the nuns full of the pictures and stories of him : he was famous for miracles and for converting 8 thousand moorish moslem infidels and 25 thousand jews, raising 28 people from the dead and curing 4 hundred sick people (just by them lying down for a moment on the couch he'd lain on when he was ill and got better on himself) and also for freeing 70 people from devils : his hat alone had done many miracles.

But my father liked most the miracle of the hostel and the wilderness.

Vincenzo had been riding through the wilderness on his donkey praying very hard and he and the donkey were near exhaustion from the prayers when suddenly they arrived at the front door of a beautiful well-appointed hostel : Vincenzo went in : it was as beautiful inside as out : he stayed in it overnight : the service, the food, the bed were all very agreeable and gave him exactly the respite he needed to go on next day with his sojourn through the wild places full of infidels and unbelievers : next morning when he got on his donkey, that same donkey was like one 10 years younger and had no fleabites and wasn't lame any more : off they went, and it was 6 or 7 miles later when the morning sun first hit his shaven head that Vincenzo realized he'd forgotten his hat.

He turned the donkey around and they went back over their own hooftracks to the hostel to fetch it : but when they got there there was no hostel and his hat was hanging on the branch of an old dead tree in the exact same place where the hostel had been.

This miracle was one of the reasons housebuilders and wallmakers wanted Vincenzo Ferreri a saint : they planned to claim him as patron.

My father prayed to him every morning.

I thought of my mother telling me the stories of some of the miracles of Vincenzo, her arms round me, me on her knee.

Vincenzo, petitioned by me, had made no difference to her going or her coming back

(clearly I had petitioned wrongly).

I thought of my mother's French-sounding name : I thought of the French shape that means the flower her name meant.

Francescho, I said.

Not Vincenzo? my father said.

He frowned.

Francescho, I said again.

My father held his frown : then he smiled in his beard a grave smile down at me and he nodded.

On that day with that blessing and that new name I died and was reborn.

But – Vincenzo –

ah, dear God –

that's who my sombre saint is on the little platform with his eyes averted and the old Christ over his head.

St Vincenzo Ferreri.

Hey : boy : you hear me? *St Vincenzo*, famed across all the oceans for *making unhearing people hear*.

Cause listen, when Vincenzo spoke, even though it was in Latin the people whether they knew any Latin or none at all knew exactly what he was saying – even people 3 miles away could hear him as if he was speaking right next to their ears in their own vernacule.

The boy hears nothing : I can't make him.

I'm no saint, am I? no.

Well good that I'm not, cause look now, here's a very pretty woman, well, from behind at least, stopped in front of my St Vincenzo

(4 to 1, and she chose me not Cosmo)

(just saying)

(not that I'm being prideful)

(another miracle, that she did, thanks be to St Vincenzo)

and since I'm no saint I can have my own close

look at her, from the back, from her bare neck just peeking through her long white-gold hair down the line of her spine to her waist then down to her bit-too-thin behind –

but so's that boy, look at him sitting up at attention, I swear he felt her come into the room cause *I* felt the hairs on *his* neck stand up when he saw her glide through the door over the floor like the room was incomplete without her, he saw her before I did, like struck by a shaft of lightning, and look at him now watching her settling her feathers in front of Vincenzo : I can't see what his eyes are doing but I bet you they're wide open and his ears and brow forward like goathead : plus I can tell from his back, he knows her already : boy in love? The old stories never change : but in love with this woman? Nowhere near his equal in years, far from it, even from behind I can tell she's decades ahead, more than old enough to be his mother : but she's not his mother, that's clear, and has no idea he's there, or his ardour, even though something between them's as strong as hatred or a ray of heat from *him* that's aimed at *her*.

Hello. I'm a no-eyed painter no one can hear and there's a boy here wants you to – I don't know – something.

She can't hear me : course she can't : but she's giving Vincenzo a good look over and Vincenzo, being saint, is averting his eyes (though the angels with the whips and bows up there are ready for anything).

She's standing with one foot up on its heel, a horsehoof at rest : so elegantly her body adjusts the weight of her head : she takes a look at St Vincenzo, up, down, up again –

then she turns on that heel and she's off

(not even a single glance at a single Cosmo by the way,

just saying)

and the boy's sprung up on his own feet like a leveret and off he goes too after her, and me too helplessly dragging after him like one foot's caught in the stirrup of a saddle on a horse I'm unfamiliar with who does not know or care for me : and as we go, out of the corner of my no-eye I see a picture by – Ercole, little Ercole the pickpocket, whom I loved and who loved me ! and wait – stop – is that, is it really? – dear God old Motherfather it's Pisano, Pisanello, I know by the dark and the way it works the light.

Look all you like, since I cannot, cause it is as if a rope attached to the boy is attached to me and has circled me and cannot be unknotted and where the boy goes I must go whether I want it or don't, through a threshold, through another room – look! Uccello! horses! –

I protest

cause this ejection is against my will : I do not choose it.

As soon as I discover to whom to complain I will do so, in a letter.

To whichever illustrious most holy interceding Excellency it concerns, this nth day of n in the year nnnn.

Most illustrious and excellent holy Lordship most inimitable and in perpetual honoured servitude : please deliver this petition of mine to God the Fathermother Motherfather One True Lord of All : I am the painter Franc. del C. who has made for Him in His honour and by His grace alone, so many works, of good materials, just saying, and done them with good honed skills, one of which said works I have witnessed is hung in His halls: and who worked alongside and as equal to other painters whose works also are hung in His halls : and here I make to Him my petition in the hope of His hearing me and granting me what little I ask : I

I what?

I, having been shot back into being like an arrow but with no notion of the target at which He is aiming me, find myself now in this intermediate place, albeit in a neighbourhood of grand houses but all the same next to a very low very poor piece of brickwork (which will not last 4 winters, by the way) with an unspeaking unseeing unhearing boy whose precipitate desires for a fine Lady he has seen in your Lord's picture halls have dragged me very much against my will to this low wall away from the beauties of His palace, a place in which I should have liked to dwell for longer : but now find myself out in the cold grey and horseless world : such state of horselessness an unfortunate luck for its people, a creatureless world I thought until I saw the doves flying up in a flock like always, the same doves though greyer, filthy, squatter than, but all the same their wings and the clatter of birds were a salve even to a heart I no longer have.

By this I recognize, most excellent Sir and Lord, that this is a purgatorium, perhaps even your picture palace is a level of this purgatorium : and my St Vincenzo Ferreri panel, for my blasphemous sin of depicting Christ as older than 33, has resulted in the being placed, both picture and painter, in purgatorium as a reminder of my prideful wrong imagining (though consider, illustrious Lordship, that if this is so, then only 1 of my pictures has ended up in purgatorium, and there are 4 of Cosmo's there, which in the end demonstrates Cosmo's work as 4 times more blameworthy than mine, just saying).

Having myself been, I can only presume, formerly until this renaissance in a heaven of

forgetfulness, am now for some unforgiven sin
reborn into a place of coldness and mystery, with
no means of practising my trade and nothing to my
name but the broken pieces of a gone life like the
breakage of a vase : each piece its own beauty in
the palm of the hand but the whole thing shattered,
nothing but air where it once was and all the air
that was enclosed in it released, now unheld by
anything, and the edges of each broken piece sharp
enough to bleed me, had I still skin to be broken

but He or His clerks will know all these things
already, so there is no need for me to note them in
my petition, which is nothing but mewling and
carping and perhaps I must just accept.

Cause I know this is not hell cause I am intrigued
not hopeless and cause I am surely put here for
some good use albeit mysterious : in hell there is no
mystery cause in mystery there is always hope : we
followed the beautiful woman until she came to the
door in the house and went through it and shut it
and left the boy, still unseen, outside, at which point
he (and I) retired to the small wall across the
thoroughfare but still in sight of that shut door,
which is where we are now : though also I did
notice, I could not fail to as we went, that the
woman, who has about her an air of some beauty
and grace, unfortunately has a walk like a swan out
of element or a flightbird forced to walk, a waddle
so unsuited to her beauty that in the end it endears

in that it mitigates that beauty : if I had paper and
a pen or a willow charcoal (and hands and arms,
even just one of each, to do it with) I would show it
with an unexpected angle, a flatness, the bodily
form appearing a touch unknowing, and it would
make her even more graced and likeable and I've
had much time and leisure to think and plan these
things cause we followed her a great distance and
were I still embodied I'd be exhausted so it's as well
I've no legs : but this boy has some stamina, will by
luck and justice live long I thought as we covered
the distance : until I felt the dip in his spirit when
the woman came to some steps and went up the
steps and in through a door and shut the door
behind her and

   (oof)

   it was a punch to the gut, a door shut on a boy
obsessed.

   It is a feeling thing, to be a painter of things :
cause every thing, even an imagined or gone thing
or creature or person has essence : paint a rose or a
coin or a duck or a brick and you'll feel it as sure as
if a coin had a mouth and told you what it was like
to be a coin, as if a rose told you first-hand what
petals are, their softness and wetness held in a
pellicle of colour thinner and more feeling than an
eyelid, as if a duck told you about the combined
wet and underdry of its feathers, a brick about the
rough kiss of its skin.

This boy I am sent for some reason to shadow knows a door he can't pass through and what it tells me just to be near him is something akin to when you find the husk of a ladybird that has been trapped, killed and eaten by a spider, and what you thought on first sight was a charming thing, a colourful creature of the world going about its ways, is in reality a husk hollowed out and proof of the brutal leavings of life.

Poor boy.

Just saying, even though these houses we're outside are grand, well appointed and many-storeyed, the boy is on a small low wall whose bricks are crying out for love : the knowing of this is the knowledge of my father turning over in his grave in his natural impatience and knocking on the lid of the box I put him in to have someone let him up and out of the ground to remake such a wall : cause if all the dead were given this chance, with their hindsight and experience this world or purgatorium would I think be better made.

I am wondering where it is, grave of my father, wondering too where my own grave, when the boy sits up, faces the woman's house, holds his holy votive tablet up in both hands as if to heaven, up at the level of his head like a priest raising the bread, cause this place is full of people who have eyes and choose to see nothing, who all talk into their hands as they peripatate and all carry these votives, some

43

the size of a hand, some the size of a face or a whole head, dedicated to saints perhaps or holy folk, and they look or talk to or pray to these tablets or icons all the while by holding them next to their heads or stroking them with fingers and staring only at them, signifying they must be heavy in their despairs to be so consistently looking away from their world and so devoted to their icons.

He holds it in the air : he is maybe saying a prayer.

Ah! I see : cause a little image of the house and its door has appeared in the tablet : which makes these votive tablets perhaps similar to the box the great Alberti had and which he displayed in Florence (I once saw) whereby the eye looks through the tiniest of holes and sees a full distant landscape formed small and held inside it.

Is it possible then that all the people of this place are painters going about their world with the painting tools of their time?

Perhaps I have been placed in a specific painters' purgatorium –

but the boy slumps beside me again, his spirit in the gutter.

No : cause these people have none of the spirit necessary for a lifelong making of pictures.

Look, boy : cheerful thing : spring flowers in a sort of bucket hanging off the top of a metal pole stuck at the side of this roadway.

Is there spring in purgatorium? Do they have

years in purgatorium? Yes, surely : given that purgatorium holds in its nature a promise of an end to it, when its inmates are judged purged, then it must have some way by which time can be measured : but I'd've thought such a place would be full of the moans and the supplicatings of thousands : no, purgatorium could surely be worse, cause look, at least there are blackbirds in it : one comes out of a hedge right now and sits along on the wall with his beak a good Naples yellow and a ring of the same yellow round the black of the eye : he sees the boy there, twitches his tail and wings back into the hedge : in the hedge he starts a song : can it really be purgatorium and not the old earth when it is so *like* the earth in the song of the bird, its everlasting unchanging fineness? Hello bird : I'm a painter, dead (I think, though I remember no going), placed here for my many prideful sins in this cold place that has no horses to watch unseen unheard unknown the back of a boy in the kind of love that means nothing but despair.

What kind of a world, though, that has no horses?

What kind of a journey can you make with no creature to befriend you to let your going anywhere reveal itself as the matter of trust and faith going somewhere always is?

Now, when I bought my horse, Mattone, he had a stupid name, Bedeverio? Ettore? something from

the stories of kings all the rage and everyone
naming their children Lancelotto, Artu, Zerbino,
and their horses too, by God : I bought him from a
woman who had fields outside Bologna, I had a
pocketful of money from the job I'd done and
hitched a ride in a cabbage cart out to her fields : I
saw him and I pointed him out, that one, I said, the
one the colour of excellent stone, can I maybe try
him? Oh he's unrideable, she said, a thrower, worse
than useless to me, he's never let anybody, and
when the slaughterer or the gypsies come he's the
top of the list : then that's the one I want, I said and
I pulled the money in a bag out of my pocket, out
came green leaves from the cart with it and fell all
at my feet and it seemed a good omen : so she went
into the field and caught him, it only took an hour
and a half, and she brought him in, he'd good feet,
was clean-haunched, most of all had a curve from
his back round to his flank that moved the heart
(cause the heart is, itself, a matter of curves) and
when I went to look at his teeth he let me put my
hand in his mouth, oh he's never let anyone do that
before, the woman said, he's bitten them all : so she
saddled him, there was a furore of kicking and
snorting when she did (and it wasn't all the horse) :
but as soon as I was up and straddling him, and
had got back on after he'd thrown me that first time
in the woman's yard, I sensed he heard what my
hands and heels were saying and he understood I'd

not do him harm, also from that first moment not just that I'd be for him *a hostelry in a wilderness* but that I would trust him to be the same for me.

So I bought him plus the tack he was wearing then and there, I hung on to his neck and leaned down without getting off (in case of difficulty of getting back on) and gave her the bag of coins, and on our way back to Bologna he only threw me the 3 or 4 times and always let me back on again without much disagreement, which was a civil thing in a horse unused to it : with my hands at the place in his neck where the warm skin folded and stretched as he walked (cause I couldn't get him to go any faster than a walk unless he had a mind to canter, at which point he would canter as he wished and I'd let him, which is a trait I felt he liked in me) so by the end of our journey 2 things had happened, it had entered my head to change his name to a more workmanlike one that suited his colouring, and it had turned out he and I were friends, this horse whose eye was still clear, for all the ill-treatment at the hands of the woman or whoever had had him before (it did not say on his bill of sale and she would not sell me a guarantee and said she could not write to sign a paper) and I don't, can't recall, ever selling him on, so I must suppose I never had cause to.

Dead, gone, bones, horsedust.

In this particular ring of purgatorium I long right

now for that smell of home, the smell of the horse I travelled the earth with and the horse who travelled it with me, with the dividing line of whiter hairs from his forehead down to the soft dark of his nostrils, cause he was a creature of symmetries and a reminder that nature is herself a bona fide artist of intent both dark and light.

Cause there was the morning when I was with the daughter of a man who'd no idea I was in the barn and his daughter there too, or that we'd been in there in each other's arms warm all the cold night, and Mattone let me know, by taking my shirt which I still had on me in his teeth and pulling it up to let the cold air in then lipping me hard in the back, not just that it was first light but that the man was up and breakfasting and his workers were in the yard, and I'd kissed the girl and was on his own back and off at a canter across the fields before the sun had the chance to melt any more of the frost, from which adventure I was left bruised, yes, but from the swift activities of our love and the biting of my own horse not from the wrath of or blows from any father or his workers, and so with dignity through the birdsong.

The blackbird in the hedge now stops his song : he darts off out and up with a chirrup and flurry cause the boy shifts : he turns in towards me : he looks at me!

No : he looks through me : it's clear that he sees nothing.

What I see for the first time is his face.

Most I see that round his eyes is the blackness of sadness (burnt peachstone smudged in the curve of the bone at both sides of the top of the nose).

It is as if he is a miniver that's been dipped in shadow.

Then I see that he looks very girl.

It is often like this at this age.

The great Alberti, who published in the year in which my mother birthed me the book for all picturemakers, and wrote in it the words *let the movements of a man (as opposed to a boy or young woman) be ornato with more firmness*, understands the bareness and the pliability it takes, ho, to be both.

The great Cennini, though, in his handbook on colours and picturemaking, finds no worth and no beauty of proportion in girls, or in women of any age – except in the matter of hands in themselves, since the delicate hands of girls and women, providing they're young enough, are more patient, he says, than those of a man, from spending so much more time indoors which makes them more suited to making the best blue.

Myself I went out of my way, then, to be expert at the painting of hands and be good at the grinding of blue *and* the using of blue, both : there were others like me, painters I mean, who could do my particular both : we knew each other when we saw each other, we exchanged this knowledge by glance and by silence, by moving on and going our own ways : and most anyone else who saw through the art of what some would call our subterfuge and others our necessity graced us with acceptance and an equally unspoken trust in the skill we must surely possess to be so beholden to be taking such a path.

In this way my father made sure of an education and an apprenticeship for me, though it maddened my brothers to be always what they considered his workshop serfs, like infidel workers compared to me they thought, carrying and working the stones and bricks that I sat and drew and calculated with, seeing to the shaping of the windows I then used as frames for seeing or sat below using the light of for reading a mathematical book or a treatise on pigments, protecting my hands.

I'm good at walls too cause I also learned from looking how to handle stone and brick and how to build a wall to last a lot longer than this one the boy is sitting on now.

But though I was descended from the men who'd made the walls which themselves made the municipal palace – the walls on which the great

Master Piero in his stay in Ferara had painted for
the Ests the victorious battle scenes
   (and from looking at whose works I learned
   the open mouths of horses,
   the rise of light in landscape,
   the serious nature of lightness,
   and how to tell a story, but tell it more than one
way at once, and tell another underneath it
up-rising through the skin of it) –
   I would paint my own walls.
   So my father, when I'd trained to what he
thought enough degree (which was not until I'd
seen 19 summers) and news reached him that there
was a need for someone to provide 3 pietà half-
figures and a quantity of painted pillars to the side
of the high altar in the cathedral, went out into the
wet night with works of mine rolled up under his
arm wrapped in treated skins to keep the rain off
and showed the priests how I could with colours
turn plain stone to what seemed marble column :
the priests, who'd seen me many times in my youth
with him and my brothers, gave me the job and
paid us good money : by both luck and justice we
all benefited and I did not formally leave my
father's tutelage till 3 years before he died, old
father, old wallmaker, by which time I had come of
age, was full grown, had been binding my chest
with linen for a decade, not too difficult being slim

and boylike then, and had been visiting the house
of pleasure with Barto for nearly as long, where
the girls taught me both binding and unbinding
and some other useful ways in which to comport
myself.

Barto.

Cause if this boy could hear me I'd tell him : we
all need a brother or a friend and at some point you
need a horse too : I had 2 brothers and admittedly
was more friends in the end with my horse : but
even better than brothers, and even than horse, my
friend Barto, whom I met after fishing barefoot out
on the stones in the river on my 12th birthday, and
though usually I caught not much, that day the fish
had been opening their mouths at the surface of the
water as if congratulating me on having been born
and I had caught 7 altogether, 3 fat carp with their
whiskers trailing and the rest were little and middle-
sized perch, the black stripes over their gold : I
knotted the lines together and hung them over my
shoulder and left my brothers to their displeasure
(they'd caught less) and was walking home through
the cow parsley along the foot of a tall wall when a
voice called down to me.

I once caught a catfish, the voice said, that was so
big I couldn't land it. In fact it almost rivered me.

I liked the word rivered so I looked up : it was a
boy leaning over the top of the wall.

I could feel from the mouth and the pull of it, he

said, that it was a lot bigger than you from head to foot, and though you're not that tall yourself it's quite long for a fish, no?

His cap was new : he was wearing a finely embroidered jacket, I saw its quality though the wall was more than 2 men high.

So I couldn't land it, he said. Cause it was a lot bigger than me too, and there was only me and the catfish, no one else, and I couldn't hold it and bring it in myself. So I cut my line and I let it escape me, I had to. But it's the best fish I've ever caught, that fish I didn't catch, cause it's a fish that will always be with me now and never be eaten, it'll never die, that fish I'll never land. I see you've done well today. Any chance you'd give me one of your hundred fish?

Catch your own fish, I said.

Well, I would, but you've taken so many it wouldn't be fair to the river, he said.

How did you get up there? I said.

I climbed, he said. I'm more monkey than man. Coming up? Here.

He leaned over the top and held out a hand but he was so far above me and his gesture so charming that I burst out laughing : I untied the smallest of the perch, separated it from its brothers and laid it in the grass.

A piece of gold for making me laugh, I shouted up.

I hoisted my other fish and my stick back on my

shoulder and waved my hand : but when I'd got a little along the path the boy called me back.

Can't you throw that fish you gave me up here to me? he said. I can't reach it from here.

Don't be lazy, I said. Come down and get it.

Frightened you can't throw a fish as well as you can catch a fish? he said.

I'd happily throw it, but I'm not meant to misuse my hands, I said, cause I plan to earn my living by them, and throwing, as the masters say in all the books, could tire or hurt them.

Scared you'll miss, he said.

You don't know it yet, I said, but you're besmirching an expert aim.

Oh, an *expert* aim, he said.

I put down my things and picked up the little perch.

Hold still, I said.

I will, he said.

I aimed it. The boy turned with languor and watched both cap and fish on their way down the other side of the wall.

There'll be trouble now, he said. I'm supposed to keep it clean. What kind of fish was it you knocked it off with?

A perch, I said.

He made a face.

Gutterfish, he said. Mudfish. Haven't you anything tastier?

Come down and we'll go to the river, I said. I'll
lend you my stick. You can catch yourself your own
taste in fish. And if what you hook's as big as the
one you caught before I'll help you.

He looked pleased when I said this : then his face
went miserable.

Ah, I can't, he said.

Why not? I said.

I'm not allowed near the river, he said. Not in
these clothes.

Take them off, I said. We'll hide them
somewhere. They'll be fine till we get back.

But then I worried for a moment in case I'd be
expected to lose my own clothes if the boy did
come down and remove his, cause I was now
become my new self in the world, which involved
taking strict pains to preserve what I appeared :
though something in me also found this idea a good
one, but in any case in the end there was no
divesting of any sort, on this day at least, cause the
boy called down –

I can't. These are clothes I have to wear. And I've
got to go in a minute. I have to attend celebrations.
It's my birthday.

Mine too! I said.

Really? he said.

Happy birthday, I said.

And to you, he said.

Years later he'd tell me it was my feet being bare

on the path as I walked that he was most taken
with, and it'd be some time, a long time, into our
friendship before he'd tell me it wasn't just cause he
was in his best new clothes that he wouldn't come
that day to the river, it was that his mother didn't
like him going near rivers cause of the brother
that had drowned before he was born, and he had
been named for the brother, the others were all
sisters.

We met whenever his family came to town,
though increasingly in secret cause he was from a
family which would have had little to do with mine,
and we went often to the river so he could doubly
defy his mother, first by going at all and second by
going without her knowledge : but he never went by
himself in case the river decided it wanted to claim
this other brother too : though truth be told I didn't
know this about him until we were both much
older.

On our first shared birthday he showed me all the
things you can do if you're balanced on the top of a
very tall wall : you can hang yourself off it by
nothing but your hands, then by nothing but one
hand : you can walk along the top of it like a cat or
a rope-walking gypsy performing : you can dance :
you can run along it like a squirrel or stand on it on
only one leg like a heron and do little jumps : you
can tuck the other leg up behind your back or kick
it openly back and fore while keeping your balance :

finally you can jump off the wall up into the air with your arms out wide like a heron taking flight.

He demonstrated all these things except the last : of the last he only spread his arms like wings to show me, as if about to.

Don't, I shouted.

He barked a laugh full of the daring of his dancing : he did one last leap in the air and landed square and safe sitting down with a thump on the top of the wall, his arms still wide : he swung his legs at me like a figure in a painting sitting half in and half out, legs over the woodframe.

You're a boy afraid of a wall, he called down at me.

And you're a boy with no idea how wrong he is, I called back at him. You'll need to know me better. And to know I'm afraid of nothing. And my father is a maker of walls, among other things, and if you can kick your legs like you're doing against one and nothing chips off it then you're lucky, it's a pretty good one. But that's far too high a wall to jump off. Any fool can calculate that.

Exactly, and I'm no fool, he said and then stood up again as if to do the jump and made me laugh again. Instead of jumping he bowed as low as was safe to.

Bartolommeo Garganelli is very pleased, on this day auspicious to both of us, to make your quaintances, he said.

You might talk as fancy as your clothes, I said. But even a common fisher of gutterfish knows you've just got that last word wrong.

1 quaintance. 2 quaintances, he said. And I've met more than 2, I've met 3 of you. Expert fisher. Expert fish-thrower. Expert in walls and their trajectories.

If you'd care to come down, I said, I'll consider introducing you to the rest of me.

Here I am again : me and a boy and a wall.

(I will take it as an omen.)

But this time the boy looks straight through me as if I've swallowed a magic ring and the ring has rendered me invisible.

(I will take this as an omen too.)

First he was all sainthood : now he's all lovelorn : what use to him is a painter?

I'll do what good I can.

I'll draw him an open threshold.

I'll put a lit torch in his hand.

For the making of pictures we need plants and stones, stonedust and water, fish bones, sheep and goat bones, the bones of hens or other fowls whitened in high heat and ground down fine : we can use the foot of a hare, the tails of squirrels : we need breadcrumbs, willow shoots, fig shoots, fig milk : we need bristles from pigs and the teeth of clean meat-eating animals, for example dog, cat,

wolf, leopard : we need gypsum : we need porphyry
for grinding : we need a travelling box and a good
source of pigment and we need the minerals which
are the source of colour : above all we need eggs,
the fresher the better, and from the country not the
town mean better colours when dry.

We can dull things down if they're too bright
with earwax which costs nothing.

We need skins of sheep and goats, clippings of
the muzzles, feet and sinews, skin strips, skin
scrapings, and a source of clear water to boil
them in.

I think of all the sketches and dessins and
paintings on panels and linens and crack-covered
walls, all the colours and the willows and the hares
and the goats and the sheep and the hoofs, all the
eggs cracked open : ash, bones, dust, gone, the
hundreds and hundreds, no, thousands.

Cause that's all the life of a painter is, the seen
and gone disappearing into the air, rain, seasons,
years, the ravenous beaks of the ravens. All we are
is eyes looking for the unbroken or the edges where
the broken bits might fit each other.

I'll tell him instead about the small boy who
wished to see the Virgin,

he prayed and he prayed, please let me see the
Virgin : let Her appear here in the flesh before me :
but an angel appeared instead and the angel said,
yes you can see the Virgin, but I don't want you to

be naïve about it cause seeing Her is going to cost you one of your eyes.

I would gladly pay an eye to see the Virgin, the boy replied.

So the angel vanished and the Virgin appeared instead and the Virgin was so beautiful the boy burst into tears and then the Virgin vanished and when She did, just as the angel had said, the boy went blind in one eye, in fact when he put his hand up to feel his face with his hand there was no eye there, just a hole like a little cave in his face where the eye had been.

But even though he'd lost the eye, he had loved seeing Her so much that he wanted nothing more than just to cast eye (not eyes, cause he only had the one) on Her one more time.

Please let the Virgin appear to me again, he prayed and he prayed until the angel got fed up listening to him and arrived in a flashing of purple-gold-white wings and stood in front of him folding these wings with a graveness that meant business and said, yes you can see Her again but you have to know – I don't want you entering into this contract naïvely – that if you do you will have to pay for it with the loss of your only remaining eye.

I rocked up and down on my mother's knees with the blatant unfairness of it, it was a story in the pamphlet of Vincenzo illustrated by the nuns, one of the stories Vincenzo liked to tell to the

multitudes who could hear every word hc spoke for
miles regardless of whether they knew his tongue
or not, and it wouldn't be till I could read for
myself, some time after my mother had gone, and I
found the pamphlet, True Happenings From The
Life Of Most Humble Servant Vincenzo Ferreri
Including Countless Miracles That Came To Pass
screwed up behind the bedhead and I unfolded it
and sat and read it to myself the first time, that I
found that my mother had never ever, in all her
tellings of it, told me the end of the story where
    1. the Virgin appears again
    2. the angel takes the second eye
    3. then finally the Virgin gives the boy back both
his eyes out of kindness,
    instead she had always left me twisting myself in
her arms on her lap with the dilemma of it.
    Will he give away both his eyes? she said. What
do you think? What should he do?
    I put my fists up to my own eyes and dug the
heels of the hands in to see if my eyes were both
still there, to torture myself and imagine them gone
while I waited for her to turn the page over from
the drawing of the boy with the black holes where
his eyes had been to the drawing which did not
scare me so, of Vincenzo curing the dumb woman :
one day Vincenzo met a woman who could not
speak : she had never been able to speak : he cured
her, after which she could speak like everybody else.

61

But before she'd uttered a word, he held up his book and his hand and he said – Yes, it's true, you can speak now. But it's best if you don't. And I'd like you to choose not to.

So the woman said Thank you.

After which she never spoke again.

My mother always laughed hard at this miracle : one day she fell off a stool she was laughing so much at it, and lay on the floor beside me next to the upturned stool with her arms holding her chest, tears coming out of her eyes, laughing in a way that meant it was fortunate we were in the thick-walled part of the house and no passers-by could hear her laugh like that, like the wild women did who lived in the forest and were shunned, cause known to do witchery.

Otherwise she held me on her knee after my bath and told me the terrifying stories like the one about the boy whose father, Apollo the sun-god, forbade him from driving the horses who drew the sun across the sky from its place of rising to its place of setting every day cause those horses were too wild for him and too strong, and she glided her arm through the air to show the horses and the sun all going their steady way : but when the boy took the forbidden horses out she shuddered her arm (the horses getting a little bit too strong) then shook and threw her arm from side to side (the horses getting stronger and stronger) then her arm threw itself wildly about as if it was a wild mad thing no longer even a part of her (the horses out of control, the reins flapping loose in the air) and the day passed and became night in a second or 2 like the whole day passing in the swoop of a bird across the sky, then horses chariot boy all dashing to the ground so fast that words can't – and here she made as if to drop me off her knee, as if I'd fall and hit the ground like them, but no, cause as soon as the fall seemed to start I'd find myself instead flung upwards not down, cause she'd stand up just as she dropped me, swing me up instead into the air very high and dangerous and free as if my heart and throat might leave my body and leap up above us both towards the ceiling   yet she never let go of holding me firm for a moment on either the down or the up, my mother.

Or the story of Marsyas the musician who was half-man and half-beast and who could play as sweetly as any god on his flute and did so until Apollo the sun-god himself heard rumours about how good the earthly musician was, came shooting down straight as a ray of light to earth, challenged him to a contest, won the contest and had the musician skinned alive as his prize.

Which isn't necessarily the injustice that it sounds, my mother said. Cause imagine, the skin of Marsyas slipped off as easily as a tomato's will in warm water to allow the red raw sweetness out of the fruit below. And the sight of such release moved everyone who saw it to a strength of feeling more than any music anywhere played by any musician or god.

So always risk your skin, she said, and never fear losing it, cause it always does some good one way or another when the powers that be deign to take it off us.

This boy is a girl.

I knew it.

I know it cause we sat on that poor specimen of wall (which will not last) until a much older woman, bent by the years, came out of the dwelling behind us making a great furore : she poked the boy in the back with the bristle end of a brush on a long wood pole and she shouted something and as we came away the boy made, I think, apology, very polite and in the unbroken undisguised voice of what can only be girl.

Also, this girl is good at dance : I am enjoying some of the ways of this purgatorium now : one of its strangest is how its people dance by themselves in empty and music-less rooms and they do it by filling their ears with little blocks and swaying about to a silence, or to a noise smaller than the squee of a mosquito that comes through the little confessional grille in each of the blocks : the girl was doing a curving and jerking thing both, with the middle of her body, she went up then down then up again, sometimes so low down that it was a marvel to see her come back up again so quick, sometimes pivoting on one foot and sometimes on the other and sometimes on both with her knees bent then straightening into a sinuous undulate like a caterpillar getting the wings out of the caul, the new imago emerging from the random circumbendibus.

Also, this girl has a brother : he is several years younger, of the same open countenance but also fatter, weller, much less shadowed at the eyes, and dancing can be as catchy as laughing and I was not alone in this knowledge cause into the room came this small boy with long and brown curling hair to dance the same dance very badly (boy I know anatomically cause bare as a bacchus cherub from the midriff down) : he danced the dance badly and laughingly half naked round her till the girl, who could not hear him and did not know he was doing it till she opened her eyes and saw him, roared like a furious African cat, hit him over the head with her hand and chased him from the room, by which I gauged them sister and brother.

She started the dance again : she performed its

strangeness with such deftness and attention that I was filled with verve by her taking of her own ups and downs so earnestly.

I've come to like this girl who will so solemnly dance with herself.

Right now she and I are outside the house that is home to her and the brother : we are sitting in a garden of shivering flowers.

Through the small window she holds in her hands we are viewing frieze after frieze of lifelike scenes of carnal pleasure-house love enacted before our eyes : the love act has not changed : no variation here is new to me.

Cold here and she's shivering too : surmise she is watching the love act repeating like this to keep herself warm.

The little brother came out here too and by a single glance in his direction she both warned him and dismissed him : this is a girl with a very strong eye : he hasn't gone far, he is behind a small wicker fence about as tall as he is, behind which there are tall black barrels hidden close to the door of the house and I think has some mischief planned : every so often he dashes out on to the grass in front of the fence and picks up a stone or twig then dashes back behind the fence and he has done this several times now without her noticing him once.

Girl, I remember it, the way the game of love makes the rest of the world disappear.

Best not to watch it through such a small window, though.

Best on the whole not to watch it at all : love is best felt : the acts of love are hard and disillusioning to view like this unless done by the greatest master picturemakers : otherwise the seeing of them being done and enjoyed by figurations of other people will always lock you outside them (unless your pleasure comes from taking solo pleasure or pleasure at one remove, in which case, yes, that's your pleasure).

Now inevitably I am thinking of Ginevra, of most lovely Isotta, of silly little lovely little Meliadusa, and Agnola, and the others into whose company I came first in my 17th year the night Barto and I, having been to see the processions in Reggio, travelled back to the city and Barto took me to what he called *a fine place to spend the night*.

What do you think, Francescho, will we go and see the Marquis be celebrated becoming the Duke? Barto'd said.

I asked permission of my father cause I'd a longing to see a throng : he said no : he said it unblinkingly.

Tell him it'll be good for your work, Barto said. We'll go a journey and see history be made.

I repeated the gist of this to my father.

There's much for a painter to see there, I said, and if you ever want me to get closer to the court and its workshops there's much I ought to know, much I ought not to miss.

My father shook his head : no.

If these fail, Barto said, tell him you're going with me and that this is an intelligent thing to let a painter do cause the more chance my family has to see your skill – you'll draw the procession, won't you – the more chance there is they'll give you work when you're fledged. And tell him you'll be away for only one night and that my parents will give you your lodging in Reggio at one of our houses.

But your houses are nowhere near Reggio, I said.

Francescho, you're green as an early leaf, Barto said.

There are a lot of kinds of green, even in just the earliest leaves, I said.

How many kinds of green are there? Barto said.

7 main kinds altogether, I said. And perhaps 20 to 30, maybe more, variations on each of these kinds.

And you're all of those greens put together, he said, cause anyone but you would already have gathered and would never have needed to be told that I've other plans for us than our spending the night at Reggio. Look at you, you're still calculating, aren't you, how to make how many greens is it?

It was true : so he laughed and threw an arm round my shoulder and kissed the side of my head.

My sweet unassuming friend, taker of things, people, birds, skies, even the sides of buildings at their word, he'd said. I love you for your greenness, and it's partly in honour of it that I want you to persuade your father to let you accompany me. So persuade him. Trust me. You'll never regret it.

Well, Barto was always wise to how to go about such things, cause sure enough the thought of a Garganelli bed with his offspring tucked in its sheets made my father blink, pause, then say the yes we needed though he gave me plenty ultimatums about behaviour and even had a new jacket made for me : I packed some things, left early in the morning and met Barto : we got to the town of Reggio and we saw it all.

We saw more people than I'd ever imagined and all packed into the square of the small town and we saw the flags, we saw the white banners with the figures painted on them : we saw it all very well too from the balcony of the house of Garganelli family friends (who were off on a Venetian ship touring to the Holy Land, Barto said, so didn't care who was on their balcony) : there were horsebacked courtiers : there were boys waving and tossing flags high into the air and then catching them : then a platform came pulled by horses so white they must've been white-leaded : on the higher bit of it there was an empty seat, tall, painted and cushioned like a throne and 4 youths stood at each of its corners draped in togas, meant to be ancient Romans of great wisdom with their faces charcoaled to make them look old and we were so close we could see the drawn lines at their brows and eyes and mouths : below them on the lower bit of the platform were 4 more boys, 1 at each corner, holding tall banners with ensigns of the town's and the new Duke's colours, that made 8 boys altogether and a 9th one too sitting at the front, and all 9 dressed-up boys struggling to keep their balance cause there was nothing to hold on to when the man leading the horses stopped them and the platform rocked to a halt below us.

The 9th was a boy dressed as Justice : he sat at the foot of the throne : he was holding such a heavy-looking sword in the air that when the platform stopped he tipped sideways, knocked into the big set of scales in front of him and nearly toppled off the platform : but he didn't, he righted himself by thumping the point of the sword off the floor of the cart : he shifted the fallen-forward fabric of his costume back up over his shoulder, used a graceful foot to tip the upended scales back to an evenness, got his breath and stuck the sword in the air again : everybody who saw it happen shouted hurray and clapped their hands, at which Justice looked mortified cause of the grimness on the face of the portly man who'd come to stand at the side of the platform facing the empty throne.

71

This man was glinting with gems : he was why we were here, he was the kindly generous charismatic Borse d'Est, the new Duke of Reggio and Modena, the brand-new Marquis of Ferara (and a pompous self-regarding fool, Barto said telling me the story doing the rounds of all the rich families who weren't Ests, about how the kindly generous charismatic Borse had been giving the Emperor gifts over many months so that everyone would know he was kindly generous and charismatic and above all much more of a gift-giver than his brother, the last Marquis, who'd known a lot of Latin, lived a quiet life then died : on the day Borse first heard that finally the Emperor was to make him Duke of Modena and Reggio (though not yet of Ferara, damn it) his attendants had seen him jumping up and down by himself in the rose garden of the palace of fine outlook squealing like a child the words over and over *I'm a Duke! I'm a Duke!*).

There were gems all over the front of him : they caught the sun like he was wearing lots of little mirrors or stars or was covered in sparks : the biggest gem, bright verdigris on the front of his coat which was vermilion, was near as big as one of his hands by which he'd been led to the front of the platform, to Justice, by a very small boy-angel (swan-feather wings, very fresh off the swan cause there was still red seepage and a shine of gristle at the bone where it met the white of the fabric on the boy's back).

Most illustrious Lord, the angel said now in a high clear voice.

The crowd in the wide square quietened.

The portly man bowed to the angel.

You see seated before you God's own Justice, the angel said and his voice rang thin as a handbell above the heads of the people.

The portly man turned from the angel and bowed with great ceremony to Justice : I saw Justice not dare bow back : the too-heavy sword wavered above them both.

The angel squeaked again.

Justice who for so long now has been forgotten! Justice who has been held for far too long in blind contempt! All the rulers of the world have closed their eyes to Justice! Forgotten and disdained since the deaths of her guardians, the wise ancient statesmen of a better time! Justice has been so lonely!

The boy dressed as Justice brought his other hand to the handle of his sword and with both hands stopped it wavering.

But rejoice cause today, illustrious Lord, Justice is dead! the angel said.

There was a shocked pause.

The angel looked stricken.

Today illustrious Lord, the angel said again. Justice is. Dead.

The portly man stayed bowed : the angel's eyes were shut, screwed up : the boys on the cart stared straight ahead. A courtier started forward from the rows of horses at the back of the platform beyond the empty throne : the portly man, without looking, raised his hand away from his side just a touch and the courtier saw and reined his horse in.

Still from his low bow the portly man mumbled something in the direction of the angel.

– Dedicating, the angel blurted. This seat. To you! Today Justice lets it be known to the world that above all others she favours – you! Justice bows – to you! Justice in her purity even declares that she is enamoured – of you! And rejoice again, cause Justice invites – you! To take the seat left empty by the deaths of the great wise ancients. The last just rulers of men. Cause Justice says, illustrious Lord, that nobody could fill this seat justly till now! This seat was empty and remained empty – till you!

The portly man, the new Duke, straightened up : his front glinted : he went to the angel : with his hand on the boy's shoulder he turned him square on so they both faced the platform.

The boy dressed as Justice still holding the sword with 2 hands let go with one of his hands momentarily to gesticulate towards the empty

throne then brought that hand back to the sword
handle quick as he could.

The new Duke spoke.

I thank Justice. I revere Justice. But I cannot
accept this honour. I cannot take such a throne.
Cause I am merely a man. But I am a man who will
do my best by my Ducal vows all my life to merit
Justice's honour and approval.

A moment of silence : then the crowd below us
went wild with cheering.

Pompous arse, Barto said. Pompous Borse.
Stupid crowd of fools.

I was inclined to join the cheering myself which
was persuasive and echoed round the great square :
also I'd heard that Borse was a man who liked to
give gifts to favoured painters and musicians and I
didn't want to think so badly of him and sure
enough the crowd seemed to hold him in favour and
could such a festive crowd be so very wrong? The
noise the people made in his honour was huge and
the new Duke was so modest : the dressed-up boys
on the cart looked soaked through by the noise of
the crowd like they'd just been driven through a
waterfall.

Only the angel with the swan wings didn't look
relieved : from above them as the new Duke bowed
again to the crowd and the crowd went on cheering,
I could see a redness at the angel's shoulder and

neck like the minium pigment which is a red that soon turns to black, it came from the hand of the new Duke gripping it hard enough to leave an imprint on it : but it is a hard thing in the world, to be modest, and must probably result in bruises for somebody somewhere along the line.

Come on, Barto said. We're going hunting.

We drove to Bologna.

At the house of pleasure in his home city Barto was already so well known that 3 girls came towards us saying his name and taking turns to kiss him before we even got through its outer doors.

This is Francescho, he's fresh from the egg. He's my dear, dear friend. Remember, I told you. He's a little shy, Barto said to a woman I couldn't quite see cause she shimmered and the rooms were dark and full of so many women as dishevelled and disarrayed as enchantresses and there was a rich smell, God knew what of, and rich colours and carpets everywhere, underfoot, on the walls and even up there soft-coating the ceiling perhaps, though I couldn't be sure cause the sweet dirty smells and air and the colours and presences made my senses spin and the floor act like ceiling as soon as we came into the inner rooms.

The woman had me by my hand : she took my coat off my shoulders : she tried to take my satchel from me but it had my drawing things in it : I hung on to it with one arm still in the sleeve of the coat.

She put her mouth to my ear.

Don't be scared, boy. And look, don't insult us, your pockets and purse'll stay full, only ever minus what we're worth or what extra you'd like to give us, you've my word on it, there are no thieves here, we're all honest and worthy here.

No, no, I said, it's not, I, – I don't mean to –

but in the saying of all the words in my ear she'd near-carried me in her arms, she was powerfully strong and it was as if I'd no will of my own, to the door of another room, made me light as a leaf and swept me in like one and shut the door behind us, I could feel the door at my back but through a lace or a curtain or some thin carpet-stuff.

I held on to my satchel and felt for a door handle with my other hand but there was none I could find : now the woman was pulling me towards the bed by the strap of the satchel and I was pulling against the strap back towards the door.

What soft skin you have, she said. Hardly even sign of a beard (she put the back of her hand on my cheek), come on, you've nothing to worry about, not even paying cause the friend you came in with, it's already arranged it's on him.

She sat on the bed still holding me by the strap of my satchel : she smiled up at me : she pulled a playful couple of times gently on the strap : I held back polite the full length of it.

She sighed : she let the strap go: she looked

towards the door : when I didn't make a dash for it right away she smiled at me again a very different way.

First time? she said unbuttoning her front. I'll take care. I promise. Don't be scared. Let me. Of you.

Now she was holding the fall and weight of her own naked breast in her hand.

Don't you like me? she said.

I shrugged.

She tucked the breast back in : she sighed again.

Jesus Mary and Joseph I'm tired, she said. Okay. Let me put myself together. We'll sort this out. We'll get you another girl. You and she can use my room. As you can see, the best room. So what do you like? Tell me. You like yellow hair? You like younger?

I don't want another girl, I said.

She looked pleased.

You want me? she said.

Not that way, I said.

She frowned : then she smiled.

You prefer a man? she said.

I shook my head.

Who do you want, who would you like to fuck? she said.

I don't, I said.

You don't want a fuck? she said. You want something else? Something special? Your friend in

78

here with a girl too? You want to watch? You want
2 girls? You want pain? Piss? A nun? A priest?
Whips? Ties? A bishop? We can do it all, pretty
much everything here.

I sat down on the bench at the end of the bed : I
opened my satchel, unrolled the paper, got out my
board.

Ah, she said. That's what you are. I should have
guessed.

The light in the room was candle-undulate : it
was best over the bed where she now was, dark and
prettily pointed of face against the bedclothes, her
nose turning up at the end, her chin dainty : older
than me by 10 years, or maybe it could even be 20 :
the years of love had worn her eyes, I could see ruin
in them : the dark of the ruin made her serious even
though she'd painted herself something quite else.

I moved a candle, and another.

You're looking at me so, she said.

I am thinking the word pretty, I said.

Well, I'm thinking the same word about you, she
said, and believe me, it's not my job to have such
thoughts. Though it's often my job to pretend
that I do.

And the word beautiful, I said. But with the word
terribly.

She laughed a little laugh down into her
collarbone.

Oh you're a perfect one, she said. Ah, come on,

don't you want to? I'd like to. I like you. You'd like
me. I'm good. I'll be good, I'll be gentle. I'm strong.
I can show you. I'm the best here, you know. I cost
double the others. I'm worth it. It's why your friend
chose me. A gift. I'm a gift. I'm the one who costs
most right now in the whole house, skilled way
beyond the others and yours for the whole of
tonight.

Lie back, I said.

Good, she said. Like this? This? Shall I take
this off?

The sleeve-ties fell as she unlaced them ribboning
over her stomach.

Stay still, I said cause the breast in and out of her
clothes was now perfect curvature.

This? she said.

Relax, I said. Don't move. Can you do both?

Like I told you, I can do anything, she said. Eyes
open or closed?

You choose, I said.

She looked surprised : then she smiled.

Thank you, she said.

She closed them.

By the time I'd finished she was sleeping : so I
had a sleep myself there on the bed by her feet, and
when I woke the beginning of daylight was coming
through the gap in the shutter through the window
hangings.

I shook her a little by the shoulder.

She opened her eyes : she panicked : she clutched for something under her pillows down the back of the bed. Whatever she'd felt for was still there : she relaxed, lay back again : she turned and looked at me blankly : then she remembered.

Did I fall asleep? she said.

You were tired, I said.

Ah, we're all tired in here at this end of the week, she said.

Did you sleep well? I said.

She looked bemused at my politeness : then she laughed and said

Yes!

as if the very thought that a sleep had been nice was astonishing.

I sat on the edge of the bed : I asked her her name.

Ginevra, she said. Like the queen in the stories, don't you know. Married to the king. What elegant hands you have, Mr —.

Francescho, I said.

I gave her the piece of paper : she yawned, barely glanced.

You're not my first, she said. I've been done before. But your kind, well. You yourself are a bit unusual. Your kind usually likes to draw more than one person, no? People in the act, or —. *Oh*.

She sat up : she held the picture closer to what morning light there was in the room.

Oh, she said again. Haven't you made me look –.
And yet it still looks –. Well, –. Very –.

Then she said, can I have this? To keep, for
myself I mean?

On one condition, I said.

You'll finally let me? she said.

She threw the sheet back from herself and patted
the bed beside her.

I want you to tell him, I said. My friend, I mean.
That you and I had a really good time.

You want me to lie to your friend? she said.

No, I said. Cause we did. Have a good time. Well,
I did. And you just said yourself, you slept well.

She looked at me disbelievingly : she looked
down at the drawing again.

That's all you want for it? she said.

I nodded.

Then I went to find Barto in the lobby which in
what daylight came through the cracked-open
shutters was very different from its night self, stale,
stained, patchy, signs of a fire gone wrong all up
one wall : Barto was sitting in an anteroom with
the house's Mistress, she was older than anyone I've
ever seen done up in white frills and ribbons, 2
servingmen filling a small cup with something, one
pouring, the other waiting to hold it to her lip :
before we left Barto kissed her white old hand.

Barto looked stale and stained and patchy too,
rough as masonry and his clothes were creased, I

saw when we came out of the house of pleasure into the sun.

I can't pay for you every time, Barto said on our way to get breakfast. Especially not Ginevra. When I'm earning or I inherit I'll treat you again. But did you have a good time? Did you use the time well?

Hardly slept, I said.

He clapped me on the shoulder.

The next time we came (cause I started to spend a couple of nights a month, my father believed, cultivating the possibility of the patronage of the Garganelli family), Ginevra met us at the door : she winked at Barto and put an arm round me, took me off to one side.

Francescho, she said. I have someone special to meet you. This is Agnola. She knows what you'll like and how you like to spend your time with us.

Agnola had long waved gold hair : she was strong at the thigh as a horsewoman though young : when we got into one of the shuttered rooms with the curtained walls she took my hand and sat me down matter-of-fact at a little table, then stood above me in a most shy way and said,

you know Mr Francescho the picture you made of Ginevra? Would you care to make another picture like it, but this time of me, for remuneration?

which I did, this time the body naked on the bedcovers to show the symmetrics, cause the great

Alberti, who graced by coincidence the year of my birth with his book for picturemakers, notes the usefulness of such study of the human body's system of weights and levers, balances and counterbalances : when I'd finished and the drawing was dry she took it, held it to the candle light, looked hard at it, looked at me to see if she could trust me, looked back at the paper again : she put it down on the bed and went to open a hidden hole in one of the walls : she got a little purse out of it and paid me a number of coins.

Then she and I lay down on the bed and closed our eyes and she woke rested, the same as Ginevra (I did too, to find I was in her arms and most content and warm, it was most pleasant), and she thanked me for both the picture and the chance to catch up on her sleep.

You're a rare client Mr Francescho and I hope you'll choose me again, she said.

I left with the coins in my pocket and bought Barto and me both our breakfasts that day.

So I went about my apprenticeship with my father and my brothers all that week thinking I was on to quite a winning thing working freelance at the house of pleasure.

The time after that it was the girl called Isotta, who was black-haired and dark-skinned, not much older than me, and who sat demure on the bed while we discussed and agreed the drawing of her

and the price she'd pay then when I turned my back
to get my paper and tools out of my satchel
sneaked silent up the bed like a cat and turned me
and kissed me full on the mouth when I didn't
expect it and had never expected such a thing to
happen with any tongue ever, to me, and then she
surprised me more by slipping (at the same time as
she kissed me, hard yet soft and full at the lip, both)
a hand down inside the front of my breeches : the
fear that went through me then when she did this
and I knew that any second she'd know me truly
was 100 times stronger than the feeling released by
the kiss, and both were the strongest things I'd felt
in all my years alive.

But what she did to me next with that hand made
me feel something *1000 times stronger* than any
fear, and when I comprehended that this girl was
now all delight, when I felt delight go through her
at what her hand had found there and then when I
opened my eyes and saw for sure this delight on her
most handsome face, well, I understood this, then :
that fear is a nothing in the world, a paltry thing,
compared.

I knew it, she said, as soon as I saw you. And I
saw you the first night you came here, though you
didn't see me. And I saw you the next, and I knew
both times, and both times I wanted you for me.

She kissed me again, and had me out of my
clothes in no time : in no time she'd taught me the

rudiments of the art of love and let me practise back on her generously : after which, I moved to the end of the bed and she stayed among the pillows and I caught her on the paper in a form both sated and ready, still tensile as a bowstring drawn back ready for its arrow, yet also as well made and completed as the circle drawn by Giotto in the legendary true story.

I gave her the work at the end as payment for the lessons : she looked at it, pleased : she kissed me back into my clothes, buttoned me up, tied me in and sent me on my way now new, all shining and courageous.

What's got into you? my father said cause all I could think of all that week was flowers for breath and flowers for eyes and mouths full of flowers, armpits of them, the backs of knees, laps, groins overflowing with flowers and all I could draw was leaves and flowers, the whorls of the roses, the foliage dark.

The next time I came to the house there were 3 new different girls all whispering in my ears at the door the promise and request of their lessons in love in exchange for my drawings (though I made sure to finish the night again with Isotta, which became my practice while she worked in that city and I visited the house she worked in).

The time after that though, Barto and I rang together at the door and there were 8 or 9, maybe more, I couldn't count them, women and girls of varying ages, their faces all round me as soon as we entered.

Francescho, Barto said in my ear, it seems you're quite the lover.

At which I knew (since far more of them had run towards me than to him) that I'd have to be a little careful : even a true friend finds a friend's talents wearing if they come too close and I loved Barto with my whole heart and really didn't want ever to cause him offence.

But art and love are a matter of mouths open in cinnabar, of blackness and redness turned to velvet by assiduous grinding, of understanding the colours that benefit from being rubbed softly one into the other : the least that the practice will make you is skilful : beyond which there's originality itself, which is what practice is really about in the end and already I had a name for originality, undeniable, and to this name I had a responsibility far beyond the answering of the needs of any friend.

This is all in Cennini's Handbook for Painters, as well as the strict instruction that we must always take pleasure from our work : cause love and painting both are works of skill and aim : the arrow meets the circle of its target, the straight line meets the curve or circle, 2 things meet and dimension and perspective happen : and in the making of pictures and love – both – time itself changes its shape : the hours pass without being hours, they become something else, they become their own opposite, they become timelessness, they become *no time at all*.

The great teacher Cennini also advises spending as little time as possible with women, who will waste the energies of a picturemaker.

I can honestly say, then, that in my training I spent what always transformed into *no time at all* with women in that pleasure house in the years of my youth.

The Mistress of the house, though, caught at me one morning by the elbow : she was more than 75 years old and she walked with 2 sticks and a helper, but precious stones caught light all over her white clothes like she'd just been out hobbling through a rainshower of them, one of which shining little stones she detached from its place sewn on to her sleeve with her canny old fingers unpicking the stitch and pressed into my hand, saying :

   You. I've had 5 women leave here cause of your pictures. What's your name? That's you. *Francescho*. Well, listen, little Francescho, whose name I hear whispered up and down my stairs and whose pictures I see being passed around and fussed over all through my house. That's 5 girls and women you owe me.

I protested that there was no way a set of pictures

done by me and given as fair payment to her girls meant I owed her anything.

The old woman pressed the jewel harder into my hand so its edges near cut me.

You little idiot, she said. Have you no idea? They look at your pictures. They get airs and graces. They come to my rooms and they ask me for more of a cut. Or they look at your pictures. They get all prowessy. They decide to choose a different life. And all the ones who've gone have left by the front door, unprecedented in this house which has never seen girls go by anything but the back. Don't you understand anything? I can't have that. You're costing me. So, it follows. I must ask you to stop frequenting my house. Or at least to stop drawing my girls.

She left a space for me to speak : I shrugged : she nodded, grave.

Good. But before you go, she said. This jewel. The one in your hand. It's yours. If you'll do me.

So I did her picture,

after which she gave me the jewel as agreed, and the next time I came to the house she took me aside and gave me a front door key she'd had her locksmith make for me.

In all these ways I gained yet more understanding of what the great Alberti, who published the book that matters most to us picturemakers, calls the function and the measure of the body, and also of the truth of the great Alberti's notion that beauty in its most completeness is never found in a single body but is something shared instead between more than one body.

But I also learned to disagree with my masters.

Cause even the great Alberti was wrong when he wrote in disapproving terms that *it would not be suitable to dress Venus or Minerva in the rough wool cloak of a soldier, it would be the same as dressing Mars or Jove in the clothes of a woman.*

Cause I met many female Marses and Joves in the house and many Venuses and Minervas in and out of all sorts of clothes.

None of them earned anywhere near her true worth in money : all of them suffered misuse, at the very least the kind of everyday misuse you hear any night through the walls of such a house, and though these women and girls were the closest thing alive I ever met to gods and goddesses, the work they did would first pock them on the surface like illness then break them easy as you break dry twigs then burn them up faster than kindling.

Ginevra I heard died in one of the blue sicknesses.

Isotta, my darling one, vanished.

I liked to think she went by her own choice.

I liked, after I heard she'd gone, to see her in my head fine and hearty in a small town or village, living in a house that was strong at the roof under

vines and figs and lemon trees in a noise of the
good unruliness of a mob of her own children :
most of all I liked to think her smiling with her eyes
and mouth both (which means love) at a lover or
friend or at least at someone whose money she
shared equally.

Agnola I heard years later was found in the river
tied at the hands and feet.

So I understood plenty of dark things too,
learned plenty of things that were the opposite of
pleasure, at the pleasure house.

Then the end of my time there did come, after
all, in our 18th year of age cause Barto had
commerce with Meliadusa, young, new to the
house, new to the work, who'd had me the
fortnight before, first, on her arrival, and had let it
slip with her guests the next few times after me that
what she expected in this house was something
better : to be brought to good climax regardless of
what they wanted, then to be allowed to sleep for a
bit, and finally to be given, in exchange for the
night's work, a very fine drawing of herself.

She told Barto laughingly about it a fortnight of
work in the pleasure house later when she found it
very funny that she'd been so misconstruing and that
the reality of life in the pleasure house was so other.

It wasn't all she laughingly told him.

Barto sat opposite me on the grass: it was early
morning : carts were coming into the city to market

behind him : he rubbed at his jaw : he was solemner than a bear : he'd maybe had a bad night, bad supper, maybe bad wine.

What? I said.

Be quiet, he said.

He leaned forwards, took one of my boots in his hands : he untied the laces and straps : he took the boot off my foot : he untied the boot on the other foot : he took it off me : he stood my boots to one side : he unsheathed his knife from his pouch : very careful with the blade not to cut me in the skin and the blade cold where it touched me, he nicked its point through my leggings at the ankle and cut in a circle all round first one, then the other.

He peeled the legging-stuff off each foot : he placed both pieces to one side : he took my bare feet in his hands : then he spoke.

Is it true? he said. You've been false? All these years?

I have never not been true, I said.

Me not knowing, he said. You not you.

You've known me all along, I said. I've never not been me.

You lied, he said.

Never, I said. And I have never hidden anything from you.

Cause there'd been many times when Barto'd seen me naked or near-naked, by ourselves swimming, say, or with other boys and young men too and the general acceptance of my painter self

had always meant I'd been let to be exactly that –
myself – no matter that in 1 difference I was not
the same : it was as simple as agreement, as
understood and accepted and as pointless to
mention as the fact that we all breathed the same
air : but there are certain things that, said out loud,
will change the hues of a picture like a too-bright
sunlight continually hitting it will : this is natural
and inevitable and nothing can be done about it :
Barto had been challenged by someone, concerning
me, and he had been humiliated by the challenge.

You are other than I thought, he said.

I nodded.

Then the fault is with your thinking, or with the
person who has changed your thinking, not with
me, I said.

How can we be friends now? he said.

How can we ever not be friends? I said.

You know I marry in the summer, he said.

That you marry makes no difference to me, I said
and this is the last thing I said that day to him cause
he looked at me then with eyes like little wounds in
his head and I understood : that he loved me, and
that our friendship had been tenable on condition
that he could never have me, that I was never to be
had, and that someone else, anyone else, saying out
loud to him what I was, other than painter, broke
this condition, since those words in themselves
mean the inevitability, the being had.

93

His hands were cold and my feet in them : he put my feet down on the grass, stood up, touched his chest where his collarbone was (cause my friend was quite the dramatist always) and turned his back on me.

I looked down at my own feet : I looked at how my taken-off boots held the foot shapes even though there weren't any feet in them : I searched around for the legging-stuff after Barto left but I couldn't find it : so I pulled my boots back on my bare feet, strapped and tied them on.

I walked round Bologna for a bit : I had a look at some churchwork, some that was finished and some being done in the early morning light, cause I was a painter before I was anything else, including a friend.

Then I went home to my father in Ferara and told him our chances of Garganelli patronage were over.

What did you do wrong? he shouted,
cause first he was furious : then he was all pride puffed up, all *no child of mine will prostitute itself* : in his fury my father looked old to me for the first time, so I took off my boots and looked at my feet which had blistered from the walking all day with nothing between skin and leather : the blisters were like little balls of unclear glass surfacing in the skin of me : how would I paint such opaqueness? What kind or what making of white would it take?

Even as I thought it I felt white all over at the loss of my friend and thought that I'd never know other colours again.

Funny to think of it now, that bleak evening : cause the biggest patrons of my short life *were* after all to be the Garganelli family, and the reason I couldn't find the legging-stuff was that my friend Barto had rolled it in his hand and put it in his pocket and taken it as souvenir, as he told me years later sitting on the stone step by my feet while I worked on the decoration for the tomb of his father in their chapel.

Girl : do you hear me?

cause although it seemed to be the end of the world to me –

it wasn't.

There was a lot more world : cause roads that look set to take you in one direction will sometimes twist back on themselves without ever seeming anything other than straight, and Barto and I were soon friends again : no time at all : many things get forgiven in the course of a life : nothing is finished or unchangeable except death and even death will bend a little if what you tell of it is told right : we were friends until I died (if I did die ever, cause I remember no death) and I trust that he remembered me lovingly till the day he died himself (if he did, cause I have no memory of such a thing).

I am watching the girl watch an old old story, the

performance of love through a too-small window : yesterday it was the theatre of saints, today it's love : albeit love performed for an audience : but an audience is only ever really interested in its own needs regardless, whoever you were or are, Cosmo, Lorenzo, Ercole, School of Unknown Painters of Ferara Workshop : *I forgive.*

Cause nobody knows us : except our mothers, and they hardly do (and also tend disappointingly to die before they ought).

Or our fathers, whose failings while they're alive (and absences after they're dead) infuriate.

Or our siblings, who want us dead too cause what they know about us is that somehow we got away with not having to carry the bricks and stones like they did all those years.

Cause nobody's the slightest idea who we are, or who we were, not even we ourselves

— except, that is, in the glimmer of a moment of fair business between strangers, or the nod of knowing and agreement between friends.

Other than these, we go out anonymous into the insect air and all we are is the dust of colour, brief engineering of wings towards a glint of light on a blade of grass or a leaf in a summer dark.

Let me tell you about the time I was seen, entered and understood by someone I was acquainted with in my life for 10 minutes only.

I'm walking along the road and I pass a fieldful

of infidel workers dressed in the white that marks them as worker and makes their skin all the darker : they're ploughing and planting : I go past freely on my way.

Further on down the road someone springs out from a copse of trees : he's one of the working men, far enough from the field to seem a touch fugitive. I pass quite close to him : his white clothes are ragged, but less from poverty, I see as I come closer, than from what seems the strength of his own body, as if it can't help but break through : his sleeves are frayed by the strength of his hands and forearms : his knees have made holes in the cloth, being so strong : the line of dark hairs above his groin sits visible : his eyes are reddened by work.

When I've gone a little distance this man calls after me, a word I don't know.

When I don't stop, he calls the word again.

It is a benign word as well as a pressing one : something in the sound of it stops me and turns me around on the road.

He is standing in the shade of the copse, perhaps so as not to be seen, maybe more for a rest from the sun, cause I can see even from the distance I'm keeping that nothing about him fears a foreman or overseer : nothing about him fears anything.

Did you mean to call after me? I say.

Yes, he says

(sure enough there's no one else on the road).

97

Tell me again, I say, that word. The word you were calling me with.

I was calling you a word in my language, he says.

An infidel word? I say.

He smiles a broad smile. His teeth are very strong.

An infidel word, he says. I don't know the word for it in your language.

I smile back. I come a little nearer.

What does your word mean? I say.

It means, he says, you who are more than one thing. You who exceed expectations.

He asks me if I can help him. He tells me he needs *a twist*.

A what? I say.

A –, I don't know the word, he says. I need to bind my clothes around me, I need a binding thing, for here.

He gestures around his midriff.

You mean a belt? I say. Something to tie?

(cause his shirt is flapping open on him except for one clasp at the collarbone, and it's March, a cold beginning to the month).

I have a length of rope in my haversack, bought in the market in Florence from a man that told me it was a lucky rope from a hanging and quartering (cause if you carry a hanging rope, it means you'll never yourself be hanged, he said) : it's a good length and a fair thickness and will probably do : I walk back towards him as he comes towards me : I hold out the rope to him : he looks at it, takes it, weighs it in his hand, then smiles at me as if to pay me with the smile.

When you've nothing, at least you've all of it.

I have never seen such a beautiful man.

He sees me see this beauty in him and it makes his nature rise.

In the copse of trees at the side of the road there I put my mouth to him and play him like the muse Euterpe plays her wooden flute : then both : he has a smell and a taste about him of grass, clean earth, bread, sweat : he makes redness at the eye a sign of something other than tiredness : he makes calloused hands a means of greater feeling when they go beneath clothes.

We stood up after and I was covered in grass and earth, so was he : he dusted me down : he picked one grass piece off my shoulder and smiled a goodbye, put the piece of grass between his teeth, slung my rope over his shoulder and walked back openly to the fields and the work he'd left.

It was all : it was nothing : it was more than enough.

Fine.

As if the girl knows I've come to the end of my story she shuts the love window down dark : the poorly performed love-acts disappear : I think they have not cheered her cause she seems very doleful.

99

She sits with the shut window on her lap.

We watch a blackbird, with 4 other blackbirds of both male and female type, chase a bird that's not a blackbird to stop it eating with them at a bush loaded with berries the red of which is the red which the great Cennini in his handbook called dragon's blood, good for parchment but not for long.

The girl gets up and crosses the patch of grass : halfway across, the brother behind the wicker divide shouts something in their language at her : she calls something back at him, something longer than a name or a *stop it*, something more like a game or a spell and she walks past the wicker heavy-browed and dismissive : then she's under a deluge of twigs and little stones and rubble, he is standing on a ledge or barrel and he has them all on a little spade and is throwing them first one lot then the next in the air so they land all over her like it's raining little stones and sticks : she stops : instead of being angry she laughs out loud.

She stands with her arms out and away from herself and from nowhere her misery is vanished, she is laughing like a child : then she puts the window down on the grass and dives behind the wicker fence, she fells her brother and drags him out on to the grass and the earth, both laughing and rolling on the ground and she tickles him into even more hilarity.

100

It is a fine thing to see a sudden happiness like that.

She is lucky in such a brother and such a love : between me and my brothers, even though there was nothing between us but air, there were invisible divisions thick as the walls of her room.

Back in that room, the room with the bed in it, back comes the sadness : she sits behind the veil of it for many whole minutes then she shakes herself to her feet and takes off her dusty shirt, shakes the dust and stuff off it out of the window : she shoulders the shirt back on, leaves its buttons unbuttoned and sits on the bed again.

There are many made pictures, all true to life in their workings, on the 4 walls of this room.

The south wall, along which the narrow bed runs, has a picture of 2 beautiful girls seen walking along like friends do : one has gold hair, one has dark but the dark of her hair is sunlit to lightness – both the heads of the girls are : they are walking along a street with awnings : it's a warm place : their clothes are mosaic gold and azzurrite : the girls are in conversational commerce and look as if between sentences : the goldener one is preoccupied : the darker-headed girl turns her head towards her in a most natural gesture in open air and so she can see the other better : her looking has about it politeness, humility, respect, a kind of gentle intent.

The picture is by a great artist surely in its

patchwork of light, dark, determination, gentleness.

The west wall has a large picture of 1 singularly beautiful woman : her eyes look straight out : *there is something just beyond you*, it says, *I can see it and it's sad, puzzling, a mystery* : this is a very clever thing to do with eyes and demeanour : one of her arms is tight around her neck holding herself, at least I think it is her own arm, and this means the curve of her hair (which is coloured between dark and light) round her face makes her face look like the mask that means sadness in Greek ancients : she is sorry I think : I think on behalf of victims : cause she is a figuring of St Monica I guess from it saying underneath in words that chance to be in my own language M O N I C A   V I C T I M S.

Behind the head of the bed the whole east wall here is all pictures, lots of pictures, of yet another woman : it is the same woman in all the pictures with the same laughing eyes : there is love in their arrangement, they are an overwhelm in this arrangement, they fall almost into and over each other : but the woman in these pictures is not the woman from the picture palace : no, this is a dark and different lady who has this warm demeanour and a finesse too about her clothes and her body in them which I admire : there are many portraits of her and at different ages like the spill of a life straight on to a wall : there are some done in greys of a small child I also take to be her.

On this last wall, the north wall, on which I can see there has been some dampwork done and plastering which has an air of recency, there is 1 picture : it is the study the girl took with her magic box tablet of the house we sat outside on the poorly made wall and were looking at until the woman with the bristles came and dispatched us.

She fixed this study of this house – the windows, a door, a gate, a high bush, the front façade – on to the wall by her bed with the earnestness I sense central to her nature.

Then she sat on the bed and stared into it with a like earnestness almost as if she wished she were of the size to enter it bodily.

Better to have a much bigger picture, lifesize and detailed, to look to with such intent.

A painter could make a larger one from a small study with ease : if I had materials or even just one arm, I'd

like when the court of the Duke of Modena and Reggio, the Marquis of Ferara, Borse (whom I'd seen those 10 and more years ago serenaded by the tiny swan-blood angel of Justice) put out a call for painters to cover the walls of the palace of not being bored with lifesize pictures of him and his world.

This longing came I think in part from the fact that his father had had a Bible made before and to rival it Borse had wanted a bigger better one of his own, filled full of tiny miniatures, a thousand small pictures of holy things and people including some pictures of local scenes : I see him in my mind's eye, Borse, sitting regarding these pages one day, each picture beautiful, each a masterpiece less than the size of the palm of his hand, and finding himself thinking how if he had such pictures made large enough, say they were the size of his own substantial body, then he could be seen by all the townspeople and all the neighbouring dignitaries to walk about inside a Bible of himself : and what better time to do such a thing than now since he was finally to be made first ever Duke of Ferara too which he'd waited for all these years, and by the Pope himself no less.

So he had a new upper floor built on the old palace his ancestor Alberto built way before any of us : the palace was quite far from the middle of town but with a new big hall in it for feasts and dancing and round that hall's walls was where he wanted painted a whole year of his own life, month by month, to show the people who'd live in the future what a good ruler he'd been.

So in my 33rd year, when I'd been in Venice and Florence and learning my trade and had made good money in Bologna and also a name in Ferara by my work at the palace of beautiful flowers, Mr de Prisciano the Falcon looked my horse and myself and my torch bearer up and down and assigned me for my talent 3 whole months of Borse's painted year, a season to myself alone, March, April, May, in fact the whole east wall : other lesser painters from the court workshop were to collaborate on the other months : it was a winter–spring job, cause the new building was brick not stone, which meant less time in the making : but as fast as you can go is best for fresco in any case.

I got the blues and golds from Venice cause skills are nothing without good materials and good materials and skill together will make for a kind of grace (and also for good payment in the end).

We stood in the new hall.

(Cosmo wasn't there.)

I knew none of the workshop workers : compared, they were mere boys : their eyes on me let me know they knew my reputation.

(Cosmo'd had a private tour of the room on a different day. Cosmo'd been *instrumental* in the *design*.)

Francescho, this is your assistant, the Falcon said.

The boy at his side looked 16 years of age and had the demeanour of a pickpocket.

(Cosmo had more assistants than Cosmo had family : most of the people in this room had been assistant to Cosmo one time or another.)

I waited till the Falcon moved off to speak elsewhere.

Were you ever assistant to Cosmo? I asked.

The pickpocket boy shook his head.

Good, I said. Cause if I'm not here and Cosmo ever tries to touch my wall, I want you to refuse him. Tell him it's by order of the Marquis, he's not to touch my wall.

Is that a lie? the pickpocket said slanting his eyes at me.

Yes, I said.

I'm a very bad liar, the pickpocket said. I need paid extra for lies.

I'll pay you what you're worth, I said.

But what about when I'm working on my own bit of wall? the pickpocket said. Cause if they think I'm any good, I'm to be let to do my own work maybe on August or September too. What if he comes in and I'm so busy I don't see him?

Not see Cosmo come in? I said. Then you've really never seen Cosmo.

Oh, you mean *him*, the pickpocket said. I know who you mean. I'll lie to *him* for nothing.

The Falcon told a boy in court clothes to climb on to a chair and stand on the mixing table in the middle of the room : then the Falcon positioned himself beneath the boy, who dipped his head and his knee to put his ear closer to the Falcon then stood straight up again in an instant on the table.

106

That way, I needn't, the Falcon said.

THAT WAY I NEEDN'T, the boy shouted as if through a horn and in a voice unexpectedly deep for such a small boy.

Raise my voice, the Falcon said.

RAISE MY VOICE, the dipping boy said.

In this way the Falcon let us know us what would be expected of us.

The walls will be THE WALLS WILL BE. Divided from left to right DIVIDED FROM LEFT TO RIGHT. Except here and here EXCEPT HERE AND HERE. Where there'll be WHERE THERE'LL BE. Gracious city scenes GRACIOUS CITY SCENES. The scenes will be THE SCENES WILL BE. Scenes of the Dukedom SCENES OF THE DUKEDOM. Of good architecture OF GOOD ARCHITECTURE. Scenes of shows and jousts SCENES OF SHOWS AND JOUSTS. And here will feature AND HERE WILL FEATURE. The Papal visit THE PAPAL VISIT. By which the beloved BY WHICH THE BELOVED. Marquis will be made MARQUIS WILL BE MADE. First Duke of Ferara FIRST DUKE OF FERARA. In celebration IN CELEBRATION. Of this historic OF THIS HISTORIC. Event in our town EVENT IN OUR TOWN. The walls of this room THE WALLS OF THIS ROOM. All the way round ALL THE WAY ROUND. Will tell this story WILL TELL THIS STORY.

The Falcon held up a hand and moved round to the other side of the table : the boy on the table stepped over to be behind him again and dipped down to hear : the Falcon gestured to my wall : down up, down up.

THE YEAR BEGINS HERE. IT BEGINS WITH MARCH. THEN APRIL HERE. THEN MAY HERE.

The boy resembled a drinking bird : the Falcon came round the table to face the north wall : the boy dipped

(later I put this boy in my month of March : I attached a lewd monkey to his lower leg)

the boy rose.

JUNE TO SEPTEMBER, the boy said. HERE, HERE, HERE. OCTOBER TO DECEMBER. HERE AND HERE. (He turned to face the west wall with the Falcon, then spun round to the south.) JANUARY IS HERE. FEBRUARY IS HERE. THE WALL SECTIONS AND MONTHS. WILL BE DIVIDED. FROM EACH OTHER. BY PAINTED PILASTERS. BUT WITHIN EACH SECTION. THERE WILL ALSO BE. ANOTHER DIVISION. CAUSE EACH MONTH. WILL BE DIVIDED. TOP TO BOTTOM. INTO 3 PIECES. AT THE TOP. THE MYTHICAL GODS. ARRIVE IN CHARIOTS. WITH THE SEASONS. MINERVA, VENUS, APOLLO. MERCURY, JUPITER, CERES.

Vulcan, and so on, the Falcon said waving his hand (cause he had no notes with him and had forgotten his order of gods).

VULCAN AND SO ON, the boy said.

At the top of the new wall we were to paint lifesize gods arriving all through the year : at the bottom we were to paint lifesize scenes of Borse's year, with the seasonal work of a common year and the illustrious Borse always at its centre.

In the middle, though, between these, there was a broad blue sky space planned.

(When I heard this I was pleased, cause I'd quality azzurrite from Venice.)

As if floating in this blue, like clouds, the Falcon wanted a frieze of astrologicals : he wanted 3 figures for each month, one symbolizing each 10 days.

GOD TAKES PLEASURE, the boy announced. AS WE KNOW. IN GIVING US THINGS. ARRANGED IN 3s. SO TO CORRESPOND. EACH MONTH WILL BE. SPLIT INTO 3. GODS THE TOP. SKY IN THE MIDDLE. EARTH DOWN BELOW. EACH BLOCK OF SKY. AT THE CENTRE. OF EACH MONTH. WILL ALSO BE. SPLIT INTO 3.

The gods, the stars, the earth, the Falcon said.

THE GODS THE STARS THE EARTH, the boy on the table shouted at us. THE GODS THE STARS THE COURT. THE GODS THE STARS

109

OUR PRINCE. GOING ABOUT THE WORLD. A
WORLD HE'S MADE. PEACEABLE AND
PROSPEROUS. IN HIS GENEROSITY. IN HIS
SPLENDOUR. IN HIS WHITE GLOVES. THE
SEASONS FRUITFUL ROUND HIM. THE
WORKERS HAPPY ROUND HIM. THE PEOPLE
FULL OF JOY. ABOVE THIS, SKY. ABOVE
THAT, GODS. IN TRIUMPHANT ARRIVALS.
ON THEIR CHARIOTS. SURROUNDED BY.
THEIR ASSOCIATED SYMBOLS. AND USUAL
ATTRIBUTES. THE DESIGN FOR THIS. CAN
BE FOUND. IN THE ANTEROOM. BEHIND
THE EAST WALL. STUDY IT CLOSELY. DO
NOT DEVIATE. FROM ITS INSTRUCTION. OR
ITS EXAMPLE. OR ITS DEMONSTRATION. IN
ANY WAY.

And for this, the pickpocket at my side said. We're
to be paid. Only 10 pence per. Bloody square foot.

I made a note to myself to ask the Falcon about
my rate of pay : the Falcon, when the speech was
done, put his arm round my shoulder and took me
over to show me my own wall.

Borse departing on hunt – here, he said. Borse
dispensing justice to aged loyal infidel – here. Borse
presenting gift to Court Fool – here. St Giorgio day
palio – round about here. Gathering of poets – up
there. Gathering of university scholars, professors
and wise men – up over there. Representation of
the Fates – here. Spring image, fertility kind of

thing, use your imagination – that area there.
Apollo – there. Venus – there. Minerva – there. All
in chariots. Minerva will need unicorns. Venus will
need swans. Apollo will need Aurora driving and
he'll need a bow and arrow. He'll also need a lute
and the delphic tripod and the snakeskin.

I nodded.

Illustrate the gods from the poems, he said.

I will, I said none the wiser.

Now, he said. The decans. For the 3 decans of
each month, check the schema in the anteroom. For
instance, as the schema shows, and this is very
important, Francescho. The first decan of Aries
should be dressed in white. He should be tall, dark,
powerful, a masterful man of great good power in
the world. He is to be the guardian not just of the
room but of the whole year. He should be standing
next to a ram to symbolize the constellation. And
next to that please put a figure which stands for
youth and fruitfulness, holding, say, an arrow, for
skill and for aim. A self-portrait maybe,
Francescho, your own fine face, what do you say?

He winked an eye at me.

And over here, April, one of the decans should
hold a key. Make the key large. And over here . . .
and here . . . on and on he went, *and one should
have the feet of a camel and one should be holding
a javelin and a baton and one should be holding a
lizard, and . . .*

111

There was no space left in all the requirements for asking about payment.

But I knew my work would speak for itself and bring when done its own due.

I began with May and Apollo : I worked hard on the horses : I invented 4 falcons all sitting on a birdframe : I added the bow and the arrow but had to give a standing girl minstrel the lute (cause Apollo's hands were already full with the bow, the arrow and the black hole of the sun which I made a little like a black seed, a burnt walnut or the anus of a cat, which is what the sun looks like if you look too long at the sun).

What was a delphic tripod?

I painted a 3-legged stool with a snakeskin draped over it.

When he saw it, the Falcon nodded.

(Phew.)

I painted all the citizens of the Ferara court, not as they looked now but as an infinite crowd of babies swarming out of a hole in the ground as if conjured from nothing, replicating by the second and all as naked as the day they were born, their teething rings around their necks on cords their only jewels and adornments, their arms cordially through each others' arms as they went their passeggiata.

When he came up on the scaffolding and saw this the Falcon laughed out loud : he was pleased enough to drop his hand to my breeches to take hold of me where something or nothing should be.

Ah! he said.

I'd surprised him.

He sobered.

I see, he said.

But he put his arm round my shoulder in a brotherly way, and I liked him all the more, the thin scholarly Falcon.

You caught me out. It's not at all what I expected after the dishevelled state of my maid when you came to my house that day, he said

(cause when I'd come to his house and drawn for him the running torch bearer, and the girl at the door had been sent finally to assure me of employment and dispatch me, I'd asked her could I borrow her cap just to have a look at and she'd taken it off, then I'd backed her gently further into the house off the street so no one could see us and I'd asked her kindly to take off some other things for me just to have a look at, which she smiling did, then I'd kissed her cause I should in the places bared, which she'd liked and had kissed me back and before I'd left she'd tied the cap sweetly in jest about my head and said *you make a very handsome girl, sir*).

So you're a little less, Francescho, than I believed, the Falcon said now.

A very little thing less only, Mr de Prisciano, I

said, and no less at all when it comes to picturemaking.

No, you're talented, true, all the same, he said.

Exactly the same, I said. No less.

I said it with passion but he wasn't listening : instead he slapped the side of his own leg and laughed.

I've just understood, he said. Why Cosmo calls you it.

(*Cosmo? talks of me?*)

Cosmo calls me what? I said.

You don't know? the Falcon said.

I shook my head.

That Cosmo, when he talks of you, calls you Francescha? the Falcon said.

He what? I said.

Francescha del Cosso, the Falcon said.

(*Cosmo.*

I forgive.)

A mere court painter, I said. I'll never be. I'll never do anyone's bidding.

Well but what are you right now, the Falcon said, but a court painter?

(It was true.)

But at least I'll never knowingly choose to be in the pay of the flagellants, I said

(cause I knew Cosmo to be making a lot of money with the images asked of him by some).

The Falcon shrugged.

The flagellants pay as well as anybody else, he said. And have you seen his St Giorgio for the cathedral organ? Francescho. It's sublime. And – didn't Cosmo train you? I thought you'd been apprentice to Cosmo.

Cosmo? Train *me*? I said.

Who then? the Falcon said.

I learned by my eyes, I said, and I learned from the masters.

Which masters? the Falcon said.

The great Alberti, I said. The great Cennini.

Ah, the Falcon said. Self-taught.

He shook his head.

And from Cristoforo, I said.

Da Ferara? the Falcon said.

Del Cossa, I said.

The brickmaker? the Falcon said. Taught you this?

I pointed down to my new assistant, the pickpocket, filling the time between plastermaking and colourgrinding by doing the drawing work I'd set him of the pile of bricks I'd made him fetch in from the gardens : I look back at my rich court babies pouring out of the hole in the stony ground into life as if the whole world was nothing but theatre and them its godgiven critics.

Since I was infant I've lived, breathed, slept brick

and stone, but you can't eat bricks, you can't eat stones, Mr de Prisciano, which is why –

(and here I got ready to ask for my money).

– on the contrary, the Falcon said. Best way to get birds to hunt well, no? Is to feed them stones

(cause it's true that this is what falconers will do to keep a bird hungry and sharp, they'll fool it into thinking it's been well fed by giving it pellets of stone so that when the hood is removed and the bird out working it's surprised by its own hunger which makes it sharper-eyed than ever in finding prey).

But it was a dodge to my question and he knew it, the Falcon : he looked askance, ashamed : he looked to my army of babies instead.

Infantile sophisticates, he said. Bare of everything, seen for what they are. Good. And I like your Apollo. Where's the lute? Ah. Yes. And I like very much the grace of your minstrels. And – these – oh. What's this?

The gathering of poets you wanted, I said, in the top corner, as required.

But – is that – isn't it – *me*? he said.

(It was true I'd painted unasked a likeness of him, in with the poets : I sensed he'd prefer to be seen as a poet rather than a scholar.)

What's that I'm holding? he said.

The heart, I said.

Oh! he said.

And this'll be, see, here, heat, I said. As if you're

examining a heart off which heat is rising like breath from a mouth on a cold day.

He coloured : then he gave me a wry look.

You're a politician, Francescho, he said.

No, Mr de Prisciano, I said. A painter, by the work of my arms and hands and eyes and by the worth of the work.

But he turned his back very quick then in case I asked about the money again.

On his way down the ladder backwards he looked back up at me.

Keep it up, he said.

Then he winked.

So to speak, he said.

(One night I came through the curtain over the month room door, it was only midnight, not late, a good damp night and very few others working cause I preferred it when quiet, but as I came down the room I saw by the shadows the swing of a torch up on one of the platforms at the far end of the room : I stayed in the dark by the foot of the scaffolding : the Falcon, I could hear, was somewhere up there speaking to someone –

Veneziano, yes. Piero, certainly. Castagno, maybe some Flems, certainly a bit of Mantegna, Donatello. But as if, your Grace, the work's soaked itself deep in them all but then washed itself new and clean and come up with a freshness like nothing I've ever.

117

Your Grace.

Yes, the other said. I'm not sure I like the way he's done my face.

There's a charm, the Falcon said. A great, I don't know what else to call it. Likeableness.

Must never underestimate charm, the other said.

Lightness of spirit, the Falcon said. Not got from anyone. Not Piero. Not Flemish.

The women's clothes are very fine, the other said. But am I well starred throughout? The auspices? And how like the gods? I mean in inference?

Very, your Grace, but very human all the same, the Falcon said. A rare thing, to be able to do gods and humans both, no?

Hm, the other said.

Look at this woman and this child here, just standing, but in such a choreography, the Falcon said. It's motherhood. But it's more than motherhood. It's as if they're in a conversation, but a conversation made of stance.

And does this particular painter do any more of me? the other said.

Yes, your Grace, the Falcon said

and I heard them move on the platform and I ducked into the shadow of the wall.

Who is he, then, the lad? the other said then as the ladder beneath him creaked.

Not a lad at all, your Grace, the Falcon said.

I held my breath.

– full-fledged painter, well over 30 years, the
Falcon said.

What's his looks like? the other said.

Youthful in demeanour, sir, the Falcon said.
Girlish, you might say. Youthful in the work, too.
Freshness all through it. Freshness and
maturity both.

What's he called? the other said.

I heard the Falcon tell him –

and not long after, since the Falcon had liked
Cosmo's St Giorgio so much, I figured him into the
fresco again, this time in the month of March (the
part of the wall my work was at its best), this time
as a falconer with his clothes winged up like the
falcon on his hand and the torch bearer drawing
he'd liked and I sat him on a horse with a stance a
bit like Cosmo's Giorgio : I made him young and
vigorous : I gave him a tasselled hunting glove :
above all I made the balls on his horse good and
large.)

Painting the months took months.

I made things look both close and distant.

In the upper space I gave the unicorns translucent
horns.

In the lower space I gave the horses eyes that can
follow you round the room, cause those are the
God eyes and whoever has them in a painting or
fresco holds the eyes of whoever looks at the work,
and this is no blasphemy, merely a reasserting of

the power of the gaze back at us from outside us always on us.

I painted the differing skies of May and April and lastly March (cause I progressed from May to March and grew more used to the plaster from each to each, which made the work flourish) : I dared paint, in Venus's upper space, with its groups of lovers standing in their 3s, women openly kissed and touched by men (to enrage any visiting Florentines who hate to see such goings-on).

Throughout I did as the great Alberti in his book suggests the best picturemakers should always do and included people of many ages and kinds, plus chickens, ducks, horses, dogs, rabbits, hares, birds of all sorts, all in a lively commerce in and about a variety of landscapes and buildings : and, cause Alberti asks in his book *that as a reward for my pains in writing this work, painters who read it might kindly paint my face into their istoria in such a way that it seems pleasant* I did this too and painted him into it in the gathering of wise men in the goddess Minerva's space : cause those who do good work should always be honoured, which is something both the greats Alberti and Cennini agree on. As a symmetric to the wise professors I placed on the other side of Minerva's chariot, where the Falcon wanted the Fates to sit, a gathering of working women and included every woman's face I could remember from the streets and workshops and the pleasure houses : I arranged them round a good loom and gave them well-made cavework as a landscape behind them.

I painted my brothers.

I painted the figure of my mother resplendent.

I painted a ram with the look of my father.

In these ways I filled the Marquis's months with those who had peopled my own on the earth.

But when I did, as can happen when you work to picture someone in paint, as soon as I'd painted them into the skin of the fresco they stopped being the people I knew : this happened especially in the colour blue meant for sky, the place between the gods and the earth.

A picture is most times just picture : but sometimes a picture is more : I looked at the faces in torchlight and I saw they were escapees : they'd broken free from me and from the wall that had made and held them and even from themselves.

I like very much a foot, say, or a hand, coming over the edge and over the frame into the world beyond the picture, cause a picture is a real thing in the world and this shift is a marker of this reality : and I like a figure to shift into that realm between the picture and the world just like I like a body really to be present under painted clothes where something, a breast, a chest, an elbow, a knee, presses up from beneath and brings life to a fabric : I like an angel's knee particularly, cause holy things are worldly too and it's not a blasphemy to think so, just a further understanding of the realness of holy things.

But these are mere mundane pleasures – I'm tempted to hire a small boy, stand him on a table and have him shout those words MERE MUNDANE PLEASURES – beside the thing that happens when the life of the picture itself steps beyond the frame.

Cause then it does 2 opposing things at once.

The one is, it lets the world be seen and understood.

The other is, it unchains the eyes and the lives of those who see it and gives them a moment of freedom, from its world and from their world both.

And I wasn't slave to this work for much longer myself cause when I neared the finish of the month of March it *was* the month of March, near New Year : one day all the assistants and the workshop painters were standing in a huddle in the middle of the room : there was passionate talk, it was about the infidel uprising, I reckoned from up on the scaffolding (cause there'd been an uprising for more food and money among the field workers, 10 men beaten cause of the actions of 1 man, and rumour that some of the 10 were near death and that the 1 who organized the rising was already cut in pieces).

But no, the talk was nothing to do with infidels :

what they were arguing so passionate about down there was their latest request to Borse for better pay.

Master Francescho! the pickpocket shouted up the side of the scaffolding.

Ercole! I shouted back down without turning.

(I was touching up the Graces.)

Let us sign your name, the pickpocket shouted up, to this petition alongside ours!

No! I shouted down

cause they had petitioned twice for more money already and the second time, instead of giving them more, Borse had had them all (me too) presented with his medal, the one with his head on one side, Justice on the other and the words on it : *haec te unum : you and she are one.*

It was a pretty medal and had an appearance of valuc, but Borse had had so many given out all over town (and not just here but in his other towns too) that they fetched very little at market.

But Borse was well known for his generosity : didn't he pay his favoured musicians handsomely? Didn't he cover Cosmo in precious stones?

True, so far I'd been paid the same rate as the others, but it was an oversight, I knew.

I intended to write to the Marquis directly and point out the oversight.

Cause I knew myself exceptional (the only painter here not working to Cosmo's cartoons, the only one brought in from outside beyond the court workshop) : and when the wrong money first came I had asked the Falcon to intercede : but the Falcon had looked at me, doleful.

Did you not get your medal, then? he said, by which I knew he had no power in this matter.

The Falcon had liked his St Giorgio a lot : I could see he liked himself as a man of action as well as a poet cause he'd flushed up red to the back of his ears.

But he'd shaken his head at the madmen from the madhouse that I'd painted running behind the horses and donkeys as if part themselves of the palio, their straitjacket tabs flying out behind them : he'd shaken his head again at the distant view of the Marquis's hunt – the Marquis and all his men on horseback heading straight towards the edge of the abyss, a dog looking coolly down into it (the abyss I'd made by painting a crack in the foreground architecture, a perspective I took great pride in).

One picture I'd made in particular made the Falcon turn pale.

Here, he was saying. No. This can't stay. You have to change it.

He was pointing at the first decan for March, at the place where he'd asked for a powerful guardian man and I'd painted him one, in the shape of an infidel.

Something like this is bad enough as it is, the Falcon was saying. Bad enough by itself. And on top of this you ask me to go to him to *get you more money*? Francescho. Can't you see? Haven't you eyes? He'll have you whipped. And if I ask for more money he'll have me whipped too. No, no, no. It's got to come off. Cut it out. Start again. Redo it.

I cowered inside my skin : I was foolish, I'd end up unpaid and dismissed and be poor for a year : I'd never get work at the court again and I was badly out of pocket cause the golds and the blues had cost half a year's money : so I readied myself to ask the Falcon, what would he like me to paint there instead?

But when I came to speak, instead of any of these words I heard myself say only

no.

The Falcon next to me gave a little start.

Francescho. Redo it, he said again.

I shook my head.

No.

That can't stay either, he was saying pointing at the Graces up in the Venus space. That Grace there. Make her lighter. Far too dark.

I had given the Graces fashionable hairstyles : I had given them fleeting bodily resemblances, Ginevra and Agnola both facing, Isotta with her back to us : I had painted them holding apples and painted some Vs in 2 spindly trees to catch and

repeat the shape of the place on the facing Graces
where all human life and much pleasure originates :
I had placed 2 birds in each spindly tree : everything
rhythmic : even the apples and breasts were
resemblances : it was the Grace I'd made like Isotta
that had caught his eye : but even she, beautiful as
she was, barely held his eye cause I saw that he
couldn't not look, kept looking again and again to
the infidel in his white work rags in the space of the
best blue.

Then – a miracle – something shifted in the
Falcon, changed in the way he stood beside me.

I saw him shake his head again but in a
different way.

He called for more light.

More light came.

He put his hands round his face.

When he took his hands away I saw that the
Falcon was laughing.

Such audacity. Well. It's true, you've done exactly
what I asked you, he said. Though I didn't ask for
such beauty. Well, let's see. I'll, I don't know, I'll fix
it. I'll redirect him to the figure of the old man here
bending the knee to him like he wanted. *Borse
giving out justice to an aging infidel.*

Thank you, Mr de Prisciano, I said.

But, in turn, do me a couple of kindnesses,
Francescho, the Falcon said. Make the bending man
a shade darker at the skin to show the new Duke's

justice as bigger than any expectation. But I'm warning you. Don't be any more of a fool. Francescho. Do you hear? And lighten up the colour of that Grace, the one with her back to us. And we might, we just might, get away with it.

Get away with it : as if I had planned a hidden satire or a sedition : but in all honesty, when I looked at my own pictures they surprised even me with their knowledge : cause at the same time as I'd been painting these questioning things I had been telling myself that the Marquis would be just, he'd naturally know and honour my worth and reward me properly for it, of course he would, even if I pictured him and his hunt all clipclopping as if blind towards a crevasse : cause the life of painting and making is a matter of double knowledge so that your own hands will reveal a world to you to which your mind's eye, your conscious eye, is often blind.

The Falcon was shaking his head at the infidel : he was no longer laughing : his mouth fell open : he put his hand to his mouth.

And if he asks anything, he said with his hand still over his mouth, I'll tell him, I don't know, I'll say it's, it's —

A figure from the French Romances, I said.

A figure from a little-known French Romance, the Falcon said. One he'd never admit to not knowing. Since we all know how well he knows them all.

Then he'd looked me in the eyes.

But I can't get you any more money, Francescho, he said. Don't ask me again.

Well then, I'd write and ask myself, direct, I thought as the Falcon descended the scaffolding : I did not need an interceder.

Master Francescho! the pickpocket called now from below.

Ercole! I called back down.

I was reworking the Graces, paler reminders now : *give, accept, give back* : but adequate Graces, still substantial : I'd sliced them out and replastered and repainted but I'd kept them human, made them all Agnolas like a triplet of herself 3 different ways.

Forgive me! the pickpocket shouted.

For what? I shouted back.

For signing the letter on your behalf! the pickpocket shouted up

(cause there had been murmurings among the assistants and workshop painters that they were being refused more money precisely cause I hadn't signed, cause I hadn't asked for more with them the times they'd asked before, which might make it look to the Marquis, they said, like I believed 10 pennies a square foot enough pay).

But not by my name, Ercole? I called back down.

But yes by your name, the pickpocket shouted up. And I can well do your hand, Master Francescho, as you know. We need paid. And the more of us asking, the better.

I brightened the apple of the farthest right Grace.

Ercole! I called down.

Yes, Master Francescho? he called up.

I leaned over the scaffolding and spoke quietly direct.

I no longer need an assistant. Pack your things. Find another master,

cause I knew it was simply a mistake, my mispayment, and Borse a man who cared above all things for *justice* : hadn't I painted his head there underneath the very word justice carved in stone under a fine garlanded stone arch in a lunette that resembled his own double-faced medal? and beneath that a scene of him dispensing justice to grateful townspeople? He cared about justice more than anything (perhaps cause his own father, Nicco, as we all knew, the same way we knew the legends of the saints and all the holy stories, had a reputation not just for favouring illegitimate sons but for *unspeakable unjustness* having decided in a temper that his second wife, the beautiful one, and his firstborn son, the handsome one, had fallen in love with each other, for which he had them both beheaded in a dungeon then buried somewhere, nobody knew where) : Borse cared so much about justice that in the anteroom on the other side of this wall on which I was brightening the apples of the Graces he was having a room made where he planned to try small matters of civic justice and we all knew he'd commissioned stucchi of Faith, Hope, Fortitude, Charity, Prudence, Temperance, but that he'd asked the French stucchi master most specifically for 6 Virtues only and to *leave Justice out* cause he was himself Justice, Justice was herself him, and when he was present in the room then Justice was present too since Justice had Borse's chin, his head, his face, his chest and moreover his stomach.

Good work, good pay, as the great Cennini says in his Handbook for picturemakers : this is a kind of justice too that if you use good materials and you practise good skills then the least you may expect is that good money will be your reward : and if it so happens that it isn't then God himself will reward you : this is what Cennini promises : so I'd write to the Marquis : I'd write now on the eve of New Year or tomorrow on New Year's Day cause it's a time of generosity (and maybe it was true, maybe the generous Borse did believe, cause I'd not signed my name on the other petitions, that I *did* think 10 pennies enough).

I saw sadness in the pickpocket's back below : you can tell many things from a back : he was packing away his tools and things in his bags : who knew, maybe if Borse were to read a letter from me

130

he'd not just right the error for me, he'd maybe be persuaded to be more generous to those lesser workers too, with a bit of luck and justice, though they'd need the luck, not being as worthy of it as me.

(I am small, sitting on stone in the smell of horse piss holding in my hand the shrunken head with the wing stuck out of it : the thing in my hand is the start of a tree, with a bit of luck and justice.

Luck, I know, is to do with chance happening.

But what's justice? I call at my mother's back.

She is on her way to the barrel full of linens.

Fairness, she calls over her shoulder. Rightness. Getting your due. You getting as much to eat and as much learning and as many chances as your brothers, and them as much and as many as anyone in this city or this world.

So justice is to do with food then, and with learning.

But what's a fallen seed from a tree to do with any of it? I call.

She stops and turns.

We need both luck and justice to get to live the life we're meant for, she says. Lots of seeds don't get to. Think. They fall on stone, they get crushed to pieces, rot in the rubbish at the roadside, put down roots that don't take, die of thirst, die of heat, die of cold before they've even broken open underground, never mind grown a leaf. But a tree is

131

a clever creation and sends out lots of seeds every year, so for all those ones that don't get to grow there are hundreds, thousands that will.

I look at how over by the brickpiles there's a straggle of seedlings in a clump, seedlings not even as tall as me : they look like nothing at all : I look up at the roof where the 3 thin twiggy arms are proof that a seed's taken root at the gutter : that's luck : But justice? And I am not a seed or a tree : I am a person : I won't break open : I haven't got roots : how can I be seed or tree or both?

I still don't see how justice is anything to do with seeds, I call.

You'll learn, she shouts back from in the barrel trampling the linens again.

In a moment I hear her singing her working song.)

Master Francescho?

The pickpocket.

Aren't you gone yet? I called down.

I've one last thing to say before I go, the pickpocket called. Can I come up?

The pickpocket had learned good pillars from me : he'd learned good rocks and bricks : he'd learned the drawn bow of a curve and the perspective behaviour of straight lines and he'd learned how lines brought together like woven threads will make a plane : I'd let him do some buildings in the lower space of May and some work on the workers there going about their daily business.

He wasn't yet 20 years old : his hair still fell over his eyes : he was good at colour and at mixing thicknesses of lime and plaster : he had the understanding that a fresco needs a wall and that at the same time the skin we apply to a wall is as sensitive as our own skin and becomes as much a part of that wall as our skin is a part of us.

I caressed the lip of a Grace : he clambered on to the platform and stood behind me and watched me work.

I know you have to let me go, he said. But you should have signed the letter. You should have signed the first 2 we wrote. It was wrong of you not to. So I signed you this time. It was for the good of us all that I did it. And Master Francescho, you should know this too. The Marquis won't be persuaded to give you any more money than us. You'll get 10 pennies per foot. He won't give you anything more.

He will, I said. It's a mistake. Cause above all Borse is fair. When he hears he will sort his mistake.

He won't, ever, the pickpocket said. Cause you should know, Master Francescho. That he likes the boys. Not the girls.

I split the lip of the Grace.

I dabbed the split away : I steadied myself on the wood.

And I should tell you too, the pickpocket was saying behind me. That when we were working on the month of May I heard him ask the Falcon to bring you to him, in the way he likes the new boys and men to be brought, cause he likes to be entertained by talent and he likes a talent to belong to him. And I heard the Falcon refuse him. Which is why you were never called to serve him in that way. But it's not the Falcon who told him anything about you, Master Francescho. The Falcon knows your worth. Now, I'll go if you still want, though I don't want to. But I'll wish you a fruitful New Year.

Behind me I heard him get back on the ladder : when I turned I saw him waiting, just his eyes and the top of his head above the platform : it was comic and sad both : but the fear I saw in his eyes let me see there was something I might do.

I'll have a bet with you, Ercole, I said.

You will? he said.

His eyes looked relieved.

I crouched down near his head.

I bet you the worth of 5 square feet of this fresco that if I write to him and ask him direct he'll give me what I ask, I said.

Okay, but if I lose that bet, the pickpocket said coming back up to sit on the platform. Though I know full well I won't, but just in case. If I do. Can we agree that I'll pay at the assistant rate? And if I win, that you'll pay at the Master Francescho rate?

Go down and grind me some black, I said, just in case I find I'll need it.

(Cause black has great power and its presence is meaningful.)

Black? the pickpocket said. No. It's New Year. It's holiday. I'm on holiday. Anyway, I'm sacked.

Make it deeper than sable, I said. Get it as deep as a lightless night.

I wrote on the Friday : I delivered the letter myself by hand to the doorman of the palace.

On the morning of the first Sunday, 2 days into the new year, the palace was cold and near-empty : I came up the stairs to the month room alone and I took the knife to March.

I peeled off the wall a small portion under the arch between the garland and *Borse giving out justice to an aging infidel* : it came away complete like marzapane off a cake.

I layered on the thin new undercoat : I went home to bed cause I planned to be working all night.

That afternoon I packed my things into my satchels except my tools, my colours and a good piece of my mirror.

That evening, alone again in the long room, I lit the torch : the faces round me flickered their hello : I climbed to the lower level by the garland and the cupids.

135

I layered the second skin over the hole in the picture below.

I replaced the lunette of Borse with a profile portrait like the one on the Justice medal : *haec te unum* : but I turned him so everyone who'd seen the medal would see he was looking the other way.

I placed next to the figure of Borse at the heart of the crowd waiting for justice a hand – with nothing in it.

Under the word JUSTICE written in the stone where the Est colours were I used black.

Above the black I whited out the letters till all you could read was ICE.

I held the mirror up to my own eyes.

Then it's down off the scaffolding and out of the palace of not being bored, out on to the street and up on to the back of Mattone and off on the hoof at speed down the streets past the smoky ghetto, under the palace tower, past the half-made castle and through the town gates for the last time cause I'd never be back and such leaving takes only a matter of minutes when the town of your birth is a small one easily passed through.

(Just a year and a half after that, as it happened, and just 6 days after the Pope made him Duke of Ferara at last, Borse would turn, blink, fall down dead, dead as an arrowed bird, the months of his year still circling regardless the walls of his palace of not being bored.)

When the town was as distant over my shoulder as the far towers in the landscapes in the work I'd just covered that wall with

(for not enough money to pay for the blues and the golds, never mind other colours)

when the morning light was up, when I'd reached the first rise of land to let the plain lie down behind me, I stopped.

I calculated my loss.

My pockets were near-empty.

I would have to hope for work.

A bird sang above me when I thought it.

I'd be fine : my arms and hands were good : I would go to Bologna where I'd friends and patrons, where there was no laughable court.

I heard through the birdsong something behind me and turned and saw a raising of dust on the line of road in the flat land : there was a horse far back, the only horse in the whole morning : no, not a horse, a pony, grey, and when it got near enough I saw someone on its back with his too-long legs sticking out at the sides : when the pickpocket drew up level with me the pony he was on was so small I looked down from a godheight.

Master Francescho, he said over the cough of the pony all out of breath from the speed it'd been made to go and the bags on its back full of all the pickpocket's worldly.

I waited till he'd got his own breath himself, as

137

covered in dust as the pony : he wiped his face with his sleeve : he readied himself to speak.

That's 5 square feet you owe me, he said. To be paid at the higher rate.

Here I am again : me and a girl and a wall.

We are outside the house of the girl's beloved and sitting by the poorly made wall : this time she is not sitting on it : she is sitting on the ground on the paving.

We have been here now many times.

I am not so sure it is a love though any more cause one of the times we were here the girl, staring with a face full of hostility, almost so that I believed she might spit like a snake, was approached direct by the woman we saw in the picture palace who came out of her house and crossed the road : and although the woman spoke to her the girl simply sat on the paving stones and looked, saying nothing, though her face was all irony, at the beautiful face of the woman : then quick as a magic trick she took out her tablet and made a study of the woman with it : the woman put her hands up over her face : she did not want a study made : she turned like that and went back inside the house : a minute later though the woman stood looking out her window at the girl across the road : at which the girl held up her tablet again and took a study of the woman in the window : the woman drew a curtain down : then the girl took a study of her doing this too, and then one of the blinded window : then the girl stayed cross-legged on the ground watching the house until the dark came down : only then she stood up, shook her limbs which will have been cold and stiff from the sitting and went.

And the next day, back again, she and I and the paving stones.

We have done this visit many days now : so many that the north wall of the room she sleeps in is covered in these small tablet studies : each study is the size of a hand and the girl has arranged them in the shape of a star, going towards its points the lighter of the pictures and the darker ones going to the centre.

The pictures are all of the house, or of the woman coming and going from it, or of other people who come and go : they are all from the same view, from in front of the poorly made wall : there are differences in the hedge leaves and tree leaves and as the season has shifted she has caught the differences in light and weather in the street from day to day.

The much older woman, the one the years have bent, who lives in the house to which the poorly made wall belongs, came out every day at first to shout things at the girl.

The girl said nothing, but on the third day simply moved from sitting on the wall to sitting on the paving stones in front of it.

The much older woman shouted then too : but the girl folded her arms over her skinniness and looked up from the ground with such calm and resolve that this older woman stopped shouting and left her in peace to sit where she chose.

One day instead the old woman said kind words to her and gave her an awning on a stick to keep rain off (there has been much rain in purgatorium) : that same day she brought a drink with steam coming off it and refreshments made of biscuit for the girl : on another colder day a woollen blanket and a large throw-over of a coat.

Today there will be blossom in the study the girl will make cause the trees in the street round this house she is looking so hard at have the beginnings in them of some of the several possible greens and some, the blossoming ones, have opened their flowers overnight, some pink along the branches, some loaded with white.

Today when the old woman came out of her house she brought nothing but for the first time sat down on her own poorly made wall behind the girl in silence and companionable.

There are bees : there was a butterfly.

That blossom will smell good to those who can smell blossom.

How the air throws it into a dance.

I had a memory of my father from not long before
he died that I could not bear : it shook me awake at
nights even 10 years after his death : as I got older
the memory got stronger : sometimes I could not
see to paint cause it came between me and what I
did and changed the nature of it : so Barto sat me
at the table and put 2 cups in front of me : he filled
1 from the jug of water : he filled the other from the
same jug of water.

Now, he said. This cup here has the Water of
Forgetting in it. This cup here has the Water of
Remembering. First you drink this. Then you wait a
little. Then you drink the other.

But you poured them both out of the same jug, I
said. They're both the same water. How can this
one be forgetting and this one be remembering?

Well, they're in different cups, he said.

So it's the *cups* of forgetting and remembering and nothing to do with the water? I said.

No, it's the water, he said. You have to drink the water.

How can the same water be both? I said.

It's a good question, he said. The kind of thing I'd expect you to ask. So. Ready? So first you drink –.

It would mean that forgetting and remembering are really both the same thing, I said.

Don't split hairs with me, he said. This one first. The Water of Forgetting.

No, cause a minute ago you said that *that* one was the Water of Forgetting, I said.

No, no, it's –, he said. Uh. No. Wait.

He looked at the 2 cups : he picked them both up and crossed the room with them : he threw the water in both of them out the open back door into the yard : he put the empty cups on the table and refilled them both from the jug again : he pointed to one, then the next.

Forgetting, he said. Remembering.

I nodded.

I was here cause Barto had come across town to see a Madonna I was painting for his friend who wanted to be painted in kneeling next to her and some saints for good money : Barto'd stared at it and shaken his head.

The people in your pictures these days, Francescho, he'd said. I mean, they're still beautiful.

But they're strange. It's like stone in their veins, where it used to be blood.

Canvas is different from wall, I said. Fresco is always much lighter looking. Materials can make things darker.

But it's the same with the work you showed to Domenico, he said

(Barto found me and the pickpocket a lot of our work in those years).

Well, he gave me the job, I said. He liked it.

A bitterness was through it, Barto said. Not like you. Like you're a different person.

I am a different person, I said.

Ha! Ercole said behind us (he was working). I wish you were. Then I'd be working for someone else.

Shut up, I said.

What's wrong? Barto said.

Master Francescho is not sleeping much, the pickpocket said.

Why not? Barto said.

Be quiet, Ercole, I said.

Bad dreams, Ercole said.

I can help with bad dreams, Barto said.

If it were only dreams, it'd be easy, I said. I could deal with only dreams.

Barto was sure, he said, of a good way to rid oneself of bad dreams and painful memories both : you had to do a ritual in the name of the goddess

143

of memory : you'd drink one water first and you'd forget everything : you'd drink the other water next and it'd give you a forceful remembering, everything crushed into 1 single huge memory boulder, a remembering the size of a mountainside.

Now I sat at the table with the 2 cups in front of me.

I don't want all my memories falling on me like avalanche, I said.

You won't know the first thing about it, Barto said. You won't even know it's happening. You'll be protected. You'll be in a trance. And then we lift you up and we carry you across the room and we put you in the special chair and you tell the oracle all the things the water's made you remember and then you fall asleep from the effort of it all. And when you wake up you find that you remember in a whole new way. You remember without fear or discomfort. You remember only what you really *need* to remember. And after it your sleep at night will be deep and good and sound and also – best thing of all – you'll find you're able to laugh again.

What special chair? What oracle? I said.

We were down in the servant kitchen : it was empty, Barto had dismissed the serving girls and the cook for the hour it would take, he said, to change my demeanour : we could hear them sunning themselves in the yard lightly complaining about the interruption : but they were used to me there :

they were kind to me too : there was always
something to eat at Barto's house if Barto was away
from home cause the kitchen was where Barto
habitually took me (to keep me out of sight of his
wife, I think, who did not like me around the house
too much : he'd promised me I'd always stand
godparent to his boys, and to *all* his boys not just
the first : and what about your girls? I'd asked,
cause I knew I'd be a great patron to girls : ah but
the girls are not so much my business, he'd said and
I'd seen from the slant away of his eyes that I was
permitted, but conditionally, to the parts of his life
over which his wife had no jurisdiction : this was
fine by me, I had more than enough grace by our
friendship : though I'd have liked all the same to be
guardian to his girls since girls got less attention
when it came to colours and pictures, which meant
the loss of many a good painter out of nothing but
blind habit : but his wife did not want her girls to
have the life of painters).

Barto leapt across to a larder, opened a corner
cupboard inside it and brought out a wrapped
honeycomb on a dish above which a small cloud of
flies appeared and congregated : he put it on the
table in front of me.

The oracle, he said.

Is there bread to go with it? I said.

He went back to the larder.

Would you prefer eggs as oracle? he said.

Can the oracle be both? I said. And can I take some of the oracle home with me?

My wife has been complaining there are never enough eggs, he said (cause she knew from her servants that I sent the pickpocket round here often : what neither of them knew was that her kitchen actually gained a lot for the eggs it happened to lose, cause the Garganelli cook had taken lessons from the pickpocket who was good with food when it came to both pictures and stomachs and who'd taught the cook how to hang and dry beef and pork in the way that enhances the flavours).

Barto set a bowl full of eggs on the table beside the honey.

And the special chair? I said (and while he looked round for a chair that would do I pocketed 5 of the eggs).

He was patting the crate of apples in the corner : he covered it with two dishcloths and patted the creases smooth.

Right, he said. Ready.

So. I drink this first, I said.

Yes, he said.

And then my memories fly off the top of me, I said, like someone putting a ladder against my walls if I were a house and climbing up on to the roof of me where all the things I remember are neatly laid like rooftiles, the first under the next under the next under the next. And then that someone jemmies each tile off, throws it down to the ground and doesn't stop till the rafters are bare. Yes?

More or less, Barto said.

And when they come off, do they stack up neatly, my memories, or do they lie broken in a heap by their fall? I said.

I can't say for sure, Barto said. I've never done this ritual before.

And then, in my new roofless state, I said, what I do is, I drink *this*, yes?

Yes –, Barto said.

– and those same old rooftiles, I said, hoist themselves off the ground again all at once, all the tiles that haven't broken and all the little broken bits, both, and they fly up like a skyful of stiff wingless birds back up to the open roof of me where they fix themselves back on, over and under all their old neighbours again? In exactly the same places?

I suppose, Barto said.

So what's the point? I said.

The point? Barto said. The point is – obviously, Francescho, *that moment*, with all the tiles, I mean the memories, gone. That moment when you're like before you were born. Like just newborn. Open to everything. Open to the weather. Everything new.

Ah, I said.

Open like a brand-new not-yet-lived-in home,

147

Barto said. Clean like a wall that's been returned to what it was like before the painting.

But then the roof, or the same old picture, lands right back on top of me again? I said.

Yes, but by the time it does you've had the moment without it, your clean moment, Barto said. And what happens in that moment is, the ritual starts its work, and I put you in the Chair of Mnemosyne, and you say out loud to the oracle on the table –

The eggs and the honey, I said –

Yes, Barto said, you tell them everything that's come into your head. After that the memory can't hurt you any more.

Ah, I said.

That's how it works, he said. That's the Rite of Mnemosyne.

Barto was my friend so he wished me well : it was a warm-hearted game, sweet, wholesome, funny and hopeful : but perhaps too, I reckoned – I suspected him of it – what he really wished was for me to forget my self so I might be *another self* to him.

More : I had seen depictions of that goddess Mnemosyne : I had seen how she would place her hand on the back of a man's head and not just pull him by the hair but get a good handful and yank him nearly off his feet by the head and suspend him in mid-air as if hanging him for a crime : she was

not a restful spirit : she was tough and wiry and
dark : the scholars and poets thought her the
mother of all the muses, even the inventor of words
themselves : I didn't want to offend in any way such
a spirit.

– then I take you home to your house, Barto was
saying, we put cushions under you, you sleep it off,
and then you wake up feeling better, Barto said.

All just from me drinking water, I said.

You'll see, Barto said.

So I picked up the first cup : but what if I did by
chance drink the forgetting and the remembering
the wrong way round? I might end up roofless and
open for ever, no memories at all of anything ever
again : what I would give, to forget everything :
cause as I know now from this place of
purgatorium this would be a kind of paradise, since
purgatorium is a state of troubling memory or the
knowledge of a home after home is gone, or of
something which you no longer have in a world
which you recognize to be your own but in which
you are a stranger and of which you can no longer
be a part.

Here, my father'd said to me once, soon after I
announced to him that I'd stop being his
apprentice, that I thought myself ready to do
without guardianship being well past 2 decades old.

He handed me a folded piece of paper which,
when I unfolded it, was worn to a thinness through

149

which actual light came cause of the too many times unfolded then folded again in its time spent as a fragile thing in the world.

I flattened it gently in my hand and I read what it said in the faded ink in an immature hand which sloped up in a curve at the ends of the lines : its writer had made no preparation for keeping his line of words steady as small children are taught to do with the mark of a straight line to follow.

Forgive my insolence if indeed it be insolence but I have held it all this time wrong of you : so much so that I have been unable some nights to sleep well for thinking on it : that you did strike me on the head that day for the pictures I had made of you in the soil and dust : honoured illustrious and most beloved of all fathers I beg of you do not think to strike me that way again : unless of course justly I deserve your wrath which in this instance I maintain it, I did not.

What is it? I asked him.

You don't remember? he said.

I shook my head.

You were small and I taught you to write, he said, and this is what you first wrote.

!

I looked at the paper in my hand : I'd have sworn my life on that I had never seen it before : yet this was my own writing.

So much we forget ourselves in a life.

I looked at how I held it, my child's hand in my adult hand, and thought how much paler the paper was in my father's : cause my own skin was light, white as any lady's compared to the skin of my father and brothers after the years of weather and work and firing of bricks, all of which will turn skin to a brown quite close to the red of the bricks themselves : my father was proud of my pale skin : to him it was achievement : with my pale hands I folded the paper again and held it out for him to take back.

It's yours, he said. If you're leaving my tutelage, then I give into your care what little I still have of your child self. It also holds your mother in it, who will have helped you fashion it, cause you were very young when you wrote this and the sentences have her turn of phrase about them, as well as – look, here, here and here – her habit of putting these 2 dots between clauses where a breath should come.

It's my habit too, I said.

He nodded. He took another paper from his sleeve pocket and held it out to me.

Yours too, he said.

What is it? I said.

The contractual agreement, he said. We made it when you were a child. Remember?

No, I said.

You sign it here, and here, he said, and I do too. We take it to the notary and he witnesses us sign it.

151

And when he does – that's it. You're *your own man* at last.

He raised both eyebrows and regarded me with comic warmth, and then me him with warmth too, and for a moment a happiness that was also made of some sadness between us.

But I was gone soon after on my new horse, I'd a life to live and a different city to work in and Florence to visit and Venice to see and was no longer apprentice to anyone.

Old father, old brickmaker.

Young gone brickshaper mother who never grew old.

3 years later I came back to the town cause I'd heard there might be work going at the palace of beautiful flowers and cause Cosmo was working on the muses and I might get the chance to work with Cosmo : I'd seen a small crowd of boys down the side of the cathedral throwing stones at a ruined serf, old man in torn cloth pulling by hand a cart loaded with the dregs of household stuff : it looked like he was stopping passers to sell them the things in the cart : he'd reach behind him, take whatever came to hand, a piece of old something, cloth, a cup, a bowl, another bowl, a footstool, a chairleg, plank of wood, and hold it up and offer it : a person took something and didn't pay : the next people pushed him out of the way : people went past him as fast as they could in a kind of panic :

except the boys : the boys followed him and threw stones and insults : he was a stranger Jew or infidel, or a gypsy or wood dweller maybe : there was fear of the blue sickness in town, there was always fear of it even when there'd been no sign of it in the people for years : but a man acting fevered always drew a sharp attention : it wasn't till after I'd gone, was a mile or 2 away, that I knew I'd recognized the last thing I'd seen him take from the cart and hold up : it had been a stonehammer : I went back along the road to the cathedral but he was gone : the boys too had gone : what I'd seen had vanished as surely as if I'd invented it.

I went to the old house : he was there, he was fine, he was sitting at the table : there was a written list of names on the wood of the table : the list went all down the long side of it where we'd sat and eaten as children : several of the names at the top end had a line scored through them : *they're the people who owe me for work done*, he said, *I'm writing to them all to absolve them of their debts, I've written to those ones there, I still have these down here to write to.*

It wasn't long after this that they came fast horse to Bologna to tell me he'd died.

In my dreams he was always younger, his arms rope-strong.

Once in a dream he told me he was cold.

But there were nights I couldn't get near any

dream cause the real things I'd seen and done, and seen and not done, fell like a shadow curtain in my way.

I came back to Ferara after he died and stood outside the empty house on the road (cause my uncle was dead and my brothers not wanting to inherit the debts had vanished and left them to me) : a woman I didn't know saw me and came out of a house opposite, she crossed the road and gave me money in my hands that Cristoforo had given her the last time he saw her saying take it, I won't need it.

4 coins : she wanted me to have them back.

(I lost that contract my father and I signed : I lost that letter my child self wrote to my father : I kept the 4 coins, and had them for the rest of my, till I

did I? die?)

I yelled it out into the kitchen.

Nothing   I remember   nothing.

Through the window I saw the 2 serving girls jump : Barto too nearly leapt out of his own skin. I threw my hands in the air like someone with lost wits : I knocked the cup with the Water of Remembering in it over : it spilled through an open crack in the table wood and hit the floor underneath : the doorways filled with Garganelli servants all wide eyes : Barto held up his hand to stop anyone coming in : he bent low over me, didn't

take his eyes off me : I looked up and through him
as if blind.

Who are you? I said.

Francescho —, Barto said.

You are Francescho, I said. Who am I?

No, *you* are Francescho, Barto said. I'm your
friend. Don't you know me?

Where am I? I said.

My house, Barto said. The kitchen. Francescho.
You've been here a thousand times.

I let my mouth fall open : I made my face empty :
I held my hand up wet from the water on the table :
I looked at it like I'd never seen a hand, like I'd no
idea what a hand was.

It's me. Bartolommeo, Barto said. Garganelli.

What place is this? I said. Who is Bartolommeo
Garranegli?

Barto went paler than autumnal fog.

Oh dear Christ dear Madonna and all the angels
and the baby Jesus, he said.

Who is Christ and dear Madonna and a baby?
I said.

What have I done? he said.

What have you done? I said.

I made to stand up, then as if I couldn't
remember what legs were for : I fell off my stool to
the ground : I fell quite convincingly : ah but then I
felt the wet of the broken eggs in my pocket.

Aw, damnt to hell, I said.

Francescho? Barto said.

Thought I'd got away with it, I said.

Is it you? Barto said.

There was sweat on his forehead : he sat down at the table.

You bastard, he said.

Then he said, Thank the Christ, Francescho.

I got myself to my feet : the wet of the eggs had made a darkness all down my coat and in the clothes on the side of my leg.

For a minute there, he said, my world ended.

I started to laugh and he did too : I put my hand in my pocket and scooped out a single yolk which had – a miracle – stayed whole in its sac in a half-shell of egg still unbroken : the other yolks were mixed up with their own whites and shells and hung off my hand in a long drip of mucus : I wiped my hand on the table and then on the face of my friend, who let me : then I upended the half-shell into my hand and held out the unbroken yolk on my palm to show him.

The oracle speaks, Barto said.

I completely forgot there were eggs in there, I said.

See? Barto said. I told you it'd work.

The girl can't sleep : or when she does sleep she shifts around in her bed like a fish not in water : in the nights I watch her writhing in the half-sleep or sitting up blank and unmoving in the dark of her room.

The great Alberti says that when we paint the dead, the dead man should be dead in every part of him all the way to the toe and finger nails, which are both living and dead at once : he says that when we paint the alive the alive must be alive to the very smallest part, each hair on the head or the arm of an alive person being itself alive : painting, Alberti says, is a kind of opposite to death : and though he knows that when we are bared back to nothing but our bones ourselves only God can remake us into humans, put faces back on our skulls on the final day and so on &c, which means there is no blasphemy in what I'm about to say –

cause Alberti said it and it is true –

all the same it's many a person who can go to a painting and see someone in it as if that person is as alive as daylight though in reality that person has not lived or breathed for hundreds of years.

Alberti it is who teaches, too, how to build a body from nothing but bones : so that the process of drawing and painting outwits death and you draw, as he says, any animal by *isolating each bone of the animal, and on to this adding muscle, and then clothing it all with its flesh* : and this giving of muscle and flesh to bones is what in its essence the act of painting anything is.

157

I now sense this girl has had a death or a vanishment perhaps of the dark-haired woman in the pictures on the south wall above her bed which are pictures she sometimes looks at for many minutes and sometimes cannot, in which the woman is both young and older, sometimes with a small infant who resembles this girl, and sometimes with another small infant who then matures to become the brother, and sometimes with strangers : in this instance the pictures mean a death : cause pictures can be both life and death at once and cross the border between the two.

Once the girl held one picture of this woman so close to a source of light, to see it more fully, as if to illuminate things in its dark, that I thought surely the picture would burn : but the lights in purgatorium are an enchanted kind of flame and nothing in the end caught fire.

Either this woman, or it is St Monica Victims who is the girl's loss? Or perhaps one of the 2 girls in the picture on the sunlit street, the 2 friends, the light one and the dark one, one in gold, one in blue : maybe it is all of them who vanished : perhaps there has been a blue sickness here and they have all died of it.

But the girl is an artist! Cause she has peeled down off her north wall all the many pictures of the house we sit and wait outside so often, and she has, on a table in the room, been making a new work out of them and I cannot help but feel I have hit target with her cause the new work is in the shape of – a brick wall.

As if each of the little studies is a brick in this wall, she has lined them up with the right irregularity and she has drawn and shaded with lead the mortar lines round and between each and cut some pictures short for each alternating brickline at the ends of her wall, just like cut or turned bricks look, it does look very like a wall! She's artisan and can very well make good things : the picture wall is very long and falls and curls off the table on to the floor and part of the way across the room as if the room is a divided territory in which

yes

here come all the memories complete with all their forgettings

doing St Vincenzo for good money in Bologna, I'd got a thick aurum musicum (cause the great Cennini, who is only rarely wrong, *is* wrong about this gold when he says it is not as good to use as other gold) : I had painted my dead father up above Vincenzo's head in the form of a Christ : not blasphemic I hoped cause my father had so loved and revered Vincenzo, the new saint patron of builders and brickmakers : my father had celebrated his saint day 8 times in the 8 years before he died

(though I liked too the notion that the Christ

159

might maybe have lived longer than they all say that he did, which, yes, is a blaspheming but worth darkening a corner of the soul for and with any luck forgivable).

The painting was full of egg : I wanted it richer and richer, especially the cloakwork and the skin of the saint.

You can't use that much, the pickpocket said. It won't set.

Wait and see, Ercole, I said.

And the lazzurrite is too thick, the pickpocket said.

Wait and see, I said again.

But I needed more of the gold so I went for a walk to stretch my eyes and to fetch more from the colourmakers, also to pay them fairly too cause I owed them a deal of money

(had done a St Lucia with more of the gold on it than I could afford at the time : she had eyes on a sprig in her hand, eyes opening at the end of the sprig like flowers will, cause the great Alberti writes that *the eye is like a bud*, which made me think of eyes opening like plantwork, cause St Lucia is the saint of eyes and light and is usually seen blind or eyeless and many painters give her eyes but not in her face, instead they put them on a platter or set them in the palm of her hand – but I let her keep all her eyes, I did not want to deprive her of any.

But Master Francescho, if the stalk has been

picked, how long will the eyes last held up out of water like that? They'll wilt and die, the pickpocket said.

Ercole, you're an idiot, I said.

No, they're every bit as fragile as real flowers, the pickpocket said. If not more so.

He looked at the picture: he looked near tears.

First of all she's a saint, so the flowers are saintly. Which means the flowers won't die, I said.

Saints are all about death. It's prerequisite, for saints, he said.

Second, it's a picture, which means the flowers can't die cause they're in a picture, I said, and third, if they do die, it'll be in the special saint world of the picture that they do and she can always pick herself another sprig from whatever bush she picked those from.

Ah, the pickpocket said.

He went on with his work but I saw him keep glancing at the slender stalk with the eyes on the end of it in the hand of the saint : from his face, all unease, and his own eyes unable not to look, I knew it would be a good picture).

On my way back from the colourmakers I was coming along the river near the place where people leave putrid things and I saw a good pair of boots lying on their sides behind a hill of bushes whose roots were all covered in rubbish and dumped guts and entrails.

161

I went to see what size they were : flies rose : as I did I saw one of the boots move by itself.

Behind the rubbish through the straggle of branches I saw hands in the air as if attached to no body : they were covered in pustules like coated in a deep soup paste made of lentils but lentils coloured blue and black : I remember the smell : the smell was strong : I came round the bushy hill and I saw that the hands were on arms and at the ends of the arms there were shoulders and a head but with this pox over everything, even the face : he was breathing : he was alive : something moved in the whites of his eyes, the eyes saw me and a mouth opened below them.

Don't come any nearer, he said.

I stepped well back : I stood in a place where I could still see the hands through the twiggy stuff.

Are you still there? the man said.

I am, I said.

Go away, he said.

Are you young or old? I said (cause I couldn't tell from looking).

I think young, he said.

You need a new skin, I said.

He made a noise a bit like a laugh.

This is my new skin, he said.

What's your name? I said.

I don't know, he said.

Where are you from? I said. Is there no one to

162

help you? Family or friends? Tell me where you
live.

I don't know, he said.

What happened to you? I said.

I had a headache, he said.

When? I said.

I don't remember, he said. I only remember the
headache.

Shall I fetch the nuns? I said.

It was nuns who brought me here, he said.

Which nuns? I said.

I don't know, he said.

What can I do? I said. Tell me.

You can go away, he said.

But what will happen to you? I said.

I'll die, he said.

I got back to the workshop and I was full of the
vision : I shouted to the pickpocket that we were to
paint strands of bush and tree, but to paint them
like they were both seeing and blind.

You mean with actual eyes on, like in your Lucia?
the pickpocket asked.

I shook my head : I didn't know how : all I knew
was I had just seen the man, the rubbish, the leaves,
the twigs of the scrubland and I had understood
pity and pitilessness both as something to do with
the push of the branches.

The imperturbable nature of foliage, I said.

Eh? the pickpocket said.

163

He painted me a branch exactly as branches look, that's right –

cause I remember everything now –

say it quick before I forget again –

the day I opened an eye, the other wouldn't open, I was flat horizontal on the ground, had I fallen off the ladder?

I found you wrapped in the old horse blanket half an hour ago, he said, no, don't – don't do that, the heat coming off you, you're sweating and it's so hot outside, Master Francescho, so how can you be cold? Can you hear me? Can you hear?

What I saw was the pickpocket above me at my forehead, he poured water on to his sleeve and put his arm on my forehead again, too cold : people ran away out of the place : everyone but the pickpocket who opened the buttons of my jacket then took a knife to my shirt then cut further, deeper, sliced open the wraps of my binding and peeled it back and open saying *forgive me, Master Francescho, it's to help you breathe and I mean you no disrespect* : I was worried, flailed my arms, furious, not about the cutting of the binding but about the prophets and the doctors we were painting on the walls and the ceiling (cause there were no real doctors brave enough for that room that day and the only doctors near me were pictures), the best work I'd done so far, not finished yet and we'd been fully paid in advance for it : I told the pickpocket to finish the prophets but to paint out the doctors altogether : he said he would : I felt better when I heard it : *never leave work unfinished, Ercole* : he got me out of that place where we were now not wanted cause of the colours that had come in my skin and carried me on his own back to a bed, I don't know where, it was next to a wall : whatever the room was it faded and sharpened and cracked round me as if a quake happened and when the whitewash cracked in the wall I saw the people –

Ercole, tell me, I said, who those fine people are who are coming through the wall. I can't make them out, quite.

What people? Ercole said. Where?

Then he understood.

Ah, them, he said, they're a troupe of young fine people, they're coming out of the woods and they've wound oak leaves and branches through their hair and round their necks and round their wrists and their ankles, they've the scent of trees all round them like a garland too as if they're dressed in tree and flowers instead of clothes, and they're carrying great overflowing armfuls of the flowers and grasses they've picked in the meadow out behind the wood, grass and flowers so scented that the fragrance of them is coming ahead like a herald, and I know that if you could have seen them properly, Master Francescho, you'd want to paint them, and if you'd painted them you'd have caught

them right cause they look the way that means
they'll never die, or more, that if they do, they
won't mind or hold it against life, shall I lower the
blind, is it too bright for you in here? he said.

I congratulate you, Ercole, I said. It is so bright
it's dark

   can't remember

   what came next

but that's what a proper burnishing of gold does :
properly done it will give out both at once
darkness and brightness : I taught the pickpocket to
burnish : I taught him hair and branches : I taught
him rocks and stones and how they hold every
colour in the world and how every colour in every
picture ever made comes from stone, plant, root,
rock and seed : I taught him the body of the son
held in the mother's arms, the last supper, the
miracle of the water and wine, the animals standing
round the stable and the day going on behind it all,
in both the foreground and background of it all,
from death to last supper to wedding to birth.

I taught him, too, how things and beings shown
to be moving upwards into the air always have about
them the most and the best vitality : he was always
loyal, sweet pickpocket : I remember now the winter
after we finished the frescoes in the palace of not
being bored sending him back to Ferara again, and
he went without complaint, cause I wanted to know
how the work was looking nearly one year dry.

He went on the Wednesday and came back on the Friday straight to the church we were restoring the Madonna in.

He's only changed one thing since we were there, one thing in the whole room, the pickpocket said. His own face.

Who has? The Falcon? I said.

Borse, of course, the pickpocket said. He's had his face redone throughout the months, including your months. I asked the man at the door, I know him, old friend of my father's. He says Borse brought in his cousin Baldass to redo it.

The pickpocket told me the doorman had welcomed him like a son and taken him through to the serving quarters where they'd all done the same and fed him and fussed over him and asked after me –

(*they asked after me?*)

– yes, he said. And listen, that's not all. Borse is away a lot these days cause he's decided to build a mountain – not just *move* a mountain, since faith can do that, easy, but *make* a mountain, a whole new one, big as an Alp, in a place there's not been one before. So there's a lot of dragging and shifting and piling of rocks at Monte Santo and a lot of stoneworkers being worked to near-death, and sometimes to actual death and when that happens Borse adds the bodies to his mountain.

But Master Francescho, the pickpocket said. This other stuff they told me. Our month room has become quite famous among folk. There's often a crowd comes to the palace from the town and when they get in there they go and stand in front of your justice scene. They just stand there and look. They never say anything out loud. Borse thinks it's that they like to come to see the picture of him, you know, giving out justice. But the doorman says the people, when they leave that room, go on their way as pleased as if someone's put money in their pockets. They come especially, his wife told me while she poured stew into my bowl, to see the face you painted in the blackness, the face there's only half of, whose eyes – your eyes, Master Francescho – look straight out at them, as if the eyes can actually see them over the top of Borse's head.

They're not my eyes, I said.

Uh huh, the pickpocket said.

You didn't tell them they're my eyes? I said.

Wouldn't matter if I had, he said. I know they're your eyes. I see your eyes every day. But they think what they like. The doorman's wife told me all the women who come to look go away talking about how the eyes are a woman's eyes. All the men who come to look go away sure the eyes are a man's. And you know how you made it only half a face, a face without a mouth? Like there are things that can't be said? People come for miles to see it and nod their heads at each other about it. And they told me this too, listen to this – that a great many workers are always coming to the palace now, infidel workers and other field workers, workers from our own south and the poor working locals too, and they knock on the door in large numbers, sometimes as many as 20 at a time, to *pay their respects*, they tell the doorman, to *show obeisance to Borse*. By which they mean they want to bow before him in person, which Borse lets them do, if he's there, and he always sees them in the virtue room.

So? I said.

Think, Master Francescho, the pickpocket said. Cause to get to the virtue room you have to pass through the month room, don't you?

So we've turned him into the popular man he wanted us to paint him as? I said.

The pickpocket laughed : he took off his travelling coat : he'd been telling me it all so fast he hadn't even put his bags down : he did now and sat on the softer of them at my feet and went on with his tale.

The story goes, the pickpocket said, that when the workers passing through the room of the months get anywhere near the far end of that room they veer towards the month of March where they stop below your worker painted in the blue and stand there for as long as they can. Some have even started coming in with their sleeves full of hidden flowers and at a given signal between them all they let their arms fall to their sides and the flowers fall out of their clothes on to the floor beneath him. When they're made to move on, they go in and they bow to Borse like they're meant to, it takes about half a minute to, then they're escorted from the palace back through the room of the months and they strain their heads round on their necks to keep their eyes on the picture for as long as they can the whole length of the room.

And one day 25 or so of them got in there and were standing below him, dust coming off them from the fields, all looking up at him, and they refused to be moved on for nearly an hour, pretended not to understand the language when asked, though in the end when they went they went quite peaceably.

And Borse hasn't had it altered? I said (and my voice came out like the squeak of a mouse).

Borse has no idea it even happens, the pickpocket said. Nobody's told him. Nobody cares to, and he's never seen it with his own eyes, has he? Since he's always on the other side of the wall squeezed into the chair in the room of the virtues waiting to be bowed to. When he's not off in Monte Santo, that is, making that new mountain.

For that moment I felt a sorrow for him, Borse the Just, whose vanity reminded me of me –

but what I really felt was frightened that

something I'd done or made might have such wild
effect.

Your stories are nothing but flattery, I said.

They're nothing but true, the pickpocket said.

I don't want to hear any more of your lies, I said.

You sent me to see. I saw. Now I'm telling you,
the pickpocket said. I thought you'd like it. I
thought you'd be pleased. You're such a vain cunt, I
thought you'd be delighted.

I hit him across the top of the head.

I don't believe you even went there, I said.

Ow! he said. Right. That's it. Hit me again and
I'm leaving.

I hit him again.

He left.

Good.

I put away all the work things : I went off home
to my rooms, to bed : I locked the door against the
pickpocket, whose habit it was to sleep at the foot
of the bed : he could sleep in the open air tonight

(he came back 3 days later,

sweet pickpocket, who'd die still young, though
long after me, of too much drink, tempus edax,
forgive me)

as for me, I lay in the bed that night by myself
and wondered if Cosmo had heard about my
pictures and about all the people coming to look
at them.

Cosmo bloody Cosmo.

I am small : I am only newly become Francescho :
I am learning to tint parchments and papers and to
mix colours for painting the range of different skin
and flesh tones in all the different lights : I'm
teaching myself from books while my father is
working on a house near the edge of the town and
one day in an empty room in the half-house I'm
leaning out of the brickwork which will become a
window and I see crossing the meadow the son of
the cobbler, everybody knows who he is cause he's
been taken on at the court : he's young, he's to
paint the pennants and horsecoats and the armour
they use in tournaments, but those who know
anything about pictures also know he is a painter
of pictures himself so full of twisting and arguing
life that they surprise everyone who sees them : as
he crosses the meadow it is as if it is revealed to me :
he is a being wholly formed of and giving off the
colour green : cause everything about him as he
walks through the high grasses (he has left the path
the people generally use to cross the land and is
making his way across a wild-grassed place instead)
is green : his head, his shoulders, his clothes are
tinted green : above all, his face is the greenest
green : it is as if his body gives out a greenness, one
I can nearly taste, as if my mouth has been filled
with leaves and grass : although I know of course it
is the meadow casting its colour on to him, all the

172

same he's the reason the grasses spread round him for miles are the green they are.

I am 18 years old : I have high hopes cause my father has persuaded the most exciting new young master the town has seen for a long time to look over some of my pictures and has gone to the municipal palace with a great many of them to show him (who isn't new at all, who's been working as a tapestry and fabric designer and painter of horsecoats and pennants there for a decade and making a name too for his pictures which are near-shocking things in their toughness, all roots and stones and grimaces and all of an astonishing arrogance, so much so that to look at them for any time will fill you with a kind of discomfort and distaste : more, Borse, the newest Marquis, has tired of his old masters, good Bono and Angelo, who weren't his but his half-brother's court painters, and word's gone round that this new painter has caught his eye and has received many gifts) : my father has decided he'd be a good man to know and that a court job could be mine easy as anything if I were apprenticed to him : I am home in the workshop my father made for me in our yard from sticks and hanging canvases, shelter from the wind but full of plain daylight, good for painting : it's a place both flimsy and serviceable and I haven't had to re-erect it this morning (my brothers like to knock the sticks out of the ground at night when

they've come home from work or drinking, but last
night they forgot to, or were kind enough not to)
and I'm hard at work on a picture as large as the
canvases that make the walls hung round me, I am
picturing a story I remember from childhood : a
musician has an argument with a god about
whose music is better : the god wins the argument
and the musician has to pay the price, which is to
be skinned and hand over the pelt to the god as a
trophy.

It's a story I've puzzled over almost all my years :
right now though I've found the way to tell it : the
god stands to one side, the unused knife slack in his
hand : he has an air near disappointment : but the
inner body of the musician is twisting up out of the
skin in a kind of ecstasy like the skin's a thick flow
of fabric coming rich in one piece off the shoulder
and peeling away at the same time from the wrists
and the ankles in little pieces like a blown upward
snow of confetti : the body appears through the
skin's unpeeling like the bride undressing after the
wedding : but bright red, crystal red : best of all the
musician catches the skin over the very arm it's
coming off and folding itself, neat.

I hear someone behind me : I turn : a man is
standing between the folds of canvas that make the
door of my workshop : he's quite young : he is
adorned : his clothes are very beautiful : he himself
inside the clothes is also good on the eye and he has

174

an arrogance that actually has a colour : I will try quite a few times after this to mix that colour but will never be able to get it.

He is looking at my painting : he is shaking his head.

It's wrong, he says.

Says who? I say.

Marsyas is a satyr and therefore male, he says.

Says who? I say.

Says the story, he says. Say the scholars. Say the centuries. Says everyone. You can't do this. It's a travesty. Says me.

Who're you? I say

(though I know quite well who he is).

Who am I? Wrong question, he says. Who are you? Nobody. No one will ever pay you, not money, for this. It's worthless. Meaningless. If you're going to paint a Marsyas, Apollo has to win. Marsyas has to display ruin and be defeated. Apollo is purity. Marsyas has to pay.

He is staring at the picture with, is it a kind of anger? He comes up closer and rubs the lower corner roughly with a thumb and first finger.

Hey –, I say

cause I am annoyed at his touching it.

He acts like he can't hear : he examines the fields and fencing and trees, the far houses, the rock formations, the people going about their day and the nothing unusual happening, the boys throwing

175

stones in the river for a dog to chase, the woman tramping the cloth in the barrel, the birds in flight, the clouds going where they're blown and the tree to which the musician was to be bound by ropes and from which the musician has twisted free.

He's as close to the surface of the painting as he can get, so close it's as if his eyelashes might be brushing the twigs and leaves of the crown on Apollo : he puts himself equally close to the place where the skin of the musician's face and neck, all that's left still attached to the body, meets the red of the underflesh : he steps back, steps back again, steps back again so he's level with me : he looks down at the colours on my table.

Who made your blue? he says.

I did, I say.

He does a shrug like he doesn't care who made that blue : he lifts his eyes and looks back at the picture again : he sighs : he gives a little disapproving shake of the head and then he disappears again through the opening in the airy walls.

2 nights later the painting went : I came out in the morning, the workshop was wrecked and ruined as usual but cause I knew my brothers liked their fun I always stored the tools and things that mattered well away : I went down to my mother's storeroom : the overgrown grass on the path down

the field had been stamped back by more feet than mine : its door was open : the painting was gone and the roll of sketches too (though my father had taken everything else with him to the palace where no one had had the time to see him so he'd brought it all back home again : it was safe in the house, in my mother's bedroom up on top of the cupboards out of the reach of the mouths of the goat and her babies).

Who knows where it went? The river? A fire? A back room, cut, rolled and squeezed into the gaps between the wall and the window or the door and the floor or hammered into the cracks in the wood or the brick to block out the damp?

(Shining Cosmo, favoured court painter who'll oust the court painters favoured before you then be ousted in turn by my own beloved apprentice pickpocket (ha!) : bright bejewelled Cosmo old and ill, writing to the last of your Dukes a letter for money cause you're too ill now for painting and the bishop and the clerk who owe you for the altarpiece and the saint panel are both ignoring your invoices : them so rich and you so poor : green forgotten Cosmo, old then dead, though quite some time after me, of poverty, yes,

but not of the cold,

cause I take my unfinished working of an old old story and unroll it over you, spread it all your length, tuck you in beneath it and fold its end down under your chin to keep you that bit warmer in the winters of being old –

I forgive you.)

The girl has a friend.

The friend has a look of my Isotta, very fine, and has arrived in here like a burst of air as if a new door opened itself in a wall where no door was suspected : there's a kin between them and their hearts are high with it : they are sharp and bright together as the skins of 2 new lemons.

The girl is holding up to her friend the wall she's made from the many small pictures : her friend is admiring and nodding : she takes a piece and looks closely at a single picture and then at how the picture has been made to become a brick.

One girl takes one end of it and the other takes the other and they measure its length by stretching it across the room : it *is* long, the wall : then into the room like a mischievous small dog comes the little brother who ducks down below the stretch of picture-wall in the middle then knocks into it with his head like a goat or a ram : both girls squeal : they gather it and swing it carefully away from him, drape it in its fragility on the table and place its ends on either side on the floor with no twists in it so it will stay whole : when this is done the girl turns and yells at the brother : he is abashed : he

leaves the room : the girls go back to fussing at the
long picture-wall : moments later the brother
comes in again carrying 2 cups with something hot
in them, steam coming off : a truce, an offering :
sure enough, there is a kind of accord : he is to be
let to sit in the room with them for bringing them
these drinks : he sits good and quiet on the bed as if
he has never been anything other.

The girls go back to examining their wall : as
soon as they forget he's there the brother dips his
head and his hands into the bag the friend has
brought with her : he has found something to eat in
there and is ripping at its wrap : both girls hear him
and turn and see and shout at him at once, then
both stand up and chase him out of the room.

But when they get back –

ruination !

They have put their too-hot cups on the surface
of the picture-wall and the cups have spilled a bit
when the table got knocked : these cups are stuck to
some of the pictures of – what are they of, again? –
so much so that to pick a cup up by a handle is also
to pick up the whole wall.

Both girls peel the picture-wall off the cups : the
studies the cups stuck to are marked from the heat
and the spill with 2 perfect circles from the shapes
of the bases of the cups.

The girl looks appalled.

She holds up the bit of the wall : she unsticks

with a little knife the 2 studies marked with the circles : she waves the studies in the air as if to dry them.

But the friend takes them out of her hands : she laughs : she holds them both up in front of her eyes like they're eyes.

Ha ha!

The girl looks astonished : her mouth opens : then it breaks into a smile : then laughter from them both : then both girls take one end of the long wall of pictures each, like they did before but now with its cut-out bricks gone from the middle and they stretch it out across the room again : this time rather than treating it with such care the girl, when the wall is at full stretch, wraps her end of it round her shoulder and tucks it under her arms like a collar or a scarf.

When she sees the girl do this the friend does the same : next moment both girls are shawling themselves in it : they twist themselves round inside the swath of wall until they are both a bristle of pictures like armour over their chests and stomachs and arms and up to their necks : then they twist towards each other as if it is the wall that is bringing them together : they meet wrapped like caterpillars in the middle of the room : but they don't just meet, they collide : at which the paper wall breaks and as it comes apart its brick-shapes fly off like rooftiles and the girls hit the floor together in each other's arms in the mess of the pictures littered round them.

I like a good skilful friend.

I like a good opened-up wall.

I'm doing a portrait now of my brown-eyed friend : what's his name? I forget his name : you know who I mean, I mean what's-his-name : his father has died which means he is the official head of his family : he owns all the land and all the ships and has come into all the money : it is an unofficial portrait though cause his wife will not have me paint him officially so to placate me he has asked me to do him too, since official versions are never true, is what he says when I ask him why

(can't remember his name but I remember pretty clearly my annoyance at his wife)

and I've sketched some ships in the far background and come back to the shape of his head again : but my friend, sitting in front of me, is even more restless today than usual : I work on the fold in the undershirt where it prettily tops his collar but with my eye on him today he can hardly sit still.

I know his frustration : I've always known it : it is almost as old as our friendship : the walled-up power, the dismay in the air round him like when a storm is unable to break.

But as ever out of kindness he pretends to me to be feeling something else.

181

He says he has been infuriated by a story.

It haunts him, he says : he can't stop thinking about it.

What story? I say.

All stories, he says, really. They're never the story I need or really want.

I ready the picture : I am quiet : I let the time pass : after a bit he speaks into this silence and tells me the bones of the story.

It's about a magic helmet which allows its bearer to turn into anything, transform into any shape he likes, all he has to do is put the helmet on his head.

But that's not the part that maddens him : he likes that part of the story : there's this other part of the story and it's about 3 maidens, guardians of a store of gold, and whoever wins the gold from them and forges it into a ring will have power over everything, over the land, the sea, the world and all its peoples : but there's a snag : there's a condition : he'll have all the power, the man who forges the ring, but to keep this power he'll have to renounce love.

My friend looks at me : he shifts about on the stool : his eyes are blunt and aimed : the everything that he can't say to me makes him even finer to my eye.

I mark behind where his shoulder will end the curve of the line for the rock where I'll put the fisherman : over here I'll put the 2 children with the fish-spear under the high rock overhang : I mark where his hand will come over the frame at the front : I mark out in rough the little circle shape for the ring his hand will hold.

I just don't see why, he is saying. Why whoever is brave or lucky enough to win the gold and make it into the ring can't have both the ring *and* the love.

I nod that I agree and that I understand.

I know now what to make of the rest of the landscape behind him.

Here I am again : me, 2 eyes and a wall.

We are outside a house, have I been here before? There are 2 girls kneeling on the paving.

An old woman, I think I

do I know her? no

has come out and is sitting on the wall watching them : they're painting, eggs? No, eyes : they're painting 2 eyes on to a wall : they take an eye each : they begin with the black for the hole through which we see : then they ring the colour round it in segments (blue) : then the white : then the black outline.

An old woman is telling them something : a girl (who is she?) bends down to a pot with white in it, reaches forward, adds a small square of white the size of the end of her fingertip then does the same in the same place to the other eye cause an eye with

183

no light is an eye that can't see, I think is what the
old woman sitting on a wall is telling
   hardly able to hear though cause there's
      something
        God knows what
             drawing me
          skin of my father?
       the eyes of my mother?
   down to
that thin-looking line
    made of nothing
      ground and grit and the
        gather of dirt and earth and
        the grains of stone
          there at the very foot of this
           (really badly made   just saying)
      wall at the place where the crumble of
    the brickbase meets the paving
  look
    the line where
      one thing meets another
the little green almost not-there weeds
      take root in it
     by enchantment
    cause it's an enchanted line
   the line drawn between planes
place of green possibles
   cause whatever they're doing up there
     eyes painted on a wall

it's nothing
             to the tiny and the many
                 variations of colours invisible
             till the eye's so close it
       becomes the place
where a horizontal line meets a
             vertical and a surface meets a surface and a
                 structure meets another which looks to
             be 2 dimensions only but is deeper than
       sea should you dare to enter or
deep as a sky and goes as deep into the
earth (the flower folds its petals down
             the head droops on the stem)
                 through layered clay on stone
             mixed by the
       worms through whose mouths
   everything passes
paddled by the many legs of
   spores so small they're much
       much finer than an eyelash and
             are colours only darkness can
       make
             veins like tracery
             look
                 the treebranch thick with
                 all its leaves before even the
             thought of the arrow
       how
                 the root in the dark makes its

way under the ground
before there's
any sign of the tree
the seed still unbroken
the star still unburnt
the curve of the eyebone
of the not yet born
hello all the new bones
hello all the old
hello all the everything
to be
made and
unmade
both

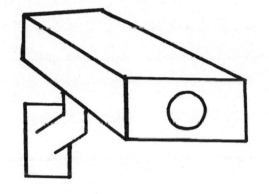

one

Consider this moral conundrum for a moment, George's mother says to George who's sitting in the front passenger seat.

Not says. Said.

George's mother is dead.

What moral conundrum? George says.

The passenger seat in the hire car is strange, being on the side the driver's seat is on at home. This must be a bit like driving is, except without the actual, you know, driving.

Okay. You're an artist, her mother says.

Am I? George says. Since when? And is that a moral conundrum?

Ha ha, her mother says. Humour me. Imagine it. You're an artist.

This conversation is happening last May, when George's mother is still alive, obviously. She's been dead since September. Now it's January, to be more precise it's just past midnight on New Year's Eve, which means it has just become the year after the year in which George's mother died.

George's father is out. It is better than him being at home, standing maudlin in the kitchen or going round the house switching things off and on. Henry is asleep. She just went in and checked on him; he was dead to the world, though not as dead as the word dead literally means when it means, you know, dead.

This will be the first year her mother hasn't been alive since the year her mother was born. That is so obvious that it is stupid even to think it and yet so terrible that you can't not think it. Both at once.

Anyway George is spending the first minutes of the new year looking up the lyrics of an old song. Let's Twist Again. Lyrics by Kal Mann. The words are pretty bad. Let's twist again like we did last summer. Let's twist again like we did last year. Then there's a really bad rhyme, a rhyme that isn't, properly speaking, even a rhyme.

Do you remember when

Things were really hummin'.

Hummin' doesn't rhyme with summer, the line doesn't end in a question mark, and is it meant to mean, literally, *do you remember that time when things smelt really bad*?

Then Let's twist again, twisting time is here. Or, as all the sites say, twistin' time.

At least they've used an apostrophe, the George from before her mother died says.

I do not give a fuck about whether some site on the internet attends to grammatical correctness, the George from after says.

That before and after thing is about mourning, is what people keep saying. They keep talking about how grief has stages. There's some dispute about how many stages of grief there are. There are three, or five, or some people say seven.

It's quite like the songwriter actually couldn't be bothered to think of words. Maybe he was in one of the three, five or seven stages of mourning too. Stage nine (or twenty three or a hundred and twenty three or ad infinitum, because nothing will ever not be like this again): in this stage you will no longer be bothered with whether songwords mean anything. In fact you will hate almost all songs.

But George has to find a song to which you can do this specific dance.

It being so apparently contradictory and meaningless is no doubt a bonus. It will be precisely why the song sold so many copies and was such a big deal at the time. People like things not to be too meaningful.

Okay, I'm imagining, George in the passenger seat last May in Italy says at exactly the same time

as George at home in England the following
January stares at the meaninglessness of the words
of an old song. Outside the car window Italy
unfurls round and over them so hot and yellow it
looks like it's been sandblasted. In the back Henry
snuffles lightly, his eyes closed, his mouth open. The
band of the seatbelt is over his forehead because he
is so small.

You're an artist, her mother says, and you're
working on a project with a lot of other artists.
And everybody on the project is getting the same
amount, salary-wise. But *you* believe that what
you're doing is worth more than everyone on the
project, including you, is getting paid. So you write
a letter to the man who's commissioned the work
and you ask him to give you more money than
everyone else is getting.

Am I worth more? George says. Am I better than
the other artists?

Does that matter? her mother says. Is that what
matters?

Is it me or is it the work that's worth more?
George says.

Good. Keep going, her mother says.

Is this real? George says. Is it hypothetical?

Does that matter? her mother says.

Is this something that already has an answer in
reality but you're testing me with the concept of it

though you already know perfectly well what you yourself think about it? George says.

Maybe, her mother says. But I'm not interested in what I think. I'm interested in what you think.

You're not usually interested in anything I think, George says.

That's so adolescent of you, George, her mother says.

I *am* adolescent, George says.

Well, yes. That explains that, then, her mother says.

There's a tiny silence, still okay, but if she doesn't give in a bit and soon George knows that her mother, who has been prickly, unpredictable and misery-faced for weeks now about there being trouble in the paradise otherwise known as her friendship with that woman Lisa Goliard, will get first of all distant then distinctly moody and ratty.

Is it happening now or in the past? George says. Is the artist a woman or a man?

Do either of those things matter? her mother says.

Does either, George says. Either being singular.

Mea maxima, her mother says.

I just don't get why you won't commit, ever, George says. And that doesn't mean what you think it means. If you say it without the culpa it just means *I'm the most*, or *I'm the greatest*, or *to me the greatest belongs*, or *my most*.

It's true, her mother says. I'm the most greatest. But the most greatest what?

Past or present? George says. Male or female? It can't be both. It must be one or the other.

Who says? Why must it? her mother says.

AUGH, George says too loud.

Don't, her mother says jerking her head towards the back. Unless you want him awake, in which case you're in charge of entertainment.

I. Can't. Answer. Your. Moral. Question. Unless. I. Know. More. Details, George says sotto voce, which, in Italian, though George doesn't speak Italian, literally means below the voice.

Does morality need details? her mother whispers back.

God, George says.

Does morality need God? her mother says.

Talking to you, George says still below the voice, is like talking to a wall.

Oh, very good, you, very good, her mother says.

How exactly is that good? George says.

Because this particular art, artist and conundrum are all about walls, her mother says. And that's where I'm driving you to.

Yeah, George says. Up the wall.

Her mother laughs a real out-loud laugh, so loud that after it they both turn to see if Henry will waken, but he doesn't. This kind of laugh from her mother is so rare right now that it is almost like normal. George is so pleased she feels herself blush with it.

And what you just said is grammatically incorrect, she says.

It is not, her mother says.

It is, George says. Grammar is a finite set of rules and you just broke one.

I don't subscribe to that belief, her mother says.

I don't think you can call language a belief, George says.

I subscribe to the belief, her mother says, that language is a living growing changing organism.

I don't think that belief will get you into heaven, George says.

Her mother laughs for real again.

No, listen, an organism, her mother says –

(and through George's head flashes the cover of the old paperback called How To Achieve Good Orgasm that her mother keeps in one of her bedside cupboards, from way before George was born, from the time in her mother's life when she was, she says, young and easy under some appleboughs)

– which follows its own rules and alters them as it likes and the meaning of what I said is perfectly clear therefore its grammar is perfectly acceptable, her mother says.

(How To Achieve Good Organism.)

Well. Grammatically inelegant then, George says.

I bet you don't even remember what it was I said in the first place, her mother says.

Where I'm driving you to, George says.

Her mother takes both hands off the wheel in mock despair.

How did I, the most maxima unpedantic of all the maxima unpedantic women in the world, end up giving birth to such a pedant? And why the hell wasn't I smart enough to drown it at birth?

Is *that* the moral conundrum? George says.

Consider it, for a moment, yes, why don't you, her mother says.

No she doesn't.

Her mother doesn't say.

Her mother said.

Because if things really did happen simultaneously it'd be like reading a book but one in which all the lines of the text have been overprinted, like each page is actually two pages but with one superimposed on the other to make it unreadable. Because it's New Year not May, and it's England not Italy, and it's pouring with rain outside and regardless of the hum (the hummin') of the rain you can still hear people's stupid New Year fireworks going off and off and off like a small war, because people are standing out in the pouring rain, rain pelting into their champagne glasses, their upturned faces watching their own (sadly) inadequate fireworks light up then go black.

George's room is in the loft bit of the house and since they had the roof redone last summer it's had a leak in it at the slant at the far end. A little runnel of water comes in every time it rains, it's coming in right now, *happy New Year George! Happy New Year to you too, rain*, and running in a beaded line straight down the place where the plaster meets the plasterboard then dripping down on to the books piled on top of the bookcase. Over the weeks since it's been happening the posters have started to peel off it because the Blu-tack won't hold to some of the wall. Under them a light brown set of stains, like the map of a tree-root network, or a set of country lanes, or a thousand-times magnified mould, or the veins that get visible in the whites of your eyes when you're tired – no, not like any of these things, because thinking these things is just a stupid game. Damp is coming in and staining the wall and that's all there is to it.

George hasn't said anything about it to her father. The roofbeams will rot and then the roof will fall in. She wakes up with a bad chest and congestion in her nose whenever it's rained, but when the roof collapses inwards all the not being able to breathe will have been worth it.

Her father never comes into her room. He has no idea it is happening. With any luck he won't find out until it's too late.

It is already too late.

The perfect irony of it is that right now her

father has a job with a roofing company. His job involves going into people's houses with a tiny rotating camera that's got a light attached to it which he fastens to the end of the rods more usually used to sweep chimneys. He connects the camera to the portable screen and pushes it all the way up inside the chimney. Then anyone who wants to know, and has £120 to spare, can see what the inside of his or her chimney looks like. If the person who wants to know has an extra £150, her father can provide a recorded file of the visuals so he or she can look at the inside of the chimney owned by him or her any time he or she chooses.

They. Everybody else says they. Why shouldn't George?

Any time they choose.

Anyway George's room, given time, enough bad weather and the right inattention, will open to the sky, to all this rain, the amount of which people on TV keep calling biblical. The TV news has been about all the flooded places up and down the country every night now since way before Christmas (though there has been no flooding here, her father says, because the medieval drainage system is still as good as it always was in this city). Her room will be stained with the grey grease and dregs of the dirt the rain has absorbed and carries, the dirt the air absorbs every day just from the fact of life on earth. Everything in this room will rot.

She will have the pleasure of watching it happen. The floorboards will curl up at their ends, bend, split open at the nailed places and pull loose from their glue.

She will lie in bed with all the covers thrown off and the stars will be directly above her, nothing between her and their long-ago burnt-out eyes.

George (to her father) : Do you think, when we die, that we still have memories?

George's father (to George) : No.

George (to Mrs Rock, the school counsellor) : (exact same question).

Mrs Rock (to George) : Do you think we'll need memories, after we die?

Oh very clever, very clever, they think they're so clever always answering questions with questions. Though generally Mrs Rock is really nice. Mrs Rock is a rock, as the teachers at the school keep saying, like they think they're the first persons ever to have said it, when they suggest to George that she should be seeing Mrs Rock, *she's a rock you know*, which they say after they clear their throats and ask how George is doing, then say again after they hear that George is already seeing her and has managed to swap PE double period every week for a series of Rock sessions. Rock sessions! They laugh at George's joke then they look embarrassed, because they've laughed when they were supposed to be being attentive and mournful-looking, and can George really even have *made* a joke, is that *done*, since she's supposed to be feeling so sad and everything?

How are you feeling? Mrs Rock said.

I'm okay, George said. I think it's because I don't think I am.

You're okay because you don't think you're okay? Mrs Rock said.

Feeling, George said. I think I'm okay because I don't think I'm feeling.

You don't think you're feeling? Mrs Rock said.

Well, if I am, it's like it's at a distance, George said.

If you're feeling, it's at a distance? Mrs Rock said.

Like always having the sound of someone drilling a hole in a wall, not your wall, but a wall like very close to you, George said. Like, say you wake up one morning to the noise of someone along the road having work done on his or her house and you don't just hear the drilling happening, you feel it in your own house, though it's actually happening several houses away.

Is it? Mrs Rock said.

Which? George said.

Um, Mrs Rock said.

In any case, in both cases, the answer is yes, George said. It's at a distance *and* it's like the drilling thing. Anyway I don't care any more about syntax. So I'm sorry I troubled you with that last which.

200

Mrs Rock looked really confused.

She wrote something down on her notepad. George watched her do it. Mrs Rock looked back up at George. George shrugged and closed her eyes.

Because, George thought as she sat there with her eyes closed back before Christmas in Mrs Rock's self-consciously comfortable chair in the counselling office, how can it be that there's an advert on TV with dancing bananas unpeeling themselves in it and teabags doing a dance, and her mother will never see that advert? How can the world be this vulgar?

How can that advert exist and her mother not exist in the world?

She didn't say it out loud, though, because there wasn't a point.

It isn't about saying.

It is about the hole which will form in the roof through which the cold will intensify and after which the structure of the house will begin to shift, like it ought, and through which George will be able to lie every night in bed watching the black sky.

It is last August. Her mother is at the dining-room table reading out loud off the internet.

Meteor watchers are in luck tonight, her mother is saying. *With clear skies predicted for the Perseid shower for much of the UK, up to sixty shooting stars an hour should be visible between late Monday evening and early Tuesday morning.*

Sixty shooting stars! Henry says.

He runs round and round the table really fast making an eeeee noise as he goes.

Sky News weather presenter Sarah Pennock, her mother says, *said showers will fade during the night giving many people a chance to see the astronomical spectacle.*

Then her mother laughs.

Sky news! her mother says.

Henry. Headache. Enough, her father says.

He catches Henry, lifts him up and turns him upside down.

Eeeeeeeeeeee, Henry says. I am a star, I am shooting, and turning me upside down will not stop meeeeeeee.

It's just pollution, George says.

You won't say that when you see them shooting so beautiful over your head, her mother says.

Fully, George says.

Every meteor is a speck of comet dust vaporizing as it enters our atmosphere at thirty six miles per second, her mother reads.

That's not very fast, Henry says still upside down from beneath his jumper which has upended and fallen over his face. *Cars* go at thirty.

Per second, not per hour, George says.

One hundred and forty thousand miles an hour, her mother reads.

Remarkably slow really, Henry says.

He starts singing words.

Cars and stars, cars and stars.

It's exciting, her mother says.

Really cold tonight, George says.

Don't be so boring, George, her mother says.

Ia, George says because this conversation takes place when she has started insisting that her mother and father, when they use her name, call her her full name.

Her mother snorts a laugh.

What? George says.

It's just that when you say that, well. It sounds like you're saying something funny from my youth, her mother says. It's how we used to do caricatures of the rich kids. D'you remember, Nathan?

No, her father says.

Yah, George, yah, her mother says pretending to be a posh girl from the past.

George can choose react or ignore. She chooses ignore.

We wouldn't be able to see anything anyway, she says. There'll be too much local light.

We'll put all the lights off, her mother says.

I don't mean our lights. I mean all the lights of the whole of Cambridge, George says.

We'll put all those lights off too, her mother says. *Brightest around midnight*. Right. I know. We can all get in the car and drive out of town to the back of Fulbourn and watch them from there, Nathan, what do you think?

Up at six, Carol, her father says.

Good, okay, her mother says. You stay at home with Henry, and me and George, I mean George yah, will go.

Georgia and I, George says. And I'm not going.

That makes three of you George yahs not going, her mother says. Okay. All three of you plus your father can stay at home with Henry and I'll go myself. Nathan, his face is going very red, put him down.

No because I *want* to see the sixty stars, Henry says still upside down. I want to see them more than anyone else in this actual room.

It says here there might even be fireballs, her mother says.

I want to see fireballs a lot actually, Henry says.

It's just pollution. And satellites, George says. There's no point.

Miss Moan, her father says shaking Henry in the air.

Ms Moan, her mother says.

Pardon my world-stopping act of political incorrectness, her father says.

He says it gently and means it both funnily and nastily.

I prefer Miss, George says. Till I'm, you know, Doctor Moan.

Too young to know the political importance of choosing to be called Ms anything, her mother says.

She could be saying this to George or her father. Her father is ten years younger than her mother which means, her mother likes to say, that they have been formed by very different political upbringings, the main difference being a childhood under Thatcher versus a late adolescence under Thatcher.

(Thatcher was a prime minister some time after Churchill and long before George was born who, according to one of her mother's most successful Subverts, gave birth to a baby Blair, someone George actually remembers being prime minister from when she was small, him in a nappy and so on but standing fully-formed and otherwise naked on a shell (not the beach kind, the missile kind) with Thatcher all puffed-out cheeks blowing his hair about and baby Blair with one hand over his crotch and the other coy at his chest and the caption underneath : The Birth of Vain Us. That Subvert, George remembers, was everywhere. It was funny seeing it in all the papers and online and knowing and not being able to tell anyone that it was her mother who'd pressed the button that sent it out into the world.)

What the age difference between her parents means in real terms though is that they've split up twice, though twice so far got back together again.

And I suppose the days of you being at least gracious to me about feminism are long gone, but I won't complain, since it won't make any difference and since the history of feminism teaches one never to expect graciousness anyway, and when you're putting that child down, try not to put him down too hard on his head or you'll break his neck, her mother says without looking up from the screen. And George. Or whatever your name is. If you miss seeing this with me you'll regret it for the rest of your days.

I won't, George says.

Not says. Said.

There was an obituary in the Independent, because although George's mother wasn't famous like people who get obituaries usually are, and although she didn't have tenure any more, she still had a quite important job at a think-tank and occasionally published opinion pieces in the Guardian or the Telegraph and sometimes also the American papers in their European editions, and a lot more people knew who she was after it was unveiled in the papers about the guerrilla internet stuff. *Dr Carol Martineau Economist Journalist Internet Guerrilla Interventionist 19 November 1962–10 September 2013 aged 50 years.* It says, in the first paragraph, *renaissance woman.* It says *childhood Scottish Cairngorms education Edinburgh Bristol London.* It says *articles and talks*

*ideology pay ratios pay differentials literal
ideological consequences spread of UK poverty.* It
says *thesis backed by IMF recognition inequality
and slowdown in growth and stability.* It mentions
her particular bugbear, *chief executive interests
workforce kept low-waged.* It says *discovery three
years ago Martineau one of the anonymous
influential satire Subverts online art movement
thousands supporters imitators.*

It says *tragic unsuspected allergic reaction
standard antibiotic.*

The last thing it says is *is survived by.* That
means dead. *Husband Nathan Cook and their two
children.*

It all means dead.

It all means George's mother has disappeared off,
or rather into, the face of the earth.

Every day before work George's mother, when
she was alive (because she can't exactly do it now
being, you know, dead), used to do a keep-fit set of
stretches and exercises. At the end of this she would
always do a dance round the living room for the
length of a song on a playlist on her phone.

She'd started doing this a couple of years ago.
Every day she put up with everybody laughing at
her doing her moves among the furniture, her
headphones bigger than her ears.

Every single day, George has decided, from its
first day onwards for this first year in which her

mother won't be alive, she will not just wear something black somewhere on her person but she will do the sixties dance for her in her honour. This is only problematic in that George will have to listen to songs while she does it, and that listening to songs is one of the things she can no longer do without inducing a kind of sadness that actually hurts in the chest.

George's mother's phone is one of the things that went missing in the panic and aftermath. It hasn't turned up, though the house is still full of all her other things exactly where she left them. She will have had her phone with her. It went missing between the railway station and the hospital. Its number has been stopped, presumably by her father. If you ring it now the message you get is the recorded voice telling you this number is currently not in use.

George thinks her mother's phone has probably been taken by someone working in surveillance.

George's father : George, I told you. I don't want to hear any more of that paranoid nonsense from you.

Mrs Rock : So you believe your mother's phone was taken by someone working in surveillance?

All her mother's playlists were on her phone. Her mother was unusually private about her phone. George only sneaked a look at it once or twice (and both times felt bad for doing so, for different reasons). She never even looked at the playlists. She only looked at a couple of emails and texts. She never thought to look at music. It was her mother's music. It was bound to have been rubbish. Now she has no idea and will never know what song or songs her mother listened to every day to do the dance thing, or on the train, or walking along the street.

But the dance her mother did was always that old sixties dance, for which there are instructions online and even several specific songs.

There is a piece of Super 8 footage her mother had transferred, of herself as a very small child in about 1965 doing this dance with her own mother, George's grandmother. George has it on her laptop and her phone.

It is a grandmother who was dead way before George, though George has seen old photographs. She looks like someone from another time. Well, she is. She is a very young woman, strict-looking but pretty, a stranger with dark hair up on top of her head. The film footage is all flickers and shadows at the top edge of it, which is where the grandmother's face tends to be because the film is really being taken of George's mother, who is much much smaller in it than Henry is now. She must be only about three years old. She is wearing a cardigan knitted in pink wool. It is the most colourful thing in the film. George can even see the detail, if she stops the frame, of the toggle buttons on its front, they're black, and behind this child who is her mother there is a television screen on spindly slanted legs, the kind from when television screens bulged like the midriffs of obese middle-aged people.

George's mother, next to the stockinged legs of her own mother, is twisting from side to side in the silence, her little arms all elbow. She looks serious and grim but she is also smiling; even then her mouth, when she smiled, was that straight line and it looks like she is already, even so young, being polite yet firm about the fact that she's having to concentrate. In the film she is *really* having to concentrate because she is so small and the cardigan is so chunky, so much bigger and thicker than she is that she looks like a small pink snowperson, like she is bound to topple over. The whole thing somehow becomes about the fact that she is balancing her self in all its wholeness, compactness and littleness against something that looks like it's going to happen and which, if it does happen, will end the dance. But it never does happen because just before the film turns into being about some swans and rowing boats on a boating pond somewhere in Scotland the dance ends, her mother (as a child) puts her arms up in the air delighted and the lady with the hair up (George's grandmother) puts her arms down, catches the child and lifts her up into the flicker and out of the frame.

The dance part lasts 48 seconds on George's laptop.

Lockjaw. Quicksand. Polio. Lung. These are some of the words that George's mother was frightened of when she was small. (George once asked.)

Tell Laura I Love Her. That's one of the records that her mother loved when she was small. One Little Robin In A Cherry Tree. To listen to these, with first their crackling needle noise then the starburst of their hokey tunes, is like being able to experience the past like you have literally entered it and it is a whole other place, completely new to you, where people really did sing songs like this, a past so alien it is like a kind of shock.

Shock of the new and the old both at once, her mother says.

Said.

One afternoon George's father brings home the new turntable and when he finally works out how to connect it up with the CD soundbox they drag the old records out from under the stairs.

A boy called Tommy loves a girl called Laura. He wants to give her 'everything' (this is funny in itself, apparently, from the way her parents fall about, though this is back when George is too young to understand why), including flowers and presents and – the thing he wants to give her most – a wedding ring. But he can't afford one, so he signs up for a stock-car race because there is a prize of 1000 dollars (idiot, George says, yes, I'm afraid so, her mother says, romantic, her father says, and Henry is too little right then to say anything). Tommy phones Laura's house. But Laura's not there. So he tells her mother instead to Tell Laura he Loves Her, tell Laura he needs her, tell Laura he won't be late, he's got something to do that can't wait (uh-oh, her mother says, it's already tragic because at one remove. Is it? George says. What does one remove mean? Romantic, her father says. That's all technology ever does in the end, her mother says. It can't do anything but highlight the metaphysical. What's metaphysical? George says. Too big a word for this song, her father says). Then the car he's in bursts into flames and as they pull him dying from the twisted remains of it he tells them to tell Laura he loves her and not to cry because his love for her will never die.

She and her mother and father all crying with laughter on the rug.

Why did you even keep this record? George asks her mother. It's so bad.

I didn't know till today but obviously I was keeping it precisely so that you, me and your father would all end up listening to it today, her mother says and they all fall about laughing again.

Thinking about that today back then in this new today right now, and in whichever stage of mourning she's in, doesn't make George feel sad or feel anything in particular.

But in case the record might do for the dance thing she went downstairs just before New Year happened, but after her father'd gone out so he wouldn't be hurt by hearing it, and found it in the pile of smaller records by the turntable (there's a name for the smaller-sized records but she can't remember what it is).

She turned the sound to very low. She put it on. It had a warp in it so the guitars in its intro sounded seasick, like the record felt sick, though George herself felt fine, or rather, nothing.

It was definitely not suitable though, being too slow.

The dance her mother did every day needs an upward beat.

At midnight on all the other New Years her mother would usually get out some really nice paper, the kind with real bits of flower petal mixed in with its texture, and give her and her father two pieces each. They would each (except Henry, asleep, which was important, fire being involved) write their wishes and hopes for the new year on to one of them and write the things they'd hated most about the old year on to the other one. Then – being very very careful not to mix the pieces up – each person would take a turn standing over the sink, strike a match, hold the flame to a corner of the piece of paper with all the things written on it that he or she hadn't liked, and watch it burn. Then when you couldn't hold it any more without hurting yourself you could drop it safely into the sink (this letting-go of it was the whole point of the ritual, her mother always said) where, when it finished burning, you could wash the burnt-up bits away.

This year George has no wishes and hopes.

Instead the piece of paper in front of her is blank except for the words WHAT'S LEFT OF XMAS HOLIDAYS DAILY SCHEDULE. She has written numbers, meaning the times of day, down one side of it. Next to 9.30 she has written DANCE THING.

This is the whole point of her looking for likely tunes, so that she will be ready to begin as soon as breakfast is over tomorrow (today).

Some time ago, George goes into her mother's study and wanders around poking at the things on top of the books on the shelves. Her mother is not dead yet. Her mother is there working. There are piles of papers everywhere.

George, her mother says without looking round.

What are you working on? George says.

Haven't you homework? her mother says.

You're working on whether I've got homework? George says.

George, her mother says. Don't move anything, stop touching stuff and go and get on with something of your own.

George comes and stands at the corner of the desk. She sits on the chair next to her mother's chair.

I'm a bit bored, she says.

Me too, her mother says. This is statistics. I have to concentrate.

Her mouth is the thin line.

Why do you keep these? George says picking up the little jar full of pencil shavings.

The jar was originally a Santorini mini capers jar, it says so on what's left of the label. Through the glass you can see the different woods of the different pencils her mother has been using. One layer is dark brown. One layer is light gold colour. You can see the paint lines, the tiny zigzags of colour made into the shapes like the edges of those scallop shells by the twist of the pencil in the sharpener.

One pencil, she can see, was once red and black (stripes?). One pencil was marbled blue. One was green, a really nice bright green. George takes out a blue-edged sharpening. It looks a bit like a wooden moth. She winds it round her finger. It is delicate and falls to pieces as soon as she twists it.

Keep what? her mother says.

George holds out the bits of shaving.

215

What's the point? she says.

Point. Ha ha! her mother says. Funny.

Why don't you just sharpen your pencils into the bin like a normal person? George says.

Well, her mother says pushing her chair back. It seems sad to, to just throw them away, I don't like to. Not until I've finished whatever project I've used them on.

Bit pathetic, George says.

Well, yes, I suppose it is, her mother says. Literally. I think it's cause they're a proof of something. Hmm. But a proof of what?

George rolls her eyes.

Proof that you once sharpened some pencils, George says. Can I borrow the dictionary for a minute?

Use your own, her mother says. Go away. Shut the door after you, you annoying and challenging little pest.

She pulls her chair back in and clicks on something. George doesn't leave immediately. She stands behind her mother, takes the big dictionary off the shelf and opens it against the wall.

Plonk piazza pelmet pathway partake pastiche pathetic see under pathos. The quality that arouses pity. Pathetic. Affecting the emotions of pity, grief or sorrow. Sadly inadequate. (Interesting: inadequate *and* sad.) Contemptible. Derisory. Applied to the superior oblique muscle, which turns

216

the eyeball downwards, and to the trochlear nerve connecting with it (*anat*).

It isn't until George has left the room and shut the door after her that she gets what she herself said and why it was funny.

Pencil sharpenings. The point. Ha ha!

She thinks about going back in and saying

I get it!

But she knows not to, so she doesn't.

(Point taken, George thinks now, on New Year's morning.)

WHAT'S LEFT OF XMAS HOLIDAYS DAILY SCHEDULE.

Under DANCE THING next to 10 a.m. she writes the word GARDEN.

This word garden here means more than just garden, because some time ago (before September) George got fed up of everybody at school always talking about the porn they'd seen on the internet. It was like doubly being a virgin, not having seen any. So she decided to watch some and make her own mind up. But she didn't want Henry seeing because he is only eight, well, he was even younger, only seven, then. This is not discriminatory on her part. He will look for himself and decide for himself when he is old enough. That is, if he gets the chance to wait that long, since kids watch this stuff pretty freely in the playgrounds of the primary schools too.

217

So she took the iPad and sat in what was left of the pergola, where she could see anyone (especially Henry) coming towards her, in case, and she clicked on the first images that came up, and it was kind of interesting, quite amazing really all the things she saw and she began to be glad she'd decided to sit out in the garden away from the house.

It was interesting at first. It was quite eye-opening.

It got boring and repetitive quite fast.

After it did, she began to be interested instead in how many of the scenarios needed to have or at least to pretend to have stories. There was one in which a long-haired blonde woman of about twenty, wearing nothing but high heels, was having her hands tied at the wrists by a much older woman wearing a quite fashionable low-cut evening dress. The older woman tipped the younger one's chin up and she took an eye-dropper and squeezed something into each of the younger woman's eyes. Apparently this now made the younger woman blind. The older woman led her into a room a bit like a gym if a gym were to be painted black and have chains hanging off its wall bars; also a bit like a gym there were machines and all sorts of apparatus in the room, as well as a semi-circle of men and women dressed in the same kind of evening clothes as the older woman, as if they'd all gone out to a prestigious formal function

218

somewhere. The younger woman didn't know any of this. She couldn't see anything because of the eye drops. At least, that was the story. At this point the film flashed forward on to lots of edits showing extreme-looking moments of what was about to happen to the blind woman, which you'd only get to see in full if you subscribed.

Could she see? Was she really blind? George was intrigued. Was it real? Or was the woman just acting? And if she was blind, had been blinded by whatever the older woman squeezed into her eyes, how long did it take before it wore off and she could see again? Or could she never see again? Maybe she was somewhere in the world right now still wandering about blind. Maybe they'd told her it would wear off, and it never did, or only partially did. Maybe something about those eye drops changed something about the way she saw. Or, on the other hand, maybe she was perfectly fine and had 20:20 vision regardless.

20:20 vision regardless! Oxymoron. Ha ha.

Then there was a film where a quite old woman, in her thirties, lay on her back and got fucked one after the other pretty briefly each time by a large number of men, most of them wearing masks like killers wear in thrillers on TV. A figure always came up on the screen every time a new one started. 7!! 8!! 9!! Then the figures flashed forward from 13!! 14!! to 34!! 35!! 36!! There were supposedly forty

219

men altogether. The whole thing was supposed to have taken exactly forty minutes, that's what the onscreen clock showed, though the film lasted about five. There was only the one woman, on her back on what looked like a coffee table, which can't have been comfortable. Her eyes were shut, she was a kind of red colour all over, and it was also as if someone had fuzzed or smudged the lens, like it had steamed up. At the end of the film the words on the screen announced that after this filmshoot *my wife* was *pregnant*. Then three exclamation marks. *!!!*

Why was it forty? George wondered sitting in the garden with the flowers all nodding round her and the occasional passing butterfly's shadow calling her eyes beyond the iPad. Was it because forty is a number that sounds like it means a lot, a magic number like forty days and forty nights, forty years in the desert, forty thieves? Open sesame! Ha ha. No, that was a bit sick. And was the woman on the coffee table really the wife of the person who made the film? And was she really pregnant after it? There was something a bit interesting about it, like watching a queen bee at work in a hive. But why had so many of the men worn the masks? Did that make it more exciting? For whom? Or perhaps they didn't want their own wives, or people at work if they went for interviews, say, after they'd taken part in this film, to know their identities.

Then one afternoon George had clicked on a particular film which made her swear to herself that she'd watch this same film (or a bit of it, since it was quite lengthy) once every day for the rest of her life.

There was a girl in it who must have been sixteen because of legality but looked much younger than George. She looked about twelve. There was a man in it who looked about forty. When he kissed this girl he took almost her whole face into his mouth. They were in a yurt-like room for a very long time doing stuff and the uncomplaining smallness of the girl alongside her evident discomfort and the way she looked both there and absent, as if she'd been drugged, given something to make her feel things in slower motion than they were actually happening to her, had changed something in the structures of George's brain and heart and certainly her eyes, so that afterwards when George tried to watch any more of this kind of sexual film that girl was there waiting under them all.

More. George found that the girl was there too, pale and pained with her shut eyes and her open o of a mouth, under the surface of the next TV show she watched on catch-up.

She was there under the YouTube videos of Vampire Weekend and the puppy falling off the sofa and the cat sitting on the hoover that hoovered by itself and the fox so domesticated that the person taking the film could stroke its head.

She was there under the pop-ups and the adverts on Facebook, and under the facts about the history of the suffragettes on the BBC site which George looked up for school.

She was there under the news item about the woman who tried to buy a burger at a McDonald's drive-thru on her horse, who, when she was refused at the hatch, got off her horse and led it into the main building and up to the counter and tried to order there. *McDonald's regrets we are unable to serve customers on horseback.*

When she'd sensed that girl there underneath even this, George went back through her own history to find the porn film. She clicked on it.

The girl sat demure on the edge of the bed again.

The man grinned at the camera and took the girl's head in his hands again.

What you doing out here, Georgie? her father asked her a couple of months ago.

November. It was cold. Her mother was dead. George had forgotten about the girl for weeks, then remembered in a French class at school when they were revising the conditional. She had come home and gone into the garden and found the film and clicked on it. She had apologized sotto voce to the girl in the film for having been inattentive.

Her father'd come out to put stuff in the bins. George was in the pergola with no jacket on. He walked up the garden. She turned the screen towards him. As he got closer he slowed down.

Jesus, George, he said. What are you doing?

I wanted to ask mum about it, George said. I meant to. I was going to. Now I can't.

She explained to her father that she had formerly watched, and intended again to watch, this film of this girl every day to remind herself not to forget the thing that had happened to this person.

But George, her father said.

She told him she was doing it in witness, by extension, of all the unfair and wrong things that happen to people all the time.

George, it's good of you, her father said. I applaud the sentiment.

It's not just sentiment, George said.

Honestly George, when I saw you out here watching something I was cheered, he said. I thought, good, Georgie's back, she's watching something on the iPad, she's interested in things again. I was pleased. But sweet heart. It's appalling, that stuff. You can't watch that. And you have to remember, it's not really meant for you. And *I* can't even *look* at it. And anyway. That girl. I mean. It probably happened years ago.

That's no reason not to do what I'm doing, George said.

She was probably very well paid for it, her father said.

George's eyes widened. She snorted.

I can't believe you just said that, she said. I can't believe I'm even related to you.

And sex isn't like that. Loving sex. Real sex. Sex between people who love each other, her father said.

Do you really think I'm that much of a moron? George said.

And you'll drive yourself mad if you keep watching stuff like that, her father said. You'll do damage to yourself.

Damage has already happened, George said.

George, her father said.

This really happened, George said. To *this* girl. And anyone can just watch it just, like, happening, any time he or she likes. And it happens for the first time, over and over again, every time someone who hasn't seen it before clicks on it and watches it. So I want to watch it for a completely different reason. Because my completely different watching of it goes some way to acknowledging all of that to this girl. Do you still not understand?

She held the screen up. Her father put the flat of his hand over his eyes.

Yes, but George, her father said. You watching it, whichever way you think you're watching it or intend to see it, won't make any real difference to that girl. It just means the number of people watching the film with her in it will keep going up. And anyway, you can't be sure of, you can never know. There are circumstances –

I've got eyes, George said.

Well, okay, well, what about Henry? her father said. What if he saw?

Why d'you think I'm out here in the cold? He won't. Not because of me anyway. I mean, obviously he'll have to do his own seeing in his own time, George said. And anyway. You watch stuff like this. I know you do. Everyone watches it.

Oh dear God, her father said. I can't believe what you just said.

He'd turned his back because the film was still facing him and was still playing. With his back to her he started to complain. Other people's children, lucky other people, normal children with normal neuroses like always having to have the same spoon to eat with or just not eating at all or throwing up, cutting themselves, whatever.

He was sort-of joking and sort-of not.

George sat back. She clicked the pause button. She waited till her father had left the garden.

She sat with her father that night watching Newsnight, the kind of programme on which massacres and injustices happened every day – if they made the news – then disappeared into old news, just weren't news any more. Her mother was dead. Her father was asleep. He was extremely tired. He was sleeping a lot. It was because of the mourning. When he woke up he switched the channel over without even looking at George to UK Border Force on the channel called Pick.

Who'd ever have believed it? George's mother says.

It is a year before she dies. George and her parents are watching rubbish on TV before going to bed, flicking channels before giving in and putting it off.

Who'd ever have believed, she says, when I was growing up, that one day we'd be watching programmes about people being checked and failed at passport controls? When did this become light entertainment?

Six months before she dies and shortly before she gets depressive about her friendship fizzling out with that woman Lisa Goliard, George's mother comes into the living room. It is a Sunday evening. George is watching a programme about the Flying Scotsman, a train from the past, on TV. But because George came in halfway through this programme and missed the beginning, and because it is an interesting programme, she is simultaneously watching it from the start on catch-up on her laptop.

On one screen the train has just broken the hundred-mile-an-hour record. On the other screen the train has just been superseded by cars. At the same time George is looking up photobombs on her phone. There are some very brilliant and funny ones. There are some you can't believe haven't been digitally enhanced, or look like they must have been set up but the people who took them swear they haven't.

You, her mother says watching her, are a migrant of your own existence.

I am not, George says.

You are, her mother says.

What's your problem, dinosaur? George says.

Her mother laughs.

Same problem as yours, she says. We're all migrants of our own existence now. In this bit of the world at least. So we better get ready. Because look how migrants get treated all over the world.

Sometimes your political correctness is so tedious that I find myself fall –, George says.

Then she mimes falling asleep.

Don't you ever want to simplify? her mother says. Read a book?

I read all the time, George says.

Think about just one thing, instead of fifteen all at once? her mother says.

I'm versatile, George says without looking up. I'm from the versatile generation. And you're supposed to be the great online anarchist. You should approve of me being so savvy.

Savvy, yes, her mother says. Always be savvy please. I'd need that from any daughter of mine. Otherwise, what with me being so politically correct and everything, I'd be sending you straight to the orphanage.

Properly speaking, that would mean both you and dad would have to die, George says.

Well, one day, her mother says. With any luck later rather than sooner. Anyway. I don't actually care how many screens you look at at once. I'm just doing my concerned-parent bit. We all have to. It's in the contract.

Blah, George says. You're pretending you're being cool about it now because online interventionism was once perceived for about three months several years ago to be cool –

Thanks! her mother says. Ratified at last.

– but really you're just as paranoid as everybody else over forty, George says, all sackcloth and ashes and stuck in the past, hitting your chests with a scourge and ringing your little bells, *unclean! Unclean! Disempowerment by information! Disempowerment by information!*

Oh, that's good, George, her mother says. Can I have that?

For a Subvert? George says.

Yes, her mother says.

No, George says.

Please? her mother says.

How much will you pay me? George says.

You're a born mercenary, her mother says. £5.

Done, George says.

Her mother takes a note out of her purse and writes on it in pencil, in the white space between the picture of Elizabeth Fry and the drawing of some of the women prisoners she helped, the words *disempowerment by information paid in full.*

Then : George spent that £5 note the day after. She liked the thought of releasing it into the wild.

Now : George wishes she hadn't spent that £5 note. Somewhere out in the world, if no one's rubbed it out and it hasn't worn off, her mother's handwriting is passing from hand to hand, stranger to stranger.

George looks at the word GARDEN under DANCE THING, in her own handwriting. The dance bit will take less than five minutes and the film of the girl is forty five minutes long, and she can't usually bear to make herself watch more than five of those terrible minutes.

Dance thing. Garden. Then Henry standing like a Victorian child from one of the sick sentimental songs about death and orphans, holding his hands in the prayery way in which he's been holding them since he saw Carols from King's on TV last week. Then her father trying to pretend he's not drunk, or getting up still drunk and sleeping it off till lunchtime on the couch, then trying to think up an excuse to go somewhere for the evenings with people who'll think the only good thing they can do for him is get him drunk, and he won't be back at work until after the weekend which means five more days of drunk.

It is only about ten past midnight. Hardly any time has passed. The fireworks are still going off sporadically outside. The rain is still drumming on the Velux. But her father is not yet home and probably won't be for ages and George has decided to wait up for him in case when he gets home he can't get up the stairs by himself.

There's a noise outside her door.

It's Henry.

He is standing in the doorway looking tearful and fevered and bizarrely a little like an illustration of Little Lord Fauntleroy now that his hair is so long.

(He is refusing to have it cut because she always cut his hair.

Henry, she's not coming back, George has said.

I know, Henry said.

She's dead, George said. You know that.

I don't want my hair cut, Henry said.)

You can come in, George says. Special dispensation.

Thank you, Henry says.

He stands at the door. He doesn't come in.

I'm really awake. I'm really bored, he says

He is near tears.

George goes over to her bed and folds down the covers and pats it. Henry comes into the room, comes over to the bed and climbs in.

Toast? George says.

Henry is looking at the photos of their mother George has put above the bed. He reaches his hand up to one of them.

Don't, George says.

He is good, because so recently asleep. He turns round and sits down.

Two slices please, he says.

With jam? George says.

No butter, whatever you do, he says.

I will bring you two slices of toast, George says. And after you've eaten them you and I together will banish boredom.

Henry shakes his head.

I don't mean bored, he says. I want to be bored. But I can't. But I really don't want to be this thing that I'm having to be instead of being bored.

George nods.

And Henry, she says. Don't touch those photos while I'm gone. I mean it.

George goes downstairs and makes a single slice of toast. She knifes over it with quite thick butter then puts the butter knife straight into the jam without washing it because no one will even notice.

She does it precisely *because* no one will, because she can leave dregs of butter in whatever jam she likes for the rest of her life now.

By the time she gets back upstairs Henry is asleep. She knew he would be. She takes the photo he's unstuck off the wall out of his hand (the picture of her mother as a teenager sitting on a statue in a park in Edinburgh right up on the back of the horse of whoever the man is the statue happens to represent) and sticks it back in its place (she has arranged them so that there is no chronology).

She sits down on the floor, leans back against her own bed and eats the toast.

It's so *boring*, she says in Italy in the palazzo in the mock-child voice they always use for this game.

Only you would come through the doors of a palace designed especially to dispel boredom and know to say out loud, by some magic understanding of the meanings of things, that you find it boring, her mother says.

But George is playing the what's-the-point-of-art game. Maybe her mother hasn't realized she's playing it.

There's nobody else in this *whole place* but us, she says still in the voice. What's the *point*, what's the *point* of it? What's it got to do with *anything*? What's the *point* of art?

Art makes nothing happen in a way that makes something happen. (That's the wording of one of

232

her mother's most retweeted Subverts.) Obviously. But this is a family game. They've played this game for years. It is one of her father's games, he plays it to make her and her brother laugh whenever her mother makes them all go to a gallery. He pretends to be a slightly mentally challenged person. He pretends it so well that sometimes people in the galleries turn and look at him, or look away in case he really might be mentally challenged.

In this case the art in this room has already made something happen – the literal cheering-up of her mother, who happened last week to see a stray photo in an art magazine of one of the pictures from here, a blue-coloured picture of a man standing dressed in ripped white clothes and wearing an old rope as a belt, at the seeing and liking so much of which her mother literally stopped being sad (she has been in a bad mood for weeks now because of her friend Lisa Goliard disappearing) then announced to the family over breakfast three days ago that they were all going to see that picture for real next week and that she'd booked a hotel.

Nathan, can you take Wednesday to Sunday off? she said.

Nope, her father said.

Fine, she said. I don't need you to look at pictures with me. George, can you take Wednesday to Friday off school?

I'll have to check with my secretary, George said,

I've got a very busy schedule. And I feel it's my duty
to inform you that it's illegal to take children out of
school just for holidays now.

How's your throat? her mother said.

Really really sore, George said. I think it's an
infection. Where are we going?

Somewhere in Italy, her mother said. Henry,
how's your throat?

My throat is very well, thank you for asking,
Henry said.

Henry, your throat is really sore, George said.

Is it? Henry said.

Otherwise you can't come to Italy, George said.

Is it good there for throats? Henry said.

Now, in the palazzo, when George says the
supposed-to-be-funny thing about what's the point
of art, Henry says, as if he thinks she means it too,

It's really pretty.

Henry is gay. He must be. Though it's true, this is
a really pretty room. At least, that part up at that
end there is, it's spectacular, or maybe it's just
better lit than the other parts of the room. Her
mother is off the whole length of the place towards
it. It is like her mother has been struck by – what?
Lightening. Her mother has lightened up since the
minute they landed in this country and the plane
door opened and the warmer air came in.

The moment they walked into this room she
lightened even more.

234

Though it is embarrassing and excruciating when someone won't play your game George gets over herself. She slips into her real self again.

Is this the place you were talking about in the car? she says. The moral conundrum?

Her mother says nothing.

She is looking.

George looks too.

The room is warm and dark. No, not dark, it's light. Both. It's like a huge dark dance hall with a lit-up picture that goes round some of its walls. There is nothing else in the room, except some low benches on which to sit and look at the walls, and over in the far corner a middle-aged lady (attendant?) on a folding seat. Apart from that, there is just the picture. It is impossible to see it all at once. Half the room is covered in it. The other half has faded picture, or no picture. What there is, though, is so full of life happening that it's actually like life, at least those bits are at the far end. And the people in the broad blue stripe which goes all round the middle of the wall, all through the middle of the picture splitting it into an above and a below, look like they're floating, or walking on air, especially in that brighter part.

It resembles a giant comic strip. Except it's also like art.

There are ducks. There's a man with his fist round the neck of a duck. The duck looks really

235

surprised, like it's saying *what the f–*. Above the duck's head there's another bird just sitting there completely free. It's sitting next to the man and it's watching him throttling the duck as if it's quite interested in what's happening.

This is only one detail. There are details like it everywhere. There's a paddling dog. George stares at its genitals. In fact, look at the largeness of the testicles on all the creatures who have them everywhere in the picture, except the one creature you'd expect it on, the bull. He doesn't seem to have any.

Then there's a monkey hugging the leg of a boy, who regards it with snobby disdain. Over there there's a very small child in a cap, in yellow, reading or eating something. An old woman holding a piece of paper is being attentive to the child. There are unicorns pulling a chariot here and lovers kissing there, and people with musical instruments here, people working up trees and in fields there. There are cherubs and garlands, crowds of people, women working at what looks like a loom up there, and down here there are eyes looking out of a black archway while people talk and do business and don't notice the looking. There are dogs and horses, soldiers and townspeople, birds and flowers, rivers and riverbanks, water bubbles in the rivers, swans that look like they're laughing. There's a crowd of babies. They look haughty. There are rabbits, or hares, no, both.

The buildings in the picture are sometimes beautiful and sometimes broken open, there are broken road slabs and bricks, broken arches up against fine architecture and plants growing through the whole and broken buildings everywhere.

It is impossible, though, not to keep looking then looking back again at the blue-coloured stripe which runs like a frieze round the room between the upper part and the lower parts of the picture and in which the people and the animals seem to float free. The blue calls your eyes every time. It gives you a breather from the things happening above and below it. In the blue there's a woman in a beautiful red dress just sitting in the air above a cheeky-looking goat or sheep. There's the man in the white rags. That's the man who was in the picture her mother saw at home. He's why they're here. Along from him, on the other side of the woman floating above the goat, there's a young man or a young woman, could be either, dressed in beautiful rich clothes and holding an arrow or a stick and a gold hoop thing, like everything's nothing but a charming game.

Male or female? she says to her mother who's standing under these figures.

237

I don't know, her mother says.

Her mother, smiling, points to the man in rags then the woman sitting on air then the playful rather dilettante richly dressed figure in turn.

Male, female, both, she says. Beautiful, all of them, including the sheep. And look at that.

She points to the top level, the level it hurts more to look at for longer because it's so high, where there are three chariots, pulled by different creatures, and a lot of people standing about, and birds and rabbits and trees and flowers and far landscapes.

In come the gods, her mother says.

Are they the gods? George says.

And nobody even notices, her mother says. Look at all the people round them. Like the gods are no big deal. In they come and nobody even bats an eyelid.

George turns on her heel to look at the other wall. Down that long side of the room there's more of the picture. It's meant to be the same kind of thing as this wall. The overall design is the same. But it's just not as good, not as eyecatching or interesting – or maybe it hasn't been as well restored.

George has a closer look at the other picture-wall.

Its figures are just not as beautiful. There are creatures, like that giant lobster there, but they're nothing compared, say, to that horse on that wall looking out almost directly, whose eyes tell you he's not at all sure about having that man on his back. There are people and flowers here too, even people covered in flowers, but they're less attractive, or more grotesque, than the people there on that end wall where the horses get fatter as the skies get bluer.

It is meant to be the seasons, is it?

She goes back to the good wall.

It is like everything is in layers. Things happen right at the front of the pictures and at the same time they continue happening, both separately and connectedly, behind, and behind that, and again behind that, like you can see, in perspective, for miles. Then there are the separate details, like that man with the duck. They're all also happening on their own terms. The picture makes you look at both – the close-up happenings and the bigger picture. Looking at the man with the duck is like seeing how everyday and how almost comic cruelty is. The cruelty happens in among everything else happening. It is an amazing way to show how ordinary cruelty really is.

There doesn't seem to be hunting or cruelty in the top parts, just the lower parts.

The unicorns have horns that look like they're made of lit-up glass.

The clothes all the people are wearing look as if breeze is blowing through them.

239

George turns towards her mother and is surprised by how young and bright she looks standing under the blue.

What *is* this place? George says.

Her mother shakes her head.

Palazzo, she says.

Then she says a word that George can't catch.

I've never seen anything like it, her mother says. It's so warm it's almost friendly. A friendly work of art. I've never thought such a thing in my life. And look at it. It's never sentimental. It's generous, but it's sardonic too. And whenever it's sardonic, a moment later it's generous again.

She turns to George.

It's a bit like you, she says.

Then she doesn't say anything. She just looks.

The place is completely silent behind them except for the lady attendant who has been charmed by Henry into leading him from picture to picture and telling him the words for whatever he points at.

Cavallo, the woman says.

Horse, Henry says.

Si! the woman says. Bene. Unicorni. Cielo. Stelle. Terra. Dei e dee e lo zodiaco. Minerva. Venere. Apollo. Minerva Marzo Ariete. Venere Aprile Toro. Apollo Maggio Gemelli. Duca Borso di Ferrara. Dondo la giustizia. Dondo un regalo. Il palio. Un cagnolino.

She sees George and her mother are both

listening to her too. She points at the blank and faded walls.

Secco, she says.

She points at the still-picture-covered walls.

Fresco, she says.

She points at the really good bright end wall.

Mando o andato a Venezia per ottenere il meglio azzurro.

I think she's saying that the blue colour is Venetian, her mother says.

George's mother goes over to speak to the attendant. She speaks in English. The attendant speaks back in Italian which her mother doesn't speak. They smile at each other and have a conversation.

What did she say? George asks her mother as they leave the room through the curtained door and go down the stairs.

I've no idea, her mother says. But it was nice to talk to her.

Afterwards they sit at an outside restaurant table in the garden of this place. Yellow sweet-smelling flowers drop off the trees on to their heads and on to the table. George notices a huge crack in the outside of the palace building up near the roof.

The earthquake maybe, her mother says. Quite recent. Last year. I think we're lucky to have got to see it at all. I think it's just reopened to the public.

Is that why some of the walls have pictures and

some just blank plaster? George says. And two of the people in the chariots on the end wall have faces and one of them doesn't?

I don't know, her mother says. I don't know much about it. It was quite hard to find out anything. But I'm finding it quite enjoyable, not knowing.

But what about the moral conundrum? George says.

The what? her mother says.

The getting paid more for the better art, George says.

Oh, yes. That, her mother says. Well.

She tells George again about the artist who did part of the room five hundred and fifty years ago, who thought his work should be paid better than everybody else's in the room and wrote a letter asking the Duke for more money.

In fact, what happened is something even more compelling, she says. Because that letter he wrote's the only reason we know anything about that artist even existing. And they only found that letter a hundred years ago. Which was more than four hundred years after he painted his bit of the walls. For four hundred years he didn't exist. No one even knew the room had frescoes in it till only about a hundred or so years ago, end of the eighteen hundreds. They'd been whitewashed over for hundreds of years. Then some whitewash fell off the walls and they found these pictures underneath The room'd been lost till then.

So if you were in a room, I mean like if you were just sitting in a room. Could the room you were actually in get – lost? Henry says.

He looks stricken.

No, George says. Don't be an idiot.

Don't call your brother an idiot, George's mother says.

You're an idiot, Henry says.

Don't call your sister an idiot, their mother says.

I didn't call him an idiot, I said nidiot, George says. Nidiot is much worse than just idiot.

You're far and away more of a nidiot than me, Henry says.

Than I am, George says.

Her mother laughs.

You can't not do that, can you? she says. It's your nature, isn't it?

Do what? George says.

Henry runs off into the cow parsley at the rough end of the garden where there are some modern-looking sculptures and the meadow has been left to grow as high as it likes. Because the grass is so high he vanishes completely.

This is like a magic place, her mother says.

It's true that it is kind of spectacular here, George thinks – and that's the second time she's thought the word spectacular – because when they walked out here a moment ago and down the garden path to this restaurant, which looked like it might be a junk shop but turns out to serve pasta and wine, a jazz track with old-fashioned piano and trumpets suddenly started playing as if by itself in the air (in reality out of one of the restaurant's speakers) as if especially for them.

Now the garden fills with Italian schoolchildren younger than George and older than Henry. They sit round the tables and talk to each other.

Did he get the money in the end? George says.

Who? her mother says.

The painter, George says. Because he really *was* better. If he painted the part of the room at the far end.

I don't know, George, her mother says. I know almost nothing about it. I only really know what I've told you, which is what it said under the picture when I saw it at home. When we get back I'll read up about it. Though, you know, it might just be that our eyes are more used to finding some parts of the room more beautiful than the others, because of what we now expect beauty to be. It might be *our* standards rather than *theirs*. But I agree. I agree with you. Some of it is really outstandingly beautiful. Some of it is breathtaking. And I find it pretty interesting that the only reason we know that the painter who did that wall existed, even lived at all, is that he asked for more.

Like Oliver Twist, George says.

Her mother smiles.

In some ways, she says.

What was his name? George says.

Her mother screws up her eyes.

You know, I knew this, George, I did know. I read it when we were at home. But right now I can't remember it, her mother says.

We came all this way to see a picture you like that much but you can't remember the name of the man who did it? George says.

Her mother widens her eyes at her.

I know, she says. But it kind of doesn't matter, does it, that we don't know his name. We saw the pictures. What more do we need to know? It's enough just that someone painted them and then one day we came here and saw them. No?

I could look it up on your phone, George says.

Then she immediately feels a mixture of things ranging from unpleasant all the way to bad.

(Guilt and fury:

– *Sing me a love song*

– *No, my singing voice went with pregnancy*

– *I wonder where it went. I bet its in a cathedral city up in some fancy cathedral ceiling hanging out with the carvings of the angels*

Fury and guilt:

— Howre your eyes today and how you doin what you doin where are you & whenll we meet)

Her mother doesn't notice. Her mother has no idea. Her mother is looking down for where her phone is, checking it is safely in the pocket of her bag.

(George's own phone is not a smartphone though she will be given one of her own in less than a year's time, at Christmas, three and a half months after her mother dies.)

Let's not look anything up, her mother says. It's so nice. Not to have to know.

Her mother is going soft.

Not that there's anything wrong with soft. Her mother, soft, forgetful, vague and loving, like other people's mothers always seem to be, is a whole new prospect.

But it is very unlike her not to try to know or to find out everything there is to know. And this morning at the hotel, when they'd been leaving the breakfast room and passing the reception, her mother had said *buona sera* to the man and the girl behind the counter, and the girl had laughed. Then that girl had realized she was being impolite, had become ashamed and had stopped herself laughing. George had never seen anyone correct herself or himself like that.

Not buona sera, madam, forgive me, the man said. But it is buon giorno. Because you are wishing us a good evening and right now it is morning.

246

Outside the hotel her mother had stopped on the pavement and looked at George.

This place is shaking loose everything I thought I knew, she said. All the things I've been taking for granted for years.

She put her arm round George's shoulder. She hugged Henry close in to her other side.

It is so bloody lovely to forget myself for a bit! she said.

She looked genuinely happy there on the pavement outside the shop selling the souvenirs and products of Ferrara.

George turns now in the palazzo garden and straddles the bench. She has noticed there's something strange about those schoolkids and she has just realized what it is. None of them is on a phone or looking at a screen. They are all talking to each other. Some of them are now even talking to Henry, or trying to. Henry is describing something. He draws a circle in the air. The kids he's talking to do the same circling thing with their arms.

George looks at her mother. Her mother looks at George. A yellow-white flower drops, brushes past her mother's nose, catches in her hair and comes to rest on her collarbone. Her mother laughs. George feels the urge to laugh too, though she is still wearing her guilt / fury scowl. Half her mouth turns up. The other half holds its downward shape.

This town they've come to is both bright and

grim. It is a place of walls and has a huge and imposing castle about which, if George were writing about it at school, she'd use the words impervious and threatening. There is this constant sense of battlement, then there are the winding high-walled little streets which look like nightmares will happen down them, that they'll definitely leave you lost. But things change in a moment here, light to dark, dark to light, and although it is so stony it is somehow also bright green and red and yellow too; all the walls and buildings go red-golden in the sun. The walls are high and blank but it sounds as if beyond them is hidden garden. There are the long straight avenues of really beautiful trees, as if it's not a city of walls at all, it's a city of trees. In fact, all the buildings and walls have bits of tree and bush and grass sprouting out of them at the tops and up the sides of their bright walls.

It smells of jasmine, then more jasmine, then the occasional sewer, then jasmine again.

It's very very strange here, her mother had said last night as they were getting ready for bed. I can't quite get a grip on it.

She looked at the map on the bed.

It's as if that map they gave us is nothing to do with the actual experience of being here, she said.

They'd been wandering about getting lost the whole day even though they had the map the hotel had given them. Things that looked close by on the map were, when they tried to get to them, actually quite far away; then they'd try to do something that looked like it'd take a very long time to do and they'd find themselves arriving almost immediately.

If her mother'd simply looked it up on Google Maps or Streetview they could've got to places with more precision and alacrity. But her mother is reluctant to look anything up, or even switch the phone on, for some reason.

Alacrity? That's a good word, George, her mother says.

From the Latin. For briskness, George says.

We don't need briskness. Let's follow our noses unbriskly for a change. It's the first modern city in Europe, her mother says as they walk back through it after seeing the palace. Because of the town planning and the walls. Though both of you are used to historic towns, growing up where you've grown up. You see stuff like this every day. It's probably no big deal to you. Anyway, the palace we just saw, with the pictures, pre-dates even the walls. It's from before this city was walled. It's that early. It's outstanding, for something that early.

Then she stops saying things like that and they simply wander in a daze looking a bit like the reprobate kids at school do after splitting, because this is nothing like home. For instance now that it's the time of day when people here come out and wander about, the streets are full of pedestrians. At

249

the same time the streets are full of people on bikes but the cyclists all mingle in with the crowds and weave round and past her and her mother and Henry and all the other people in a way that seems effortless. It is miraculous that no one ever hits anyone and that people can cycle so slowly and not topple. Nobody topples. Nobody hurries, even in the rain. Nobody rings a bike bell (except, George notices, the tourists, who are easy to spot). Nobody shouts at anybody to get out of the way. Even very old ladies cycle here wearing black with their bicycle baskets full of things wrapped up in paper and tied with ribbons or string, as if being old, going to a shop and buying things and bringing them home are all completely different acts here.

A boy the same age as George passes them at a crossroads with his bare arms on either side of a pretty girl lightly perched holding on to nothing on his handlebars.

George's mother winks at George.

George blushes. Then she is annoyed at herself for blushing.

That night the noise of the summer birds swooping round the roofs near their hotel gives way to a noise of drums and trumpets. They follow this new noise to a square where a crowd of quite young people, older than George but still young, some of whom wear historical costumes tabard-like slung over their jeans and T-shirts, or have leggings like

250

the people in the pictures they saw earlier, one leg one colour, the other a different colour, are taking turns to do marching dances or dancing marches where they throw huge flags on sticks up in the air, flags which unfurl to be bigger than bedspreads as they go up then fold themselves round their sticks again as they come down. The flag throwers walk with them held at their backs against their shoulders like folded wings, then they wave them about in the air like outsize butterfly wings while other members of their teams (it seems to be a rehearsal for a flag-throwing contest) blow long medieval-looking horns and thump their drums.

She and her mother and Henry stand on an old historic staircase with the other people, above two tall sign boards which say on them TALKING WALLS (you can download a walking tour from each board and one will tell you about where a film director her mother likes grew up, and the other about Giorgio someone, her mother says a novelist who lived here in the past). It is so loud, the rehearsal, that it literally shakes these boards.

But George watches a dog cross the square through the noise and stop to sniff at something then amble off again as if nothing unusual is happening, so maybe something like this just happens here every week. Then, above the heads of everyone in the city, above the highest-tossed of the flags, church bells here and there announce midnight and as if they've been enchanted the next team after that to do a routine does it without drums and bugles but with its musicians humming instead, in tuneful voices and with a gentleness that seems sweet and absurd after the great din of the teams that have gone before.

If only all ceremonials and pomp got hummed like that, her mother says.

Do you remember when

Things were really hummin'.

Full stop.

Is her mother really dead? Is it an elaborate hoax? (All hoaxes, on TV and the radio and in the papers and online, are described as elaborate whether they're elaborate or not.) Has someone elaborately, or not, spirited her mother away like on an episode of Spooks and now she's living a life elsewhere under a new name and just isn't allowed to contact people (even her own children) from her former life?

Because how can someone just vanish?

George had seen her contorted in the hospital bed. Her skin had changed colour and was covered in weals. She could hardly speak. What she did say, in the last part of whatever was happening to her and before they put George outside the door to wait in the corridor, was that she was a book, I'm an open book, she said. Though it was also equally possible that what she'd said was that she was an *un*open book.

I a a u opn ook.

George (to Mrs Rock) : I'm going to tell you this thing, and I think after I tell you you'll suggest I get sent for a stronger type of therapy than the kind you're giving me because you'll think I'm completely paranoid and hysterical.

Mrs Rock : You think I'll think you're paranoid and hysterical?

George : Yes. But I want to tell you now, before I say it, that I'm neither paranoid nor hysterical, though ostensibly it might sound like I am, and I want to make it clear that I thought it way before my mother died, and so did she, she thought it herself.

Mrs Rock nodded to let George know she was listening.

What George told Mrs Rock then was that her mother was under surveillance and had been being monitored by spies.

Mrs Rock : You believe your mother was being monitored by spies?

That was what counsellors were trained to do, to say back to you what it was you said, but in the form of a question so you could ask yourself why you'd thought or said it. It was soul-destroying.

George told Mrs Rock anyway. She told her

about the time five years ago that her mother was walking past the big glass windows of an expensive and stylish hotel in central London. People were having supper in there; the windows were restaurant windows, and her mother had seen, sitting with a group of people quite prominently in one of the windows, a politician or spin person and at this point her mother had been furious at some politicians. George couldn't remember which politician it was in the window, only that it was one of the politicians or spin people her mother held responsible for something. Anyway her mother had got her lip salve out of her rucksack and then she'd started to write on the glass of the window with the lip salve above this man's head like a halo (that's how she described it).

She was writing the word LIAR. But by the time it took to write the L, the I and the A, George said, there were security people coming at her from several directions. So she legged it. (Her words.)

Mrs Rock was writing things down.

After that, George said, two things happened. Well, three. Mail that came to our house for my parents, and even for me and for Henry, it was around the time when he had a birthday, began arriving looking like it had already been opened. It would arrive in these see-through Sorry Your Mail Has Been Damaged bags that the mail people use if something gets ripped. And then someone revealed in the papers that my mother was one of the Subvert interventionists.

One of the what? Mrs Rock said.

George explained about the Subvert movement and how, by using really early pop-up technology pretty much before anyone else was, they'd been able to make things appear on whatever page someone accessed like adverts do now all the time. Except, a Subvert took the form of a random visual or a piece of information.

My mother was one of the original anonymous four people who made up the things to send out, George said. Eventually there were hundreds of them. She was kind of minor to start with, then she got more minor. It's actually really hilarious because she's completely computer illiterate. I mean, you know, was.

Mrs Rock nodded.

Anyway, it was her job to subvert political things with art things, and to subvert art things with political things. Like, a box would flash up on a page about Picasso and it would say did you know that 13 million people in the UK are living below the poverty line. Or a box would flash up on a politics page and it would have a picture in it or some stanzas of a poem, stuff like that. Then it got revealed in the papers, George said, that she was a part of the Subvert movement, and then after that, whenever she published anything in the papers about money or

255

economics, the people who disagreed with her called her gauche and politically partisan.

Inside George's head as she says this her mother is laughing out loud about being called politically partisan. There isn't a single person in this world who isn't it, she says. She says it exactly as if she's singing a pretty tune, tra la la. And gauche, she says, is one of my favourite words. Always be gauche, George. Go on. I dare you.

Mrs Rock : And what was the third thing that made you think your mother was being monitored by spies?

[Enter Lisa Goliard]

George : Oh no, nothing. There were only the two things.

Mrs Rock : Didn't you say there were two, but then change it to three?

George : For a minute I think I thought there were three. But then I realized I really meant two.

Mrs Rock : And these are the two things that mean you believe your mother was being monitored by spies?

George : Yes.

Mrs Rock : And your mother believed it too?

George : She knew she was.

Mrs Rock : You think she knew she was?

George : We talked about it. All the time. It was a kind of a running joke. Anyway, she quite liked it. She liked being watched.

Mrs Rock : You think your mother liked being watched?

George : You think I'm insane, don't you? You think I'm just making it all up.

Mrs Rock : You're worried that I think you're making it up?

George : I'm not making any of it up.

Mrs Rock : Is what I think, or others think, very important to you?

George : Yeah, but what *do* you think, Mrs Rock? Are you thinking right now, dear me, this girl needs to be sent for much heavier-duty therapy?

Mrs Rock : Do you want to be sent for 'much heavier-duty therapy'?

George : I'm just asking you to tell me what you think, Mrs Rock.

Then Mrs Rock did something unexpected. She departed from her usual technique and script and started telling George what she actually maybe thought.

She said that in the ancient times the word mystery meant something we're unused to now. The word itself

– and I know this will interest you, Georgia, because I've gathered from talking to you how interested in meanings you are, she said –

– Well, I was, before, George said.

– you will be again, I think it's safe to say that about you, though I'm going a bit out on a limb

257

here and taking a risk saying it, Mrs Rock said. Anyway. The word mystery originally meant a closing, of the mouth or the eyes. It meant an agreement or an understanding that something would not be disclosed.

A closing. Not be disclosed.

George got interested in spite of herself.

The mysterious nature of some things was accepted then, much more taken for granted, Mrs Rock said. But now we live in a time and in a culture when mystery tends to mean something more answerable, it means a crime novel, a thriller, a drama on TV, usually one where we'll probably find out – and where the whole point of reading it or watching it will be that we *will* find out – what happened. And if we don't, we feel cheated.

Right then the bell went and Mrs Rock stopped talking. She'd gone bright red up under her hair and round her ears. She stopped talking as if someone had unplugged her. She closed her notebook and it was as if she'd closed her face too.

Same time next Tuesday, Georgia, she said. I mean, after Christmas. First Tuesday after the holidays. See you then.

George opens her eyes. She's slumped on the floor leaning back against her own bed. Henry is in her bed. All the lights are on. She'd fallen asleep and now she's woken up.

Her mother is dead. It's 1.30 a.m. It's New Year.

There's a noise downstairs. It sounds like someone is at the front door. That's what woke her.

It will be her father.

Henry wakes up. His mother is dead too. She sees the knowledge cross his face about three seconds after he opens his eyes.

It's okay, she says. It's just dad. Go back to sleep.

George goes down the first flight then the next flight of stairs. He will have lost his keys or they will be in a pocket he is too pissed to put his hand in or remember he even has.

She looks through the spy bubble in the door but she can't see anyone. There's no one there.

Then the person outside moves back into view to knock again. George is amazed.

It is a girl from school, Helena Fisker.

Helena Fisker with her shoulders dark from the rain, her hair looks quite wet too, is standing on the other side of George's front door.

She knocks again and everything about George, because she's standing so close to the door, literally leaps. It is as if Helena Fisker is knocking on George.

Helena Fisker had been there in the girls' toilets when George was being hassled by the moronic Year 9 girls with their mania for using their phones to record the sound levels of other girls urinating. What happened was: if you were a girl you would go to the toilet, then in the next class you'd go to everybody would be laughing at you because they'd all had the sound of you urinating sent to their phones with a film of the toilet door then the door opening then you coming out. Then Facebook. A couple of them even got put on YouTube and lasted several days there.

All anyone, including the boys, talked about for a while when they talked about someone (if the someone happened to be a girl) was how loud or how quiet her urinating was. This had started a separate mania among all the girls, an existential panic about whether their urinating was silent enough. Now they went to the toilet in twos so that there'd be someone to listen and make sure their urinating wasn't too audible.

One day George had opened a toilet door and outside it there'd been a huddle of girls she vaguely recognized but didn't know any of, all crowded round a girl holding up a smartphone.

On cue as if they'd rehearsed, like a little choir, they all started making disgusted noises at her.

But behind them, at the main door, she'd seen Helena Fisker come in.

Most people in the school were pretty respectful of Helena Fisker.

Helena Fisker had been reprimanded, most recently, George knew from people in art, for designing the school Christmas card. She was known for being really good at art. The picture of the robin she'd presented them with was apparently such a cute one that they'd simply let her place the order and stamped the form for the printer. It was paid for and printed up with the name of the school on the back. Five hundred had arrived from the printer in a huge box.

When they'd opened the box they'd found, instead of the robin, a picture of a really ugly massive blank concrete wall in the sun.

Helena Fisker, the story goes, had smiled at the Head as if she couldn't understand the fuss when she was called to his office and made to stand on the carpet in front of his desk.

But it's Bethlehem, she'd said.

Now this gang of girls was standing in front of George and filming and squealing at her with no idea that Helena Fisker was standing behind them. Helena Fisker caught George's eye over the tops of their heads. Then Helena Fisker shrugged her eyes.

Her doing just that knocked everything those girls were saying and doing into the land-of-not-meaning-anything-much.

Helena Fisker reached her hand over the tops of those little girls' heads and plucked the phone out of the main girl's hand.

All the girls turned round at once.

Hi, Helena Fisker said.

Then she told them they were a silly little bunch of wankers. Then she asked them why they were all so interested in urine and what their problem was. Then she pushed past them and held the smartphone over the bowl of the toilet that George had just flushed.

All the girls squealed, especially the one whose phone it was.

You can choose. Delete or drop, Helena Fisker said.

It's waterproof, you ethnic cow, one of the girls said.

Did you just call me an ethnic cow? Helena Fisker said. Great. A bonus.

Helena Fisker slammed the front of the smartphone on the edge of the toilet door. Bits of plastic flew off.

Now we can test your phone's waterproofing *and* we can test the school's policies on racism, she was saying as George left.

Thanks, George had said later when they were queuing up outside history.

She had never actually spoken to Helena Fisker before.

I liked that speech you gave in English that day, Helena Fisker said then. That story you told about the BT Tower.

(It had been George's turn, in the going-round-
the-room order, to give a three-minute talk about
empathy. She'd had no idea what to say. Then Ms
Maxwell had said in front of the whole class,
though in a quiet and nice way, it's okay if you
don't want to talk today, Georgia. This had made
George even more determined to do it. But when she
stood up her mind went blank. So she'd said some
things her mother was always saying about how
near-impossible it was to inhabit anyone else's shoes,
whether they lived in Paraguay or just down the road
or were even just in the next room or the next seat
along from you, and ended it by telling the story of a
pop singer who was having her lunch in the
restaurant of the BT Tower when it was called the
Post Office Tower in the 1960s and was so outraged
at the way the maître d' was bossing one of the
underwaiters around that she took the bread roll
she'd just been given off her side plate and threw it at
the maître d' and hit him on the back of the head.)

That's all she and Helena Fisker have ever said to
each other.

A couple of times since that thing in the toilets
happened, though, George has caught herself
thinking something unexpected. She has caught
herself wondering whether those girls, that girl with
the phone – if the phone memory had survived –
had deleted or maybe kept the film.

If that film still existed it meant there was a recording of her somewhere and in it she was looking straight over their heads into the eyes of Helena Fisker.

George opens the door.

Thought you maybe weren't in, Helena Fisker says.

I am, George says.

Good, Helena Fisker says. Happy New Year.

Henry sits up in the bed when George and Helena Fisker come into George's room.

Who are you? Henry says.

I'm H, Helena Fisker says. Who are you?

I'm Henry. What kind of a name is that? Henry says.

It's the initial of my first name, Helena Fisker says. The people who don't really know me tend to call me Helena. But I know your sister. We're friends at school. So you can call me H as well.

It's the same initial as my first name, Henry says. Did you bring a present?

Henry, George says.

She apologizes. She explains to Helena Fisker that since their mother died whenever people come to the house they generally tend to bring Henry a present, sometimes several presents.

Don't you get them too? Helena Fisker says.

Not as many as he gets, George says. I think they

think I'm too old for presents. Or they're more scared of trying to give me anything.

Did she bring a present or not? Henry says.

Yes, Helena Fisker says. I brought you a cabbage.

A cabbage isn't a present, Henry says.

It is if you're a rabbit, Helena Fisker says.

George laughs out loud.

Henry, too, clearly thinks this is very funny. He curls into a laughing ball in the bedclothes.

Your hair's all wet, he says when he stops laughing.

That's what happens when you walk through the rain with no hat or hood or umbrella, Helena Fisker says.

George takes her over to the bookcase and shows her the leak and the rain dripping every few minutes on to the cover of the top book on the pile.

At some point, George says, this roof will stave in.

Cool, Helena Fisker says. You'll be able to look directly out at the constellations.

There'll be nothing between me and them, George says.

Except the occasional police helicopter, Helena Fisker says. The great lawnmower in the sky.

George laughs.

Two seconds after she does she realizes something and she is surprised.

What she realizes is that she has laughed.

In fact she has laughed twice, once at the rabbit joke and once at the lawnmower.

The thought of it pretty much surprises her into another laugh, this time inside herself.

That makes it three times since September that George has laughed in an undeniable present tense.

The first time H comes to the house again after
New Year she hands George the A4 envelope she's
carrying under her arm. She takes off her jacket
and hangs it up in the hall.

George holds the envelope back out for her
to take.

It's for you, H says.

What is it? George says.

I brought you some stars, H says. I printed them
up off the net.

George opens it. Inside there's a photograph on
thick paper. It's summer in the picture. Two women
(both young, both between girl and woman) are
walking along a road together past some shops in a
very sunny-looking place. Is it now or is it in the
past? One of them is yellow-haired and one of
them is darker. The yellow-haired one, the smaller

of the two, is looking at something off camera, off
to her left. She's wearing a gold and orange top.
The dark-haired taller girl is wearing a short blue
dress with a stripe round the edging of it. She is in
the middle of turning to look at the other. There's a
breeze, so her hand has gone up to hold her hair
back off her face. The yellow-haired one looks
preoccupied, intent. The dark one looks as if
something that's been said has struck her and she's
about to say a yes.

Who are they? George says.

French, H says. From the 1960s. I was telling my
mother about your sixties kick and I told her that
story, the one you told in Maxwell's class about the
BT Tower and she wanted to know which singer it
was and then she started looking up singers she'd
liked, especially ones *her* mother'd liked, and she
got annoyed that I didn't know any of them and
made me look them all up on YouTube. Then,
when I did, I thought this one (she points at the
blonde one) looked a bit like you.

Really? George says.

My mother says they were both huge stars, H
says. Not together, separate stars. They both had
huge careers and changed the music industry in
France. My mother went on and on about it.
Actually she went off on a tangent, I told her about
your mother at one point and she went all (H starts
doing a lightly French accent) *it is not fair for your*

268

friend, she is not going to get the important boredoms and mournings and melancholies that are her due and are owing to her just from being the age that she is, for now it will be interrupted by real mournings and real melancholies, anyway then I thought I'd bring the picture round to get away from her going on about it, then I thought I could ask you if you want to come out to the car park with me.

A car park? George says.

The multi-storey, H says. Want to come?

Now? George says.

I guarantee it'll be really boring, H says.

George looks out of the window. H's bike is leaning against the wall outside. Her own bike is in the shed still with last summer's puncture. In her head she can see the tyre useless in the dark, the bike all lopsided against the gardening stuff.

Okay, she says.

They walk towards town with H wheeling her bike between them. When they get to the multi-storey George goes towards the lift door but H puts a finger to her mouth then points at the glass-walled security cubicle. There's a man in a uniform in it with what looks like a newspaper for a head. He's asleep under it. H points at the fire doors that lead to the stairs. She opens one of the doors with great care. It's heavy. George props it with her foot. When they've both squeezed through, H eases it closed.

It's a Monday night in February so there aren't many cars. There's only one solitary four-wheel drive parked up on the top deck, which is the roof of the car park and is open air, open to the sky, its concrete flooring wet from the rain and shining under the car park lights.

George and H lean as far over the top deck wall as they can (they make them this high so it'll be less inviting to suicides, H says). They look down at the roofs of their city, the streets near-empty, shining too after the rain. An occasional car passes below. Nobody much is out.

This is what the town will look like when I'm dead too, George thinks. And if I were to jump, right now? Nothing about it would change. They would just clean up whatever mess I'd make and then the next night it would rain or not rain, the street surface would be shiny or matt, the occasional car would pass below and on the busy days the traffic would queue up down there to park in here so people could go to the shops, this deck would fill with cars then later it'd empty of cars, and the months would pass one after the other, February coming round again, and again, and again, February after February after February, and this historic city would carry on being its historic self regardless.

She stops thinking it because H has fetched, by herself, by dragging it up the steps in the stairwell, the shopping trolley they passed on the way up which someone'd abandoned at the lift doors on the floor below.

It's quite a new trolley. It crosses the concrete without too much noise.

Here, H says. Hold it steady for me.

George holds it still while H climbs into it, no, not so much climbs as vaults. All she has to do is take hold of the side and flick herself into the air and she's in. It is pretty impressive.

How's your chariot-driving? she says.

Put it this way, George says. There's only one car up here and if I push you, no matter what direction I intend to push you in, you'll hit it. And if you're fortunate enough not to hit *it* –

She points at the steep entry and exit slopes that dip in real suddenness down to the next floor.

Ski-jump, H says. The ultimate challenge.

She glances above her head at where the security camera is. Then she jumps out of the trolley as easily as she jumped in.

Right, she says. You first.

She nods at George then nods towards the trolley.

No way, George says.

Go on, H says. Trust me.

No, George says.

We won't do the slope, H says. I promise. I'll be careful. I think we've time for one. If there's time for two and he stays asleep and no one comes up I'll get you to do me too.

271

She holds the trolley steady.

She's waiting.

There's nowhere for a foothold so George has to balance herself on the sides of it and sort of roll into it and turn herself the right way up again (ouch).

Ready? H says.

George nods. She braces herself against the sides of the trolley and equally as much against the fact that she isn't the kind of person who usually does something like this.

Want me to keep hold of it all the way across or just to push it really hard then let it go? H says.

The latter, George hears herself say.

She is quite surprised at herself.

Latter. Fortunate. You use words, H says, that I never hear anyone else using ever. You're wild.

Literally, George says inside the cage of the trolley.

Latter. Fortunate. Literally. Here goes, H says.

H swings the trolley round so George is facing the expanse of the car park roof. She angles it away from the exit slopes. The next thing George knows is the way she's forced backwards by a forward shove so strong that for a moment it's like she's going in two directions at once.

Later, back at home, George goes downstairs to make coffee and leaves Henry in her room talking to H.

Yeah, that's her, H is saying. The heroine of the Anger Games.

It's Hunger Games, Henry says.

Catnip, H says.

Her name's not Catnip, Henry says.

By the time she gets back upstairs Henry and H are engaged in a kind of verbal ping-pong.

Henry : As blind as?

H : Houses.

(Henry laughs.)

Henry : As safe as?

H : A bell.

Henry : As bold as?

H : A cucumber.

(Henry rolls about on the floor laughing at the word cucumber.)

H : Okay. Switch!

Henry : Switch!

H : As keen as?

Henry : A cucumber.

H : As pleased as?

Henry : A cucumber.

H : As deaf as?

Henry : A cucumber.

H : You can't just keep saying cucumber.

Henry : I can if I want.

H : Well, okay. Fair enough. But if you can, I can too.

Henry : Okay.

H : Cucumber.

Henry : Cucumber what?

H : I'm just playing it your way. Cucumber.

Henry : No, play it properly. As what as a what?

H : As cucumber as . . . a . . . cu–

Henry : Play it properly!

H : Likewise, Henry. Like plus wise.

When H goes home at eleven George literally feels it, the house become duller, as if all the light in it has stalled in the dim part that happens before a lightbulb has properly warmed up. The house becomes as blind as a house, as deaf as a house, as dry as a house, as hard as a house. George does all the things you're meant to do before bed. She washes, she brushes her teeth, she takes off the clothes she's been wearing in the daytime and puts on the clothes you're meant to wear at night.

But in bed, instead of the usual jangling nothing in her head, she thinks about how H has a mother who is French.

She thinks about how H's father is from Karachi and Copenhagen and how, H says, according to her father, it is actually perfectly possible to be from the north and the south and the east and the west all at once.

She thinks this is maybe where H gets her eyes from.

She thinks about the picture of the two French singers on her desk. She thinks about how she might be said to resemble a French girl singer from the 1960s.

She will put that picture up by itself, give it a whole wall like she's done with the poster her mother bought her of the film actress when they went to the museum in Ferrara and saw the exhibition about the director her mother liked who always used this actress in his films.

She thinks about how she's never cycled two on a bike before, where one person does the cycling by standing on the pedals and the other person sits on the seat and holds on to her at the waist but loosely enough so that she can continue to move quite freely up and down.

She thinks about how polite H was when she apologized to the security man at the car park. In the end he had seemed rather charmed even as he'd threatened them with the police.

Finally she lets herself think about how it feels:

to be so frightened that you almost can't breathe

to speed so fast and be so completely out of control

to know the meaning of helpless

to spin across a shining space knowing any moment you might end up hurt, but likewise, all the same, like plus wise you just might not.

Then she wakes up and for once it's morning and she has slept right through without any of the usual waking up.

The next time H comes to the house George isn't expecting her and is in her mother's study. She has sneaked in there where she's not meant to be and is sitting at the desk with the big dictionary open looking to see if LIA, without the R, happens to be a word in its own right.

(It doesn't.)

She looks at the list of words that begin with LIA. She imagines her mother in the dock in a courtroom. Yes, your honour, I did write the word above his head, but I wasn't writing the word you imagine. I was writing the word LIANA and a liana, as I'm sure you know your honour, is a twisting woody tropical plant which can hold the weight of a man swinging through the trees, familiar to us for instance from the Tarzan films of my youth. From this it should be easy to deduce that the word I was writing would have been meant finally as a compliment.

Or

Yes, your honour, but it was going to be the word LIATRIS, which your honour may or may not already know is a plant but can also mean a blazing star, from which it should be easy to deduce etc.

No. Because her mother would never have lied like that about what she was writing. Lying and equivocating are what George, not her mother,

276

would do if she'd been caught writing some word on a window above someone important's head.

Not that her mother was caught.

Though George probably would have been.

Her mother, instead, would have said something simple and true like, yes your honour I cannot tell a lie, I believe him to be a liar which is precisely why I was writing the word.

I cannot tell a lie. It was me who chopped down the cherry tree. Now that I've been so honest, make me a precedent. No, not president. I said precedent.

That'd maybe be worth £5 for a Subvert, if her mother were here.

(But now that she isn't, does that make it worthless?)

There are also the possible words LIAS, LIANG, LIARD. A sort of stone, a Chinese weight measure, a greyish colour *and* a coin worth very little (it is interesting to George that the word liard can mean both money and a colour).

There is the word LIABLE.

There is the word LIAISON.

(*I bet its in a cathedral city up in some fancy cathedral ceiling hanging out with the carvings of the angels.*

I bet its

its)

Wrong.

The wrongness of it is infuriating.

The George from after can still feel the fury at the wrongness of things that beat such huge dents into the chest of the George from before.

She turns on the chair. H is in the doorway.

Your dad let me in, she says. I went up to your room but you weren't there.

H had decided earlier that day at school that a good way to do revision would be for them to transfer what they needed to remember into song lyrics and learn to sing them to the tune of some song they both know. This, H says, will make information unforgettable. They both have a test next week in biology and George also has a test in Latin.

So what we can do, H said, is : I'll make up the biology version and we can learn it off by heart then you can translate it into Latin for double the benefit.

They'd been standing in the corridor outside history.

What do you think? H had said.

What I'm thinking is, George said. When we die.

Uh huh? H said.

Do you think we still have memories? George said.

This was her test question.

H wasn't even fazed. She was never fazed by anything. She made a face, but it was a thinking face.

Hmm, she'd said.

Then she'd shrugged and said,

Who knows?

George had nodded. Good answer.

Now H is here, turning on one foot and looking at all the piles of books and papers and pictures.

Wow. What a place, she says. What's this place?

What's this place? George turns on the swivel chair her mother specially bought for this study and catches, at the corner of her eye, the framed and printed-out first-ever Subvert. It's a list of the names of all the women art students who went to an art college in London over three years at the end of the nineteenth and the beginning of the twentieth centuries. This list with no explanation attached flashed up for a month on the online pages of anyone who looked up the word Slade (including people who'd chanced to be looking up things about the band with all the old men in it who wrote that Christmas song). It came about because George's mother had been reading a biography of a quite famous artist from the turn of that century and had become more and more interested in what had happened to his wife, whom he'd met at the same art school. She'd been a student too but had died really young after having more children than her body could handle having (George's mother is a feminist). (Was.) Before this woman died (well obviously) she had had a friend called Edna who was also a student at the school. In fact Edna'd been one of the most talented artists in the place. Edna had gone on to marry a well-to-do type. One day this well-to-do type had come home to find Edna's paints and brushes spread out on the dining-room table and had told Edna to put all this rubbish away. It was before Henry was born. George and her mother and father were on holiday in Suffolk staying in a cottage. Her mother had been reading this book. She got to the page where this happened to Edna and she burst into tears in the garden. That's the story. George has no memory of it but the story goes that her mother raged round the cottage's garden like a mad person and that the letting agency had sent a bill afterwards for some of the plants she'd wrecked. Your mother is a very passionate person, her father always said whenever the story got told. Anyway Edna's life hadn't been so bad after all in the end because the husband had died quite early on and she herself had gone on to live till she was a hundred and to show lots of pictures in galleries and even to be called, by a reputable newspaper, the most imaginative artist in England (though she did have a nervous breakdown at one point, and at another point in history her studio got hit by a bomb and totally destroyed along with lots of her work).

All of this information flashes through George's head in that fraction of a second it takes to do the single swivel round towards H in her mother's chair and say the words:

It's my mother's study.

Cool, H says.

She puts a piece of paper with her writing all over it down next to George on the desk. She picks up a picture off the top of a pile of letters. George looks to see what she's picked up.

She liked that picture so much, George says, that we went all the way to Italy to see it.

Who is it? H says.

I don't know, George says. Just some man. On a wall. In a kind of blue space.

Who did it? H says.

I don't know that either, George says.

She looks down at the song she's meant to translate into Latin. She has no idea what the Latin for DNA will be.

To The Tune Of Wrecking Ball

(Verse 1)

Herr Friedrich Miescher found it in / some pus in 1869 / Crick, Watson and Ros Franklin saw / the two strands intertwined like vine. / Double helix in 1953 / X-Ray photo '52. / Franklin died before Nobel Prize Award / Life not one strand but two.

(Chorus)

G - A - T - C and D - NA / Deoxyribonu-cleic / Guanine-adenine-thymine cytosine / Supercoil can be both / Po - o - si tive / Yeah and /Ne - e - g a tive.

(Verse 2)

Plants fungi animals make up / The eukaryotes /
Bacteria and archaea / The prokaryotes / It's A&T
or it's G&C that's the / Only way it will do / Two
long chromosomes, codons three letters long / I will
always want you.

H is still standing looking at the picture of the man in rags.

That last line's just there for scansion, she says. While I decide what else to use.

She holds up the picture of the man.

When in history is this from? she says.

It's from a palace, George says. If you look up the words Ferrara Palazzo in Images, Ferrara's the place we saw it, you'll probably find it.

She looks at the song again.

I don't think I can translate much more than three or four lines of this into Latin, she says. A lot of it also already looks pretty Greek.

Do the last line first, H says.

She is sort of grinning. She is looking away, still looking at the picture of the ragged man.

The one line we're not going to need or use and that's the one you want first in Latin? George says.

I'd just quite like to hear it in Latin, H says.

She is grinning broadly now and still looking away. She sits down on the floor.

She's waiting.

282

Okay, George says. But can I ask you something first?

Yep, H says.

It's a hypothetical, George says.

I'm not much good with them, H says. I've been known to faint whenever I see a needle.

George gets off her mother's chair and comes and sits opposite H cross-legged on the floor too.

If I were to say to you that while my mother was alive she was being monitored, she says.

For health, or? H says. For diet, or what?

George speaks a little more quietly because her father doesn't like her saying this stuff, *she made it up to distract herself from her life and how do you think that makes me feel, George? And you're making it up to distract yourself from her death. She was being adolescent. So are you. Get a grip. Interpol and MI5 and MI6 and MI7 were not interested in your mother.* He has specifically instructed her to stop it, and has been known to lose his head about it if George does mention it, even though he's being generally self-consciously gentle at most other times, what with everything being so post-death.

By people in, you know. Like on TV, George says. Except not like on TV, there weren't bombs or guns or torture or anything, there was just this person. Sort of keeping an eye on her.

283

Oh, H says. That kind of monitored.

If I were to say it, George says. Would you think words like deluded and paranoid and needs to be put on some kind of medication?

H thinks about it. Then she nods.

You would? George says.

Not living in the real world, H says.

Something inside George's chest falls. It is a relief, after all, the kind of relief where everything feels both bruised and released.

H is still speaking.

More likely that your mother was being minotaured, she is saying.

It isn't a joke, George says.

I'm not joking, H says. I mean, it's not like we live in mythical times. It's not like we live in a world where the police, say, would ever minotaur the people whose son's murder they were supposed to be investigating, or the press would minotaur famous people or even dead people to make money out of them.

Ha, George says.

It's not like the government would minotaur *us*, H says. I mean, not *our* government. Obviously all the undemocratic and less good and less civilized ones would do it to *their* citizens. But our own one. I mean, they might minotaur the people they needed to know about. But they'd never do it to ordinary people, say through their emails or mobiles, or

through the games they play on their mobiles. And
it's not like the shops we buy things from do it to us
either, is it, every time we buy something. You're
deluded and insane. There's no such thing as a
minotaur. It's mythical. And your mother was,
what? Quite a political person? Someone who
published stuff about money in the papers? And did
disruptive stuff on the net? Why would anyone want
to monitor her? I think your imaginings are
dangerous. Someone should monitor *you*.

She looks up.

I'd do it, she says. I'd have done it, if it was you.

If it had been you, George says inside her head.

I'd have minotaured you for free, H says.

She looks George laughingly and seriously right
in the eye.

Or maybe, if it were you, George thinks.

She lies down flat on her back on her mother's
carpet. Her mother got this carpet at an antique
shop off Mill Road. Well, antique. Junk shop,
really.

H lies down next to her so that their heads are
level.

Both girls stare at the ceiling.

The thing is, doctor, H says.

George hears her from the miles away where she's
thinking about what the differences might be, and
what her mother would have said they were,
between antiques and just old junk.

I have this need, H is saying.

What need? George says.

To be more, H says.

More what? George says.

Well, H says and her voice sounds strangely altered. More.

Oh, George says.

I think I might be, by nature, H says, a bit more hands-on than hypothetical.

Then one of her hands reaches and takes one of George's hands.

The hand doesn't just take George's hand, it interlaces its fingers with it.

This is the point at which all the words drain out of the part of George's brain where words are kept.

H's hand holds her hand for a moment, then H's hand lets go of her hand.

Yes? she says. No?

George doesn't speak

I can slow down, H says. I can wait. I can wait till it's right. I can do that.

Then she says,

Or maybe you don't –.

George doesn't speak.

Maybe I'm not –, H says.

Then George's father is at the door of the room, he's been there for God knows how long. George sits up.

Girls, he says. George. You know I don't want

you in there. Nothing's sorted. There's a lot of important stuff, I don't want anything messed with in there. And I thought you were organizing supper tonight, George.

I am, George says. I will. I'm just about to.

Is your friend staying for supper? her father says.

No, Mr Cook, I've got to be home, H says.

She is still lying on her back on the floor.

You're very welcome to stay, Helena, her father says. There'll be plenty.

Thanks, Mr Cook, H says. It's really nice of you. I'm expected at home.

You can stay for supper, George says.

No I can't, H says.

She gets up.

See you, she says.

A minute later she is not in the room any more.

A moment after that George hears the front door of the house closing.

George lies back down flat on the carpet again.

She is not a girl. She is a block of stone.

She is a piece of wall.

She is something against which other things impact without her permission or understanding.

It is last May in Italy. George and her mother and Henry are sitting after supper at a table outside a restaurant under some arches near the castle. Her mother has been going on and on to them (well, to George, because Henry is on a computer game) about fresco structure, about how when some frescoes in a different Italian city were damaged in the 1960s in bad flooding and the authorities and restorers removed them to mend them as best they could, they found, underneath them, the underdrawing their artists had made for them, and sometimes the underdrawings were significantly different from their surfaces, which is something they'd never have discovered if there hadn't been the damage in the first place.

George is only half listening because the game Henry is looking at on the iPad is called Injustice and George thinks Henry is far too young for it.

What game is it? her mother says.

It's the one where all the cartoon superheroes have turned evil, George says. It's really violent.

Henry, her mother says.

She takes an earphone out of one of Henry's ears.

What? Henry says.

Find something less violent to do on there, his mother says.

Okay, Henry says. If I must.

You must, his mother says.

Henry puts the earphone back in and clicks off the game. He clicks on a download of Horrible Histories instead. Pretty soon he is giggling to himself. Not long after that he falls asleep at the table with his head on the iPad.

But which came first? her mother says. The chicken or the egg? The picture underneath or the picture on the surface?

The picture below came first, George says. Because it was done first.

But the first thing we see, her mother said, and most times the only thing we see, is the one on the surface. So does that mean it comes first after all? And does that mean the other picture, if we don't know about it, may as well not exist?

George sighs heavily. Her mother points across the way, to the castle wall. A bus goes past. Its whole back is an advert for something in which there's a Madonna and child picture as if from the past, except the mother is showing the baby Jesus how to look something up on an iPad.

We're sitting here having our supper, her mother is saying, and looking at everything that's round us. And over there. Right there in front of us. If this was a night seventy years ago –

– yeah, but it *isn't*, George says. It's *now*.

– we'd be sitting here watching people being lined up and shot against that wall. Along from where those seats for the café bar are.

Uch. God, George says. *Mum*. How do you even *know* that?

Would it be better, or worse, or truer, or falser, if I didn't? her mother says.

George scowls. History is horrible. It is a mound

of bodies pressing down into the ground below cities and towns in the unending wars and the famines and the diseases, and all the people starved or done away with or rounded up and shot or tortured and left to die or put up against the walls near castles or stood in front of ditches and shot into them. George is appalled by history, its only redeeming feature being that it tends to be well and truly over.

And which comes first? her unbearable mother is saying. What we see or how we see?

Yeah, but that thing happening. With the shooting. It was aeons ago, George says.

Only twenty years before me, and here I am sitting here right now, her mother says.

Ancient history, George says.

That's me, her mother says. And yet here I am. Still happening.

But *it* isn't, George says. Because that was then. This is now. That's what time *is*.

Do things just go away? her mother says. Do things that happened not exist, or stop existing, just because we can't see them happening in front of us?

They do when they're over, George says.

And what about the things we watch happening right in front of us and still can't really see? her mother says.

George rolls her eyes.

Totally pointless discussion, she says.

Why? her mother says.

Okay. That castle, George says. It's right in front of us, yes?

So I see, her mother says.

I mean, you can't *not*, George says. Unless your eyes don't work. And even if your eyes didn't work, you'd still be able to go up to it and touch it, you'd be able to register it being there one way or another.

Absolutely, her mother says.

But though it's the same castle as it was when it was built way back when, and it has its history, George says, and all the things have happened to it and in it and round it and so on ad infinitum, that's nothing to do with us sitting here looking at it right now. Apart from it being scenery because we're tourists.

Do tourists see differently from other people? her mother says. And how can you have grown up in the town you've grown up in and not consider what the presence of the past might mean?

George yawns ostentatiously.

Best place in the world to learn how to ignore it, she says. Taught me everything I'll ever need to know. Especially about tourism. And growing up around historic buildings. I mean. They're just buildings. You're always talking such crap about things meaning more than they actually mean. It's like some drippy hippy hangover, like you were inoculated with hippiness when you were little and now you can't help but treat everything as if it's symbolic.

That castle, her mother says, was built by order of the Estense court, the d'Estes being the family who ruled this province for hundreds of years and the people responsible for so much of the art and poetry and music. And therefore for the art and writing and music that followed it, which you and I take for granted. If it wasn't for Ariosto, who flourished because of this court, there'd be a very different Shakespeare. If there'd even be a Shakespeare at all.

Yeah, maybe, but it's hardly relevant *now*, George says.

You know, Georgie, nothing's not connected, her mother says.

You always call me Georgie when you want to patronize me, George says.

And we don't live on a flat surface, her mother says. That castle, this city, were built all those irrelevant centuries ago by a family whose titles and hereditaries come down in more or less a direct connection to Franz Ferdinand.

The band? George says.

Yes, her mother says. The pop band whose assassination in Sarajevo in 1914 brought about World War One.

World War One is like a whole hundred years ago

next year, George says. You can hardly call it relevant to us any more.

What, the Great War? in which your great-grandfather, who happened to be my grandfather, was gassed in the trenches not once, but twice? Which meant he and your great-grandmother were very poor, because he was too ill to work and died young? And meant I inherited his weak lungs? Not relevant to us? her mother says. And then the break-up of the Balkans, and the start of the territorial trouble in the Middle East between the Israelis and the Palestinians, and the civil unrest in Ireland, and the shifts of power in Russia, and the power shifts in the Ottoman empire, and the bankruptcy, economic catastrophe and social unrest in Germany, all of which played a huge part in the rise of Fascism and in the bringing about of another war in which, as it happens, your own grandmother and grandfather – who happened to be my mother and father – both fought when they were just two or three years older than you? Not relevant? To us?

Her mother shakes her head.

What? George says. *What?*

A well-heeled Cambridge childhood, her mother says.

She laughs a laugh to herself. The laugh infuriates George.

Why did you and dad choose to live there, then, if you didn't want us to grow up there? she says.

Oh, you know, her mother says. Good schools. Proximity to London. Buoyant housing market that'd always hold its own in recession. All the things that really matter in life.

Is her mother being ironic? It's hard to tell.

Very good food-bank system for when you leave school and your father and I can't afford to send you to university *and* eat, and for later too for you when you come out of university, her mother says.

That's such an irresponsible thing to say, George says.

Well but at least it's new and contemporary, my irresponsibility, her mother says.

The tables round them are emptying. It's late and quite a bit cooler. There's been rain beyond the arches while they've sat here eating and arguing. Her mother puts a hand into her handbag and pulls out a jumper. She gives it to George to put round Henry's shoulders. Then she gets her phone out of her bag. She switches it on. *Guilt and fury*. After a moment, she switches it off. George feels so guilty she is nearly sick with guilt. She formulates, quick, the kind of question she knows her mother likes to answer.

You know that place we went to earlier today? George says.

Uh huh, her mother says.

Do you think any women artists did any of it? George says.

294

Her mother forgets the phone in her hand and immediately holds forth (just as George knew she would).

She tells George how there are a few renaissance painters they know about who happen to have been women, but not very many, a negligible percentage. She tells her about one called Catherine who was brought up by the court here, in that castle right there, because she was the daughter of a nobleman and one of the women of the Estense court took her under her wing and made sure she had a superb education. Then Catherine had gone into a nunnery, which was a good place to go if you were a woman and wanted to paint, and while she was there she became a celebrated nun and she wrote books and painted pictures on the side, about which nobody really found out until after she died.

Her paintings are quite lovely, her mother says. And you can actually still see Catherine today.

You mean through sensing her personality by looking at the paintings etc, George says.

No, I mean quite literally, her mother says. In the flesh.

How? George says.

In a church in Bologna, her mother says. When they made her a saint they dug her up – there's all sorts of testimonials about how sweet the smell was when they dug her up –

Mum, George says.

– and they put her in a box in a church dedicated to her, and if you go there you can still see her, she's gone black with age and she's sitting in the box and holding a book and some kind of holy monstrance.

That's insane, George says.

But other than something like that happening? her mother says. No. It's pretty unlikely that women worked on much that's extant, certainly on anything we saw today. Though if I had to, I don't know, write a paper about it or try to make a thesis about it, I could make a pretty good one about the vaginal shape here –

Mum, George says.

– we're in Italy, George, it's all right, no one knows what I'm saying, her mother says drawing a diamond shape at her own breastbone, the vaginal shape here on that beautiful worker in the rags in the blue section, the most virile and powerful figure in the whole room, much more so than the Duke, who's supposed to be the subject and the hero of that room, and which must surely have caused a bit of trouble for the artist, especially since that figure's a worker or a slave and also clearly black or Semitic. And how the open shape at his chest complements the way the painter makes the rope round his waist a piece of simultaneously dangling and erect phallic symbolism –

(her mother did an art history degree once)

296

– and as to the constant sexual and gender ambiguities running through the whole work

(and a women's studies degree)

– at least the part of it that this particular artist seems to have produced, well. Or if we want to be more detailed about it. The way he used that figure of the effeminate boy, the boyish girl, to balance the powerful masculine effect of the worker, and how this figure holds both an arrow and a hoop, male and female symbols one in each hand. On this alone I could make a reasonably witty argument for its originator being female, if I had to. But as to likelihood?

How does she even remember *seeing* all these things, George thinks. I saw the same room, the exact same room as she did, we were both standing in the very same place, and I didn't see *any* of it.

Her mother shakes her head.

Slim, George, I'm sorry to say.

That night in their hotel room before they go to bed her mother is brushing her teeth in the bathroom. This hotel used to be someone's house in the years when people made frescoes. It is called the Prisciani Suite and was the actual house of someone who had something to do with the making of the frescoes at the palace where they went to see the pictures earlier (it says so at the door in a long information panel which George,

297

who doesn't speak Italian, has tried to decipher).
There are still some bits of the original frescoes the
man from back then will have lived with on the
walls of this room – George has even touched them.
They go right the way up the wall, up past the
mezzanine where Henry is asleep above them on a
small single bed. You can touch them if you like.
Nothing says not to. Pellegrino Prisciani.
Pellegrino, like the bottles of water, she'd said. And
the bird, her mother'd said. What bird? George had
said. The peregrine falcon, her mother'd said,
pellegrino means a pilgrim, and at some point it
also morphed into what we know as the name of
the bird.

Is there anything her mother doesn't know about?

The hotel is full of art. Above the bed she and
her mother will sleep in is a modern piece by an
Italian artist from now. It is shaped like a giant eye
but with a propeller at one end like an aircraft,
except the propeller looks like it's been made with
giant sycamore seeds. The strip of metal or whatever
it is that's meant to be the pupil has a snail shell
stuck to the upper curve of it and the whole thing
moves very slowly in the air above the bed so that it
almost seems possible the snail might also be
moving, even though it's obvious it's not. There is a
panel on the wall about the artwork. Leon Battista
Alberti regalo a Leonello d'Este un manoscritto in
cui compariva il disegno dell'occhio alato. Questa

298

raffigurazione allegorica rappresenta l'elevazione
l'intellettuale : l'occhio simbolo della divinita, le ali
simbolo della velocita, o meglio della conoscenza
intuitiva, la sola che permette di accedere alla
contemplazione e alla vera conoscenza. Leon
Battista Alberti, whoever he was, regaled Leonello
d'Este (important if he was an Este since they were,
George has gathered, like the royals of Ferrara) a
manuscript in which, something about comparing,
and design, and some words George doesn't know.
But that one, occhio, might be eye or eyes, not just
because the artwork is obviously an eye, but
because of the word oculist. A refiguring allegory
and represent and intellectual elevation, the eye
symbolizes divinity, something symbolizes velocity,
blah, intuition, permitting, contemplation –

George gives up.

Her mother's phone, in its pouch, is on the
bedside table.

Guilt and fury. Guilt and fury.

There is something her mother doesn't know
about, George thinks looking up at that eye.

The giant eye turns on its own in the air above
the bed and George glows and fades below it like
her whole self is a faulty neon.

George is tired of art. She is fed up of its always
knowing best.

I want to come clean about something, she says
when her mother comes out of the bathroom.

Uh huh? her mother says. What would that be?

It would be something I did that I shouldn't have done, George says.

What? her mother says stopping halfway across the room, the moisturizer jar in one hand and its lid in the other.

I've been feeling bad for months, George says.

Her mother puts the stuff in her hands down and comes over and sits on the bed next to her.

Sweet heart, she says. Stop worrying right now. Whatever it is. Everything is forgivable.

I don't know that this *is* forgivable, George says.

Her mother's face is all concern.

Okay, she says. Tell me.

George doesn't tell her mother about the time she looked at the phone and saw the text conversation about losing your voice and the carvings of angels. But she does tell her about the day when her mother's phone had flashed on, on the sideboard in the kitchen, and George had seen the name Lisa Goliard lighting it up.

Uh huh? her mother says.

George decides to leave out the bit it said about her mother's eyes.

It said How you doin what you doin where are you & whenll we meet, George says.

Her mother is nodding.

And the thing is, George says. I sent a reply.

Did you? her mother says. A message from you?

A message from you, George says.

From me? her mother says.

I wrote it pretending to be you, George says. I've been feeling really bad about it. I know I shouldn't have looked. I should never have invaded your privacy. And I know I shouldn't have pretended to be you under any circumstances.

What did I say? Can you remember? her mother says.

By heart, George says.

And? her mother says.

I'm ever so sorry Lisa but I am very busy spending quality time with my family and am so taken up with all the loving things happening with my husband and two children that I'm afraid I won't be able to meet with you for some considerable time, George says.

Her mother explodes into laughter. George is stunned. Her mother is laughing like it's the funniest thing she's heard in a long time.

Oh you're a beauty, George, you really are, you're a perfect beauty, she says. Did she write back?

Yes, George says. She wrote back and said, like, Are you all right you don't sound like you.

Her mother slaps the bed in delight.

And I wrote back, George says, and said I am very well thank you just very busy with important and time-consuming private family matters but so busy that I no longer have much time even to look at this phone. I will be in touch with you so please don't get in touch with me. Goodbye for now. And then I deleted my messages. And then I deleted her messages.

Her mother laughs so loudly and so delightedly that Henry, asleep above them, wakes up and comes downstairs to see what's happening.

When they've got Henry back to bed and settled again they get into bed themselves. Her mother puts the lights off. They listen for Henry's breathing to regulate. It soon does.

Then this is the story her mother tells her quietly in the dark:

One day I was waiting at a cash machine in King's Cross and there was this woman ahead of me, about the same age as me.

As I am, George says.

George, her mother says. Whose story is this?

Sorry, George says.

She gave me a smile because we were both waiting our turn. The bag she had at her feet was open, it was full of things that interested me, rolls of artisan paper and a big ball of green yarn or wool or gardening string, and a great many pens and pencils and some metal tools and rulers. Anyway her turn came and she was putting her numbers in and then she started patting all her pockets and riffling through that open bag and looking at the ground all around her feet and I said, are you looking for something? can I help? And she clapped her hand to her forehead and she said *when did I become the kind of person who panics about where her bank card is when she's at a cashpoint in the middle of getting money out of it when the card is right there in front of her, it's just that she's forgotten she's actually put it into the machine?* Which made me laugh because I recognized myself in it. And we had a chat and I asked her about the rolls of paper in her bag and she told me she made books, one-offs, like artworks, books that were themselves also art objects. You know me. I was interested. We swapped emails.

About a fortnight later there was a message from this woman in my inbox, all it said was : *what do you think?* and when I opened the attachment it was some photos of a beautiful little book, all colours and swerving written lines and figures, sort of like if Matisse had written it, and I wrote back and told her I really liked it, and she emailed me back saying *but should I be doing something different with my life?* and I was struck by the intimacy of the question, from a stranger to a virtual stranger. I wrote back and said, *do you want to do something different with your life?* Then I didn't hear anything and I forgot about her again. Until one day she left me a voicemail inviting me to lunch, which was odd because I didn't remember ever giving her my phone number, you know me, I never give it out. The voicemail said she had something to show me and invited me to come to her workshop first.

It was pretty exciting going there. There was lots of printers' type, drawers of it open and half open, and inks and paint everywhere, and machines for cutting, and an old press, and bottles full of who knows what, fixatives, colours, I don't know. I loved it.

The thing she wanted to show me was a glass box. She was making a set of books for a commission for someone who wanted her to make three of these books then deliver them to him sealed in a glass case. So these books would be full of beautifully decorated pages that no one'd ever be able to look at, without breakage at least.

And she sat there and said, so my quandary is, Carol, do I even bother to fill these books with beautiful text and pictures or do I just rough up their edges so it looks like there's something in them, you know, wear them out and smudge them about a bit so it looks like they've been well worked, and deliver them to him and get paid and get away with doing much less work myself? Do I choose to be a charlatan or do I make quite a lot of work that the risk is no one will ever even see?

We went for lunch and we got quite drunk. She said, *this is exciting for me because I get to watch you eat*, and I said, what? really? something like that excites you?

But all the same. How flattering. Someone wanted to watch me eat.

Weird, George says.

Her mother smothers a laugh to herself.

I liked her more and more, she says. She was repressed and respectable and anarchic and rude and unexpected, she was trivial and wild both at once, like a bad girl from school. And she was lovely. She was attentive, sweet to me. And there was something, some glimmer of something. She'd look at me and I'd know there was something real in it, and I liked it, I liked how she paid attention to me, my life. Like she personally cared how I was feeling from day to day or what I was doing from one hour to the next. And she did kiss me, once. Properly, I mean against a wall, a real kiss –

Oh God, George says.

That's exactly what your father said, her mother says.

You told dad? George says.

Of course I did, her mother says. I tell your dad everything. Anyway sweet heart, after that I knew it was a game. You always know where you are after a kiss. It was a pretty good kiss, George, I liked it fine. But all the same –

(*I will never forgive her*, George is thinking)

– I knew after it something didn't quite ring true, her mother says. She was always so curious, about where I was, what I was doing, who I was doing it with, who else I was meeting up with or working with, especially that and what I was working on, what I was writing about, what I thought about this or that, it was constant, and I thought, well, *that's* a bit like love, that obsessiveness, when people are in love they need to know the strangest things, so maybe it *is* love, perhaps it just feels this odd to me because it's the kind of love that can't be expressed unless we both choose to really mess up our lives. Which I'd no intention of doing, George. I know how good my life is. And, I presumed, neither had she, any such intention, she has a life too, a husband, kids. At least I think she does. At least, I saw some photos once.

But then there was the day I went to see her in her workshop without telling her I was coming, and I knocked on the door and a woman came to the door, she was wearing overalls, and I asked for Lisa and she said who? And I said Lisa Goliard, this is her bookmaking workshop, and the woman said, no, that's not my name, I'm whatever, and this is *my* bookmaking workshop, can I help you? And I said, but you sometimes let your workshop to other printers or bookmakers, yes? and she looked at me as if I was crazy and said she was really busy and was there anything she could help me with, and it's as I was walking away that it came to me that the whole time I'd known Lisa, which was by then a couple of years, I'd never see her once make or do anything in that workshop. We'd just sat around in it, talking. I'd never seen her write anything, or bind anything, or print anything, or cut anything.

And then when I got home I looked her up online and there were the same couple of web pages that I'd looked at before, a page still saying Site Coming Soon and a link to a bookseller in Cumbria, but not much else. In fact nothing else. Not a trace.

She almost didn't exist, George says. She only just existed.

Not that an absence online means anything, her mother says. She definitely existed. Definitely exists.

If this was a film or a novel, she'd turn out to be a spy, George says.

I know, her mother says.

She says it quite happily in the dark next to George.

It's possible, she says. It's not at all impossible. Though it seems improbable. It wouldn't surprise me. I did meet her rather oddly, it did all happen very oddly. It's as if someone had looked at my life and calculated exactly how to attract me, then how to fool me once my attention was caught. Quite an art. And she's quite a nice spy. If she is one.

Is there such a thing as a nice spy? George says.

I wouldn't have said so before, her mother says.

We even had conversations about it, we had a running joke. I'd say, you're in intelligence, aren't you, and she'd say I'm afraid I can't possibly answer that question.

Did you tell her you'd rumbled her workshop? George says.

I did, her mother says. I told her I'd gone and it hadn't been her workshop the day I went. She laughed and said I'd met the other person who worked there occasionally, and how this person owned the building and was fearful that the authorities, the council, would know she was letting space to other people so always swore no one used it but her whenever she was asked. And when she told me that, I thought, well, that's perfectly feasible, that explains *that*, and at exactly the same time I could feel myself thinking, well, that explains that *away*. I think this double-think is the reason I started to see much less of her.

But George, what I'm about to say, I don't expect you to understand it till you're older –

Thanks, George says.

No, her mother says. I'm really not being patronizing. But understanding something like what I'm going to say takes having a bit of age. Some things really do take time. Because even though I suspected I'd been played, there was something. It was true, and it was passionate. It was unsaid. It was left to the understanding. To the imagination. That in itself was pretty exciting. What I'm saying is, I quite liked it. Even if I was being played. And most of all, my darling. The being seen. The being watched. It makes life very, well I don't know. Pert.

Pert? George says. What kind of a word is pert?

The being watched over, her mother says. It was really something.

But by a spy and a liar? George says.

Seeing and being seen, Georgie, is very rarely simple, her mother says.

Are, George says.

What? her mother says.

Are very rarely simple, George says. Did you tell dad she was a spy? What did he say?

He said (and here her mother puts on a voice that's supposed to be her father), Carol, nobody is monitoring you. It's a sub-repressed expression. You're attracted to her middle-classness. She's attracted to your working-class origins. It's a classic class-infatuation paranoia and you're both making up an adolescent drama to make your own lives more interesting.

Does dad not know about how there are no longer just three but a hundred and fifty different social classes to which it can be decided that we belong? George says.

Her mother laughs in the dark next to George.

Anyway, sweet heart. Games run their course. I

got a bit tired of it. I stopped being in touch with her back in the winter.

Yeah. I know, George says.

I was a bit down about it, her mother says. You know?

We all know, George says. You've been awful.

Have I? her mother says and laughs gently. Well, I missed her. I still miss her. It felt like I had a friend. She *was* my friend. And God, George, something about it made me feel permitted.

Permitted? George says. That's insane.

I know. Allowed, her mother says. Like I was *being allowed*. It made me laugh, when I realized it. Then it made me feel rather, well, special. Like a character in a film who suddenly develops an aura of light all round her. Can you imagine?

Frankly? No, George says.

Can we never get to go beyond ourselves? her mother says. Never get to be more than ourselves? Will I ever, as far as you're concerned, be allowed to be anything other than your mother?

No, George says.

And why is that? her mother says.

Because you're my mother, George says.

Ah, her mother says. I see. Anyway. I quite enjoyed it, while it lasted. Am I mad, George?

Frankly? Yes, George says.

And at least now I know why the texts asking

why I wasn't in touch stopped coming. Ha ha! her mother says.

Good, George says.

How funny, her mother says.

Your Lisa Goliard, or whoever she really is in the real world when she's not pretending to be someone else, can fuck off back to spy-land, George says.

There is a short disapproving silence in which George senses she's gone too far. Then her mother says

Please don't use language like that, George.

It's okay. He's asleep, George says.

He might be. But I'm not, her mother says.

Said.

That was then.

This is now.

It's February now.

But I'm not.

Her mother's now not anything.

George lies in bed with her hands behind her head and remembers the one time in her life she ever saw Lisa Goliard in the flesh.

They were all on their way on holiday to Greece, they were in the airport pretty early, half past six in the morning, they were getting breakfast in a Pret and she turned to ask her mother to get her a tomato and mozzarella hot thing. But her mother wasn't there. Her mother'd fallen back, was behind them talking to a woman with long white-looking hair though the woman was young, and beautiful, which George could tell even just from looking at her back; and something about her mother was most strange, she was sort of standing on tiptoes, was she? as if straining upwards, like trying to reach something just too high off a tall shelf, a very high apple off a tree. The person leaned forward and put her hand on George's mother's shoulder and kissed her on the cheek and as she turned to say a final goodbye George caught the moment of her face.

Who was that? George asked her mother.

Her mother went on and on. Coincidence, the friend who makes books, what are the chances of, well that was a surprise.

George watched her mother's colour rise and change.

It took a long time for her mother's colour to return to normal. It took half the plane journey – most of northern Europe – before her mother's colour had calmed down.

The minotaur is a bull-headed half-man who's been placed at the centre of a dastardly labyrinth. Every so often the king, whose wife gave birth to this monster, has to feed it live youths and maidens as a sacrifice. The monster is defeated by a hero with a sword and the labyrinth is defeated by a simple ball of string. Isn't that how it goes?

George gets up and goes over to the door and gets her phone out of the pocket of the jeans hanging on the back. It is 1.23 a.m. It is a bit late to text anyone.

She texts H.

– *There is something I need to know.*

There's no answer. George texts again.

– *Did you do that minotaur joke because you think that me thinking she was being monitored is a load of bull?*

Dark.

Nothing.

George hunkers down in the bed. She tries not to think about anything.

The next day at school, though, H won't really speak to George. Not in an unpleasant way but in a polite and nodding and turning-away way. It is possibly because she does think George is paranoid and mad. George speaks and it's not that H doesn't reply, but she doesn't really speak back and tends to end her sentences by looking away, which doesn't make for easy continuous conversation.

This gets particularly complicated because they have been paired up on the empathy / sympathy project in English and are meant to be discussing ideas, and it's got to be finished and the talks are to be given to the rest of the class on Friday. But H keeps getting up and going to another table where the printer is and printing things out, and it's on

313

the side of the classroom where there are three girls with whom H is friendly but George is less friendly. Then when she comes back she turns side-on and makes notes and only replies if George asks something direct. She does it nicely but quite definitely uninterestedly.

It is a Tuesday, so there's Mrs Rock.

I think I might not be a very passionate person, George says.

Mrs Rock, since Christmas, has stopped repeating back to George what George says. Her new tactic is to sit and listen without saying anything, then very near the end of the session to tell George a sort of story or improvise on a word that George has used or something that's struck her because of something George has said. This means that now the sessions are mostly George in monologue plus epilogue by Mrs Rock.

I asked my father this morning, George says, did he think I was a passionate person and he said I think you're definitely a very driven person George and there's definitely a lot of passion in your drive, but I know he was sort of fobbing me off. Not that my father would know whether I was or I wasn't passionate anyway. Anyway then my little brother started making kissing noises on the back of his hand and my father got embarrassed and changed the subject and then when we went out the front door to go to school my little brother was standing next to my dad's van in the drive and going on about how there was a lot of passion in this drive, how this drive was full of passion, and I felt stupid, like an idiot, for having said anything out loud at all to anyone.

Mrs Rock sits there silent as a statue.

That makes two people who won't really speak to George today.

Three, if you count her father.

George feels a stubbornness come over her sitting there in Mrs Rock's student easy chair. She seals her mouth. She folds her arms. She glances at the clock. It is only ten past. There are another sixty minutes of this session still to go (it is a double period). She will not say another word.

Tick tick tick.

Fifty nine.

Mrs Rock sits next to her table in front of George like a mainland off an island for which the last ferry boat of the day is already long gone.

Silence.

Five minutes pass in this silence.

Those five minutes alone pass like an hour.

George considers risking looking insolent and getting her earphones out of her bag and listening to music on her phone. But she can't, can she? Because this is her new phone and she hasn't downloaded any music on to this phone yet, though she's had it for nearly two months and there's nothing on it except that song H downloaded for her to which H wrote the words for the DNA revision yesterday.

I will always want you.

Want is quite a complicated word there, because there's volo, which means I want, but it's not usually used with people. Desidero? I feel the want of, I desire. Amabo? I will love.

But what if I will never love? What if I will never desire? What if I will never want?

Numquam amabo?

Mrs Rock, do you mind if I send a text? George says.

You want to send a text to me? Mrs Rock says.

No, George says. Not to you.

Then I do mind, Georgia, because this is a session in which we have decided to spend the duration talking to each other, Mrs Rock says.

Well, George says. It's not like we're doing any talking, we're just sitting here not saying anything.

That's your choice, Georgia, Mrs Rock says. You get to choose how to use this time with me.

You mean this time in which it was decided by whoever decided it in some school meeting, George says, that I should come and sit in your room so you can all minotaur me to see how I'm doing after my mother dying.

316

Minotaur you? Mrs Rock says.

I'm sorry? George says.

You said minotaur you, Mrs Rock says.

No I didn't, George says. I said monitor. You're monitoring me. You must have heard that other word inside your own head and decided I said it for some reason of your own.

Mrs Rock looks suitably discomfited. She writes something down. Then she looks back up at George with exactly the same blank openness as before the conversation.

And anyway, literally, if I get to choose how I use this time, then I can choose to send a text in it, George says.

Not unless it's to me, Mrs Rock says. And if you do, you'll be in trouble. Because, as you know, if you get your phone out of your bag and I see you using it on school property at a time that's not lunch hour, I'll have to confiscate it and you won't get it back till the end of the week.

Does that rule hold even in counselling? George says.

Mrs Rock stands up. It is quite shocking that she does. She takes her coat off the back of the door and opens the door.

Come with me, she says.

Where? George says.

Come on, she says.

Will I need my jacket? George says.

They walk down the corridor and past all the classrooms full of people doing lessons, out of the main school doors then along the front of the school to the school gate, which Mrs Rock walks through. George follows.

As soon as they're beyond the gate Mrs Rock stops.

You can now get your phone out, Georgia, without breaking any rules, she says.

George gets her phone out.

Mrs Rock turns her back.

You can send that message now, Mrs Rock says.

– *Semper is always*, George writes. *Or there is a good word, usquequaque. It means everywhere, or on all occasions. Perpetuus means continual or continuous and continenter means continuously. But I can't mean any of them because right now for me they are just words.* Then she presses send.

When they get back to Mrs Rock's room, there's ten minutes of the session left.

This is the point at which you sit forward and tell me the story or whatever you've decided to tell me about and with which you want to round off the session, George says.

Yes, but today, Georgia, I think you should round the session off, Mrs Rock says. I think the theme which arose for us today was talking and not talking, and the whens and the wheres and the hows of both of these. Which is why I think it was important that we detoured a little out of the school structure, so that you could make the connection you so clearly felt it was urgent to make.

Then Mrs Rock talks for a bit about what saying things out loud means.

It means a decision to try to articulate things. At the same time it means all the things that can't be said, even as you make the attempt to put some of them into words.

Mrs Rock means well. She is very nice really.

George explains that when she gets out of here and checks her phone she'll see that the message Mrs Rock just went so out of her way to let her send will have the little red exclamation mark and the sign next to it saying not delivered, because there is no way you can send a message to a phone number that no longer exists.

So you sent a message knowing that your message would never reach the person you sent it to? Mrs Rock says.

George nods.

Mrs Rock blinks. She glances at the clock.

We have two minutes left, Georgia, she says. Is there anything else you'd like to bring to the session today, or anything else you feel you need to say?

Nope, George says.

They sit in silence for one minute and thirty seconds. Then the bell goes.

319

Same time next Tuesday, Georgia, Mrs Rock says.
See you then.

When George gets home, H is waiting on the
front step.

This is the third time H has come to the house.

*I thought you weren't talking to me / what if I
will never love / never want / never desire / I think I
might not be a very /*

Hi, George says.

Hi, H says. I'm really. I'm.

It's okay, George says.

I was feeling really lousy today, H says. I wasn't
much up to it.

Then H tells her that she found out last night
when she got home that her family is moving to
Denmark.

Moving? George says. You?

H nods.

Away? George says.

H nods.

For good? George says.

H looks away, then looks back at George.

Can you just take a school student out of a
school year like that? George says.

H shrugs.

When? George says.

Beginning of March, H says. My father's work.

He's in Copenhagen now. He's found us a fantastic apartment.

She looks miserable.

George shrugs.

Empathy sympathy? she says.

H nods.

Brought my ideas, she says.

They sit down at the downstairs table. H switches on her iPad.

She has had an idea that they should do a presentation on the painter who did the painting which George's mother liked enough to go all the way to Italy to see. She has found some other pictures by him and a bit of biography.

Not that there's much, she says. The thing it always says about him, in the hardly-anything-there-is when you do look him up, is that very little is known about him. They don't know for sure when he was born and they only know he died because there's a letter that says he did, maybe in the plague, and he was 42 the letter says, which means they can work out a rough birthdate, but no one's sure exactly which years, it could be one or the other. And there's the letter he wrote himself, that your mother told you about, that he wrote to the Duke about wanting higher pay. There's one of his pictures in London in the National Gallery and there's a drawing at the British Museum. There are only fifteen or sixteen things by him in the whole world. At least I think so. A lot of what I was looking at came up in Italian. I google-translated it.

H reads something out.

Cossa was the victim of the plague that infierti in Bologna between 1477 and 1478 . . . the 78 would be the most likely date, jackets in this year's disease came of rawness.

Jackets what? George says.

Jackets in this year's disease came of rawness, H says again. I wrote it down exactly. That's what it said.

She reads another bit.

The few early works do not leave almost predict doing compositions so innovative imaginative –

then she says a word that sounds like annoy or paranoia.

She shows it to George on the page.

– so innovative imaginative Schifanoia.

That's it. That's the place we went to, George says when she sees the word.

(Her mother is saying it next to her in the car in Italy right now, months ago. It is the place to which they are on their way.

Skiff. A. Noy. A., she is saying. Translated, it means the palace of escaping from boredom.

I'll be the judge of that, George is saying back.

They pass a roadsign that makes George laugh

because it points the way to somewhere called
Lame.

They pass another. It says

> Scagli di vivere
> non berti la
> vita

Is that what it said? Something to live, not
something the life? It went past so fast.)

H has decided that they could do the empathy /
sympathy exercise about this painter precisely
because there's so little known about him. This
means they can make a great deal of it up and not
be marked wrong because nobody will know
either way.

Yeah, but will Maxwell expect us to do all that
dreary historical imagine you are a person from
another time stuff? George says. *Imagine you are a
medieval washerwoman or wizard who's been
parachuted into the 21st century.*

He'd speak like from another time, H says. He'd
say things like ho, or gadzooks, or egad.

I don't think they knew about the word ho, I
mean about what it means in rap songs, in Italy in
the whenever it was, George says.

I expect they had their own word for it, H says.

George goes upstairs. She goes into her mother's

study and gets the dictionary off the shelf. In it, it says ho was already a word in 1300 when it meant an exclamation of surprise and also the call of a boatman. Now, apart from a prostitute and a shout of laughter, it can stand as a police term for a Habitual Offender and as a government term for the Home Office.

Ho ho ho, H says. Lots of ho's in Shakespeare. Heigh-ho, green holly. Most friendship is feigning, most loving mere folly.

(H worked last year at the Shakespeare Festival in the summer as a ticket-seller and cleaner-upper for £10 a night.)

Wouldn't it be better if we just imagine him talking like *we* do? George says. More empathetic?

Yeah, but the language would definitely have been different, H says.

Yeah, it'd have been Italian, George says.

But Italian *then*, H says. The way they said things then. Which would be different from it now. Imagine. Him wandering in his whatever they wore up and down the stairs in, I don't know. The multi-storey. What would he make of cars?

Little prisons on wheels, George says.

Little confessionals on wheels. Everything for him would've been about God, H says.

That's good, George says. Write that down.

He'd be like an exchange student, not just from another country but from another time, H says.

He'd be all *alas I am being made up really badly by a sixteen-year-old girl who knows fuck all about art and nothing at all about me except that I did some paintings and seem to have died of the plague*, George says.

H laughs.

You can't just make stuff up about real people, George says.

We make stuff up about real people all the time, H says. Right now you're making stuff up about me. And I'm definitely making stuff up about you. You know I am.

George blushes, then is surprised to find she's blushing. She turns away. She thinks something else quick; she thinks how typical it'd be. You'd need your own dead person to come back from the dead. You'd be waiting and waiting for that person to come back. But instead of the person you needed you'd get some dead renaissance painter going on and on about himself and his work and it'd be someone you knew nothing about and that'd be meant to teach you empathy, would it?

It's exactly the kind of stunt her mother would pull.

There's an advert on TV right now for life assurance and someone's dressed up as a plague victim in that, because the advert wants to suggest that its life assurance company has been around for centuries and that nothing's not insurable.

But what would it have been like, she wonders, to die of plague? To be buried in a pit full of other people's bones, someone fearful of catching it shovelling you in before you're even cold, then shovelling all the other dead people on top of you? For a moment she thinks of bones under a cold floor, under flagstones in a church maybe, or under nondescript town buildings that people are living and working in right now with no idea that the bones are there below them. The bones agitate. They shift amongst themselves at her imagining them. They're the bones of the man who painted that truly shocked duck with the hunter's fist round its neck, painted the gentle eye of the horse, the woman who could float in the air above the back of the sheep or goat with its cheeky face, that strong dark man in the rags her mother found so astonishing and which H has brought up on to the screen right now.

It's kind of better in real life, George says.

It says online it's an allegory for laziness, H says. I suppose because his clothes are torn and he looks poor.

If my mother were still alive she'd make a Subvert out of them saying that, George says. She'd have a heart attack if she heard someone call that picture laziness.

The same place it says he's an allegory of

326

laziness, it also says this one's an allegory of activity, H says.

She brings up the picture of the rich youth with the arrow in one hand and the hoop in the other.

I mean if she weren't already, you know, dead, George says. I saw that one there too. Along from the ragged man. In the flesh.

H has also found three other pictures by this painter, which aren't in the Ferrara palace. There is one in which an angel is kneeling to tell a Virgin Mary she's going to give birth. Above them both, far away in the sky, there's a floating shape. It's God. He is shaped oddly, like a shoe, or a – what?

Then George notices a painted snail at the bottom of the picture, crossing it as if it's a real snail crossing a picture. The snail shape is nearly the same as the God shape.

Does that mean that God is like a snail? Or that a snail traversing a picture is like God?

It has a perfect spiral in the shell.

Another is a bright gold picture. It is of a woman holding a thin-stemmed flower. The flower has eyes instead of flowerheads.

Wild, H says.

The woman holding the flower-eyes is smiling very slightly, like a shy magician.

The last picture H has found is of a handsome man with brown eyes. He is holding a gold ring. He is holding it like his hand is coming right out of the picture over the edge of its frame and into the real world like he's literally saying, here, it's for you, do you want it?

He is wearing a black hat. Perhaps he is in mourning too.

Look at that, H says.

She points to the rock formations in the background, behind the man's head, where an outcrop of rock shaped a bit like a penis is pointing directly at a rocky bank opposite – across a small bay and on the other side of the handsome man's head – which has an open cave set back in it.

Both girls burst out laughing.

It is both blatant and invisible. It is subtle and at the same time the most unsubtle thing in the world, so unsubtle it's subtle. Once you've seen it, you can't not see it. It makes the handsome man's intention completely clear. But only if you notice. If you notice, it changes everything about the picture, like a witty remark someone has been brave enough to make out loud but which you only hear if your ears are open to more than one thing happening. It isn't lying about anything or feigning anything, and even if you weren't to notice, it's there clear as anything. It can just be rocks and landscape if that's what you want it to be – but there's always more to see, if you look.

They stop laughing. This is the point at which H

leans towards George as if to kiss her on the mouth, yes, that close, so close that George for a second or two is breathing H's breath.

But she doesn't kiss George.

I'll come back, she says.

George doesn't say anything.

H moves her head away again.

She nods at George.

George shrugs.

It's half an hour later. George and H are in George's room. They have decided that talking about a painter they don't know anything about will take too much explaining and be too much hard work, that they might too easily get caught out not knowing about things people knew about then, like how to grind the colours of paints out of beetles etc, or like about popes and saints and gods and goddesses and mythic and delphic whatever (delphic what? George says; delphic, I don't know, tripods, H says; what are delphic tripods? George says; see? we've no idea, H says).

Instead they will demonstrate the difference between empathy and sympathy with a simple mime.

For empathy, H will pretend to trip and fall over in the street and George, acting as a passer-by seeing her do this by chance, will trip over her own feet too simply because she's seen someone else do it. For sympathy, H will pretend to trip again but this time George will go over and ask her if she's all right and say things like, poor you etc. Then H will pretend she's really out of it on drugs and George, seeing this, will act like she's starting to feel dizzy and woozy and high too. Then they will take a poll of the class as to whether this last bit, the drugs bit, is a demonstration of empathy or sympathy.

They will call their presentation Empathy and Sympathy Take a Trip.

H is admiring the spread of the damp. George is now hiding it with pictures of the kinds of things her father would never suspect there'd be damp behind. There are some pictures of kittens and a couple of the bands people at school right now are listening to, about which George doesn't give a toss and which she doesn't mind being ruined by what's under them.

Who's she? H says looking across the room at the picture on the far wall.

An Italian film actress, George says. My mother bought it for me.

Is she good? H says.

I don't know, George says. I've never seen anything she's in.

H looks at the picture of the French girl singers and at the arrangement of photographs above the pillows on the bed of George's mother as a woman, a girl and a child and even a very small black and white baby. She sits on George's bed and looks at them.

Tell me about her, she says.

You tell me something first, George says. Then I will.

What? H says. What kind of thing?

Anything, George says. Just something you remember. Something that came into your head tonight at some point.

When? H says.

Whenever, George says. When we looked at the pictures. Whatever.

Oh, okay, H says. Well. That thing about jackets and rawness.

She tells George about the festival she was working at last summer, she was selling and tearing tickets for As You Like It at St John's. She was doing a double shift and for the evening showing the audience was unexpectedly huge, there were nearly three hundred people – about seventy was usually more like it.

So I was ripping tickets like mad, she says, and doing my eleven and fifteen times tables, fifteen was full price and eleven was concession and we started with almost no change, two five-pound notes, one single pound coin and a handful of pennies, which meant that for a bit I could only really sell tickets to people who had the right money. And it was a really cold evening so the people queuing were cold as well as furious, I know exactly how cold it was because I had no jacket.

Raw, George says.

Yeah, but wait, H says. After the tickets I had to serve two hundred and seventy five people polystyrene cups of mulled wine from the urn and they all wanted it because it was so cold, and there was only me, and the urn would only work if you tipped it, which was quite hard because it was heavy and really hard to hold a cup to without it just emptying out all over the cup and my hand. And I'd seen As You Like It one and a half times that day already, I'd seen the last half in the morning and the whole run-through in the afternoon and wanted to go home but I couldn't because my next job was to hold the torch after the second half to show people where to walk in the dark and how to get to the exit. So I spent a lot of the second half trying to keep warm next to the urn, actually with my arm round the urn a lot of it, and trying to read though it was nearly dark and I wasn't allowed to use the torch because it would distract from the performers.

The girl playing Rosalind had this habit of getting into her Ganymede character by walking about behind the audience pretending to be a girl then pretending to be a boy to get her stance right, and she was in a very bad mood that night not just because she was also having to slip off in the breaks and cover for someone ill by playing Ophelia at Trinity but because at her afternoon performance of the Hamlet someone had exploded a bottle of cherryade just as she started doing her rosemary for remembrance speech and she'd forgotten her lines. Anyway she was walking up and down and up and down in the half-dark pretending to be one and then the other and from where I was sitting I could sort of see her, I was half watching her and half trying to read, and then something else caught my eye, it was a small fast thing, at first I thought maybe she'd forgotten which play she was in, had dipped into being Ophelia and had got down on all fours, which I knew she actually did do in her mad scene, but the thing moving was too fast and too small for that and anyway I could hear her, she was out front, had been on for some time, was doing the line I really like about how you can't shut doors on wit, and whatever the four-legged thing was darted behind the audience then back again and I saw it was a fox, it had something in its mouth, it had lifted a coat or jacket from the back of the audience and run off with it. And five minutes later it did it again, darted in and this time it came away with what looked like a handbag. And then when the play was over I stood on the road and held up my torch to show people where to go

333

and the three or four people whose things'd been taken wandered about the gardens looking for them and then left the gardens not knowing. I knew. They didn't. But I didn't want to tell them. It'd be like betraying the fox. And then on my way home I realized I'd stopped thinking about the cold and that this had happened when I saw the thing happen with the fox.

Jackets in this year's disease came of rawness, George says. I suppose it means skin.

How? H says.

Where it says jackets, George says. It could be something about the raw way the disease that year made the skin go. And talking of coming and going. And rawness.

She asks H when her family plans to leave.

First week of March, H says.

New school, George says.

Fifth in four years, H says. You might say I'm used to change. It's why I'm so well balanced and socially adept. Your turn.

What? To be socially adept? George says.

To tell me something you remembered, H says. When we looked at the pictures.

It is last May. It is Italy. They are in the hire car on the way back to the airport.

Skiffa what was it? George says.

Noia, her mother says.

Henry starts singing in the back of the car. Skipannoy, Skipannoy. Ship ahoy, Ship ahoy.

Really annoying, Henry, George says.

Her mother starts singing the words of a Pet Shop Boys song.

They were never being boring, she sings. *They dressed up in thoughts, and thoughts make amends.*

It's not thoughts, George says. It's fought.

No it isn't, George's mother says.

It is, George says. The line goes: *we dressed up and fought, then thought, make amends.*

No, her mother says. Because they always write such intelligent words. Imagine. Dressing up in thoughts because thoughts make amends. *Thoughts make amends*. It ought to be a figure of speech. If I had a shield, that's what I'd want it to say in Latin on it, that'd be my motto. And I've always thought it a beautiful philosophical explanation and understanding of precisely *why* they were never being boring.

Your version doesn't make sense, George says. You can't dress up in thoughts. It's *fought*. It's obvious. You're mishearing it.

I'll prove it to you, her mother says. Next chance we get we'll play it and listen.

We could look up the lyrics online right now, George says.

Those online sites are full of mistakes, her

335

mother says. We'll use our human ears and listen together to the original when we get home.

I bet you fifty pounds I'm right, George says.

You're on, her mother says. Prepare yourself for a substantial loss.

Francesco de what? the woman behind the information desk had said.

Cossa, George said.

Cotta? the woman said.

Cossa, and it's del, George said. With an l.

Della Francesca, the other woman, coming over, said.

No, George said. Francesco. Then del. Then Cossa. Francesco del Cossa.

The second woman shook her head. The first one shook her head.

It's a picture of St Vincent. St Vincent of Ferrara, George said.

Actually, George had been wrong about that. It's not Ferrara. It's a painting of a saint called Ferrer and nothing to do with the place George has been to in Italy.

But even so, neither of the women at the information desk in the gallery back on that first day George went to see St Vincent Ferrer recognized the name of the painter or the picture. Probably no one ever asks about anything here except the really famous paintings, which makes it fair enough, not to know, because a person can't be expected to know about every single painting in a gallery of hundreds, no, thousands, even if he or she works on the information desk of what's just one wing of it.

And when George first looked at the painting herself she'd thought it wasn't anything much. You could easily walk past it and glance at it and think you'd seen all you wanted to. Most people, most days, as George has seen day after day, do. It is not what you'd call an immediately prepossessing picture. It had taken a bit of looking to get past her own surface reaction to it. It's not like those ones in the palace in Italy, or it doesn't seem to be, at first look.

If you wouldn't mind spelling it, thank you, one of the women said.

She typed what George said into a computer. She waited for a result. When it came, both women looked amazed, like they'd really pulled something off, and then delighted like George's asking and their being able to answer her had made their day better.

It's in Room 55! the first woman said.

She looked like she might even want to shake George's hand.

That was three weeks ago near the start of March. Since then, twice a week, George has been getting up, putting her clothes on, having breakfast, making sure Henry's ready for school, seeing him off on the bus, going into the front room and doing the dance thing in honour of her mother to whatever random French song comes up on the playlist, putting her jacket on, going to the old bureau and filching the Subverts bank card (her father has forgotten about this account) then leaving the house as if to go to school but doubling back round the other side of the house where her father can't see which direction she's taking and cycling to the station instead, where she hangs around in the ticket place or the waiting room for the hour it takes till the cheaper fares kick in. Then George, travelling below surveillance cameras like people in novels from the past used to pass below the leaves or bare branches of trees and the eyes and wings of birds, nods to the tower there on the city horizon like a mega insect antenna, where fifty years ago the singer threw the bread roll at the maître d', goes down into the Underground and comes up again in a different place not far from the wing of the gallery where the only painting in this country done by the painter her mother liked is.

Francesco del Cossa
   (about 1435/6–about 1477/8)
   Saint Vincent Ferrer   about 1473–5
   Saint Vincent Ferrer was a Spanish Dominican
preacher, active throughout Europe and ardent in
the conversion of heretics. Here he holds the gospels
and points upwards to a vision of Christ displaying
his wounds. Christ is flanked by angels holding
instruments of his Passion. This is the central part
of an altarpiece from a chapel dedicated to Saint
Vincent in San Petronio, Bologna.
   Egg on poplar   NG597   Bought 1858.

The gallery knows more about the man in the
picture than it does about the painter who painted it.
About. There is nothing here about the painter except
the fact that they don't know for definite the year he
painted this picture or the years he died and was born.
   The painting is in a room of other pictures by
painters from around the same time. At first all
these pictures by the other people look more
interesting than this one, which just looks like
another religious picture (first reason not to look)
of a rather severe-faced monk (second reason not
to look) who's ready and waiting with his finger up,
holding a book up and open in his other hand, with
which, both finger and book, it looks like he'll
probably admonish anyone who does stop and look
at him (third reason not to look).

But then you notice that he's not looking *at* you. He's looking past and above you, or into the far distance, like there's something happening beyond you and he can see what it is.

Then there's the stone road off to the side of him which seems to be changing from road into waterfall as you look, the paving stones literally morphing, stone to water.

That lets you start to see that the picture is full of things you'd not expect. There's a Jesus at the top in a sort of gold arch, he looks weirdly old, a bit rough and ready for a Jesus, a bit friendly, like a well-worn human being or a tramp who's been dressed up as Jesus. He's wearing salmon pink which somehow makes him (Him?) look like nothing else in the picture and he's surrounded by angels who are floating, but very unostentatiously, on clouds. Their wings are bright red or purple or silver. They could all be either male or female. They're holding torture implements like the people in an S&M session online but really unlike an S&M session in their calmness, or is it sweetness? The information placard says they're holding 'instruments', which is apt because it's quite like they're about to play music on them, like a small orchestra waiting to tune up.

Then you notice that the saint is standing on a little table. The table is like a tiny theatre stage. This makes the black cloak-like thing he's wearing start to look like theatre curtain too. You can see through the table legs to the base of the pillar behind him and it's like a behind-the-scenes revelation, like it's all theatre, but at the same time the wrinkles in the skin of the wrist that's holding the book up are real-looking. They act exactly like the skin of a hand that's holding something heavy up does.

Best of all, up at the level of his head, the pillar's had its top broken off and there's what looks like a miniature forest growing out of it.

There are very small people in the background behind the saint's legs. They're meant to be small because of perspective but at the same time it makes it look like this man is a giant and sure enough, when you look away from this painting at the others in the room it's like they've all been dwarfed. After this painting they look flat and old-fashioned, as if they're stale dramas and pretending to be real. This one at least admits the whole thing's a performance.

Or perhaps it is just that George has spent proper time looking at this one painting and that every single experience of looking at something would be this good if she devoted time to everything she looked at.

George has now been seven times. Each time she's visited, the monk has seemed less severe. He has started to look unruffled, like he's not bothered by anything – the other paintings in the room, the stuff happening in them, the people passing back and fore in front of him every day with all their different lives, the whole rest of the gallery, the square, the roads, the traffic, the city, the country, the sea, the countries radiating out beyond the gallery and away. Look at the wide-open arms of the God up there a bit like a baby in a womb in an old cross section of a pregnant woman's body, a very old wise baby. Look at the cloth of the cloak of the saint which opens wide too and changes from dark to silver right in the middle of the saint's body. His pointing finger has stopped being about being told off and started to be about looking up, and not really at the God, which is what the gallery placard says he's pointing at, but more at the way the blue in the sky gets darker and bluer as it rises, or at the way a forest will grow out of stone, or at how what's meant to be a torture instrument is really powerless, nothing but a museum piece, a stage prop for some old drama whose horror's all long gone.

George has become more and more interested in spite of herself and in spite of how little this picture – or any of the pictures in this room, all made more than five hundred years ago – seems on first glance to have to do with the real world. Now when she comes into Room 55, it's weird, but it's like she is meeting an old friend, albeit one who

343

won't look her in the eye because the saint is always looking off to the side. But that's good too. It's good, to be seen past, as if you're not the only one, as if everything isn't happening just to you. Because you're not. And it isn't.

A friendly work of art. That was when her mother said the thing about how the art they were looking at was *a bit like you.* Generous but also, what was it? Something else.

Sarcastic?

George can't remember.

At first, coming here, she knew consciously all the time that she was seeing a picture her mother never even knew existed or might well have walked past without seeing, like people do, on their way to see the more famous pictures.

Today what she sees is the way the rockscape on one side of the saint is broken, rubbly, as if not yet developed, and on the other side has transformed into buildings that are rather grand and fancy.

It is as if just passing from one side of the saint to the other will result if you go one way in wholeness and if you go the other in brokenness.

Both states are beautiful.

She looks across at the picture to the left of the saint, past the open door. It's of a woman sitting on a fancy throne holding a sprig of cherries, by a painter called Cosimo Tura, and it has those little glass or coral balls in it too, on a string above her head. So

344

does the one to George's left, which is a Virgin Mary and Baby and is by Cosimo Tura as well.

The coral and glass balls on the St Vincent picture are by far the brightest and most convincing.

Maybe there was a glass and coral ball school where the painters all went to learn to do these things.

Today is Wednesday. She is missing double maths, English, Latin, biology, history, double French. Today instead she is going to count the number of people who pass through Room 55 in a given half-hour (she will start at noon) and how many of those people stop to look at the Francesco del Cossa picture and for how long.

From this she will be able to form a statistical study of attention spans and art.

Then she will get herself some lunch, then off back to King's Cross and home in time to be there for Henry getting out of school.

Then she will slip the bank card back into its place as usual and go out into the garden, if it's not raining, and say the daily hello and how are you today that she's pledged to the girl in the yurt. She'll come in and make supper and hope her father comes home in not too bad a shape.

It is lovely, being intoxicated, her father said the other night. It is like wearing a whole fat woolly sheep between me and the world.

The smell of an old sheep in the house, George thought when he said it, its fleece all grassy, matted with excrement, would be hugely preferable to the smell of her father after he's been drinking.

It was the weekend. She was watching a film on TV. It was about four teenage girls, friends who'd been devastated to find that they were all going to have to spend their summer holidays in different parts of the world. So they made a pact that they'd share a pair of jeans, meaning they'd send the jeans by post from one to the next to the next and so on as a sign of their undying friendship. What happened next was that the pair of jeans acted as a magic catalyst to their lives and saw them through lots of learning curves and self-esteem-getting and being in love, parents' breaking up, someone dying etc.

When it got to the part where a child was dying of cancer and the jeans helped one of the girls to cope with this, George, sitting on the floor in the front room, howled out loud like a wolf at its crapness.

She decided she'd watch instead one of the DVDs H brought round before she left.

The league of mothers has got your back, H had said handing her a small pile of films all in different languages which her mother had sorted out, in the moving, *for your poor friend who likes the 1960s and who is mourning for real.*

346

Mourning for real, George liked the phrase. The top one on the pile next to the DVD player had the actress whose picture is on George's wall in it. It was about some people who go to a near-deserted island on a boat. Then one of them goes missing. She literally disappears. The people spend the rest of the film looking for her and falling in and out of love with each other, but they never find out where she's gone or what's happened to her. George watched it without moving from where she was sitting on the floor from beginning to end. Then she ejected it and took the next film off the top of the pile.

It was called, in French, A Film Like The Others. It had no subtitles and when it started it looked like a bootleg, fuzzy, as if copied from dodgy video.

Her father came into the room and sat in the chair behind her.

She could smell him.

What's the film, Georgie? he said.

George was about to tell him the title but then she realized that if she told him what it was called he'd think she was being cheeky. This made her laugh.

It's French, she said.

Nice to hear you laugh, he said behind her.

The film began with some footage of two young men making very small brick walls. They seemed to be learning how to bricklay, could that be it? Over the top of this a lot of people were speaking in a French which George couldn't really follow. It seemed to be about politics. Then it cut to some young people sitting talking in long grass. There was footage of what looked like strikes and protests, which made George think about the students here, how long they'd lasted in the university building and the stories that went round school about how rough the police and private security men had been to them, which her mother had made her tell her and some of the telling of which she'd sent out in phrases and paragraphs via Subvert.

Her father was maundering on now about the film and song which had made her mother decide to call George her name.

I said but what if you ended up looking like the girl in the film. She's a bit plain, a bit of a loser. But your mother was right. She liked the notion of an anti-hero. Anti-heroine. She was of the belief that people can be who they really are and still come up trumps against the odds. Including me, I hope. Eh? Eh, Georgie?

Yup, George said.

She sighed. She hated the song from which her name had supposedly come.

Her father started whistling it then singing the bit about how the world would see a new Georgie girl. The people in the film, whose faces you never got to see, just their arms and legs and torsos, sat round and talked about God knows what. The film showed them talking like all that mattered was that they *were* talking. While they talked they played with stems of the grass they were sitting in. They'd break little bits off it. They'd knot it. They'd split it as if to whistle through it. They'd hold up a stem and burn it with the end of a cigarette as they talked, holding the lit end to it till the bit of grass burnt through and fell off, then starting again further down the stem or with a new bit of grass. Then the film cut to a wall with words sprayed on it. PLUTÔT LA VIE.

You know, her father said behind her, you'll be leaving me soon, don't you?

George didn't turn round.

Purchased that ticket to the moon for me already, have you, then? she said.

Silence, except for the French people all talking years ago. She turned. Her father looked grave. He didn't look misted or sentimental. He didn't even look drunk, though the room round him smelt like he couldn't not be.

It's the nature of things, her father said. Your mother, in some ways, is lucky. She'll never have to lose you now. Or Henry.

Dad, George said. I'm not going anywhere. I'm sixteen.

Her father looked down. He looked like he might start to cry.

Perhaps the day will come, George thought, when I will listen to my father. For now though, how can I? He's my father.

As she thought it, she felt mean. So she gave in, fractionally.

Oh yeah, and dad, she said. My room's got a leak.

You what? her father said.

He sat up.

The roof's been leaking, she said. It's possible that it's been like that for some time. It was happening behind posters and stuff so I didn't notice. Not till earlier today.

Her father leapt up off the chair.

She heard him take the stairs two at a time.

George left the interesting / boring French film running and opened her laptop. She typed in Italian Film Directors. She clicked on Images.

Up came a photograph of a man in the dark whose face she couldn't see, wearing a lit-up picture on his chest. No, not a picture. Someone was literally projecting a film on to the man using him as a screen.

George clicked on the link. It was about a director who'd sat in an art gallery in Italy while an artist projected one of the director's own films from start to finish on to his chest.

It said that not long after this art act this man was found dead on a beach.

It said rent-boy, assignation, murder, conspiracy theory, Mafia, Vatican.

It had a photograph of people letting off fireworks where his body'd been found.

She heard her father thumping about upstairs. Imagine if someone projected films on to the side of your house. Would what those films were about affect your living space, she wondered, or your breathing, say, if they projected them on to your chest?

No, of course they wouldn't.

But imagine if you made something and then you always had to be seen through what you'd made, as if the thing you'd made became you.

George sits among the pictures from all the centuries ago and looks hard at a picture by the painter who disappeared then reappeared centuries later by the skin of his teeth. His teethskin. The painter who wanted more money because he was greedy. Or the painter who wanted more money because he knew his worth. The painter who thought he was better than everybody else. Or the painter who knew he deserved better.

Is worth the same as money? Are they the same thing? Is money who we are? Is it how much we make that makes us who we are? What does the word make mean? Are we what we make? *It is so*

*bloody lovely to forget myself for a bit. We saw the
pictures. What more do we need to know?* The
banking crisis. The food-banking crisis. The girl in
the yurt. (*She was probably very well paid for it.*)

Consider, for a moment, the moral conundrum.

She shakes her head, which is like it's full of rattling
hard grimy things like the way her room, in November
one afternoon when the wind had lifted the Velux up
and open on its own, had filled with grimy sycamore
seeds and shreds of wing and old leaf off the trees at
the backs of the houses, all over the desk, the bed, the
books, the floor, bits of city filthiness scattered all over
the last of her clean clothes.

Galleries are not much like life. They are such
clean places, generally. Something about this one
that they haven't thought to mention in any of the
brochures or online information, but that is
actually a selling point for George, is that it smells
nice, at least in this new wing it does, George
doesn't know about the old wing. It smells of wood
in here. It can shift from quiet to full quite
suddenly. You can be sitting here on the bench and
there can be no one in the room but you (and the
attendant) though you can always hear the footfall
in the other rooms because all the floors
throughout are creaky. Then from nowhere a huge
group of tourists from Japan or Germany,
wherever, will fill the place, sometimes kids,
sometimes adults, usually passing time till it's their

turn to see the Leonardo cartoon out in the hall for which there's usually more of a queue.

She gets her phone out and texts H.

– *Did you know Leonardo da Vinci was a cartoonist?*

Then she readies her notebook and pen for the statistical experiment.

H has texted straight back.

– *Yeah and he was so ahead of his time he invented Helix the Cat*

H has moved to a town in Denmark that sounds like someone Scottish saying the word whorehouse. The day she left she started sending texts. The texts seemed pretty random. They weren't about where H was or what it was like there or what H was feeling or doing; not once has H mentioned any of the stuff that people are usually meant to tell you. Instead they came, with no accompanying explanation, like information arrows aimed through space at their target, which was George.

The first one said,

– *His mother's name was Fiordelisia Mastria*

Then, much later,

– *His father built the belltower of the cathedral*

The next day,

– *He sent a letter on 25 March 1470 to a Duke called Borso d'Este to ask for more money for those pictures you went to see*

After that one, George (who wasn't replying to

any of these because every time she took her phone in her hand to try to, she'd type in half a word or a couple of words then she'd stop and delete it and in the end send nothing) knew they were about the something real between them.

Two hours after, another text,

— *The Duke wrote on the bottom of it in pencil in Latin, Let him be content with the amount already decided*

Late that night,

— *He left in a sulk and went to work elsewhere*

Then, next day, over the whole day,

— *The 25 March 1470 was a Friday*

and

— *They thought for years all his paintings were done by someone else*

Then H clearly ran out of information about the painter.

Instead, over the next few days, she fired mysterious little arrows at George in Latin:

— *Res vesana parvaque amor nomine*

— *Adiuvete!*

— *Puella fulvis oculis*

— *Quem volo es*

— *Quingenta milia passuum ambulem*

On the second day of the Latin texts, George worked out that I would walk five hundred miles was also the name of the Scottish song by the geeky eighties twins with the glasses.

354

She downloaded it and listened to it.

Then she'd downloaded the songs called Help!, Crazy Little Thing Called Love and Brown-Eyed Girl. She listened to them all. She made up a playlist – the first one she'd made on her new phone – and listed them by their Latin names. When she worked out that Quem volo es was maybe meant to be the song called You're The One That I Want, she laughed out loud.

They were pretty good. And H didn't do Latin so the fact that they were actually quite good Latin meant even more.

It also means that when she hears songs, just in passing, for instance when she's doing shopping and they're played like they always are over the loudspeakers at Asda, she doesn't mind any more. This is useful. Almost everywhere you go songs are invariably being played and just hearing songs in the air, in shops or cafés or on adverts on TV, has been one of the hardest things to deal with.

There is also the bonus that these songs H has made her listen to are the kind that play everywhere. But not just that. When you listen properly to them they are also pretty good songs. Even more strange and fine is the fact that someone has wanted her to hear them, and not just someone, but Helena Fisker.

It is like having a conversation without needing to say anything. It is also like H is trying to find a

355

language that will make personal sense to George's ears. No one has ever done this before for George. She has spent her whole life speaking other people's languages. It is new to her. The newness of it has a sort of power that can make the old things – as old as those old songs, even as ancient as Latin itself – a kind of new, but a kind that doesn't dismiss their, what would you call it?

George sits in the new wing of the National Gallery in front of an old painting and tries to think of the words for it.

Their classic status?

She nods. That's it. Whatever is happening makes them new and lets them still be old both at once.

After she'd downloaded the songs, she'd sent her first reply to H.

Let's helix again, like we did last summer.

She followed it immediately with a text saying

(*Helix : Greek for twist.*)

Back came a text that pierced whatever was between the outside world and George's chest. In other words, George literally felt something.

It's good to hear your voice

What is great about the voice of that singer called Sylvie Vartan (whom George, apparently, may even resemble a little) is that there's almost no way it can be made gentle, or made to lie. Also, although it was recorded decades ago, her voice is always, the moment you hear it, rough with its own aliveness. It is like being pleasurably sandpapered It lets you know you're alive. When George wants something fierce and sad in her ears she listens to the song where Sylvie Vartan howls like a wolf on the words *dreamed* and *read* in French. One day last week with this song on repeat in her ears she cycled out towards Addenbrooke's which is the place her mother died, then way past the hospital and out into the countryside because on her way to London, the morning before, she'd seen from the train a metal structure, a sculpture thing shaped very like a double helix.

It *was* a DNA structure after all, a sculpture of one, and it marked the start of a cycle trail you could follow for two miles along the little different-coloured rectangles painted on the tarmac, each standing for one of the 10,257 components there are in a single human gene.

She sat in a clump of grass at the side of the path in the early spring sun. The grass was wet. She didn't care. There were bees and flies out and about. A small bee-like creature landed on the cuff of her jacket and she flicked it away with a precise flick of her thumb and first finger.

But a fraction of a second after she did she realized the impact her finger must have had on something so small.

It must have felt like being hit by the rounded front of a giant treetrunk that's been swung through the air at you without you knowing it was coming.

It must have felt like being punched by a god.

That's when she sensed, like something blurred and moving glimpsed through a partition whose glass is clouded, both that love was coming for her and the nothing she could do about it.

The cloud of unknowing, her mother said in her ear.

Meets the cloud of knowing, George thought back.

So she cycled the length of the single gene holding her phone camera out and towards the ground. She took a photo of the other double helix sculpture that marked the end.

She looked at the picture on her phone then back up at the artwork itself.

It resembled a joyful bedspring or a bespoke ladder. It was like a kind of shout, if a shout to the sky could be said to look like something. It looked like the opposite of history, though they were always going on at school about how DNA history had been made here in this city.

What if history, instead, *was* that shout, that upward spring, that staircase-ladder thing, and everybody was just used to calling something quite different the word history? What if received notions of history were deceptive?

Deceived notions. Ha.

Maybe anything that forced or pushed such a
spring back down or blocked the upward shout of
it was opposed to the making of what history
really was.

When she got back to the house she downloaded
the film and the photos and she sent them.

When you come back we will cycle the length of
one thirty-thousandth of the human genome, she
wrote. *If we ever want to cycle the whole thing it*
will take us four years, that's if we do it without
stopping and unless we split the task and do half
each, which will mean it will take two years each
but be a lot less interesting. It will be like cycling
round the earth 15 times, or seven and a half if we
do half each.

Halfway through writing this email George
noticed that she'd used, in its first sentence, the
future tense, like there might be such a thing as a
future.

!

And did you know (you probably did) that
Rosalind Franklin nearly didn't get credited for the
double helix discovery? Though she took the
original X-ray that meant Crick and Watson could
make their discovery, and was clearly on the way to
the same discovery herself. And that when Watson
saw her giving a talk about her research he thought
she ought to have been warmer and more frivolous
in her lecture about diffraction (!) and that he might

359

have been more interested in what she was saying if she'd taken off her glasses and done something with her hair. So we need to add a whole new verse to that wrecking ball song. It is only sixty three years ago that this happened, and that's less than the age of your grandmother and only eleven years before my mother happened. It is the kind of historic fact that opposes the making of true history. Anyway in the film here the green bars are for adenine, the blue for cytosine, the green for guanine and the red for thymine.

Oh yeah and also, if you remember. You asked, and te semper volam.

Please remember, she thought as she sent it.

Sardonic! That was the other word, along with generous, that her mother'd said she was. Not sarcastic.

When I remember, it is like an earthquake, Henry said yesterday. Sometimes I don't remember, for almost all day. And then I do. Or I remember maybe a different thing that happened. Like when we went to that shop and bought the pipe that when you blew down it the very long bubbles came out of it.

Henry is doing a project on earthquakes and tsunamis at school. The schoolbook from which he is making his drawings and getting his facts has a picture on its cover of a motorway that looks like it's been lifted by a giant hand and put back down on its side instead and all the trucks and cars have slid off it and are on their roofs, wheels-upward, at the foot of it.

Strange, but the photo is beautiful. The photos all through this book are beautiful, of roads with crevasse cracks splitting through them, of a clock face at the top of a tower split in half so only the roman numerals for seven to eleven survive and the rest of the face is just sky. There is one picture of a small girl holding a teakettle and standing against a backdrop of aid tents. It's a natural disaster and it looks a bit like a fashion shoot. Well, almost all photos of roughed-up places, so long as there are no actual dead people in them, look like a fashion shoot.

Sooner or later, George's mother said in her head, *the ones with the dead people in them will look like a fashion shoot too.*

Fashion shot. Ha ha.

That would make a good Subvert.

George saw that her little brother, sitting at the breakfast bar over his earthquakes and tsunamis book, was hanging his head like a done flower.

She pulled up a chair beside him.

You're a rift, she said.

I'm a what? he said in a little voice.

You're a fault, she said.

I am not, he said.

You are, you're a San Andreas fault. You're a tectonic plate, she said.

361

You're a tectonic plate, he said.

Sticks and stones may break my bones, she said. But names will never harm me. You're a drifting continent.

You're a drifting continent, he said

You're a drifting incontinent, she said (though the subtlety of this pretty much went over Henry's head). You're a Richter scale. A scaly Richter. A nidiot.

Sticks and stones, Henry said.

He was singing now to himself with his face sad.

May break my bones. Sticks and stones.

George went out to the garden. She collected some pebbles and bits of hedge, a few twigs. She came back into the kitchen and she flung them at Henry. Little twigs and leaves stuck in his hair. Gravel went everywhere, into the sugar, the butter, the cutlery drawer.

Henry looked at the debris all round and all over him and then up at her in astonishment.

Did your bones break? she said. Well?

She tickled him a bit.

Is that one broken? she said. Is that one? That one?

It worked. He lightened, he gave in, he laughed and twisted in her arms.

Good.

She scooped the gravel out of the butter and sugar with a spoon. She wiped the twigs and leaves and grit into a J-cloth and cleaned the table. She made them eggs for supper. (Egg on poplar. Like something made in a chic restaurant. What would it taste like? Think of all the paintings made with all the eggs laid all the hundreds of years ago and the blips of life that were the lives of the warmblooded chickens who laid them.)

Henry was still finding the sticks and stones joke funny, and she was still finding the grit in his hair, when she bathed him and put him to bed.

The earth is made of rock. It is more than four and a half billion years old. Five hundred years is a nothing. It is about the length of an eyelash. Less.

At level four to five, things fall off walls and shelves.

At level six, walls themselves fall.

There are thousands of earthquakes all over the earth, every year, most so small no one notices them.

But these are the signs for which people have learned to watch. Dogs will bark. Frogs will leave the area. The sky will fill with strange lights.

Mrs Rock, George had said the last time she'd seen Mrs Rock, I am between you and a hard place.

Mrs Rock almost smiled.

So I have decided to veer towards you rather than towards the hard place, George said.

Mrs Rock looked slightly panicked.

Then George told Mrs Rock how she was sorry she'd lied.

363

That day when I said the word minotaur then pretended you'd misheard me, George said. You didn't mishear me. I did say it. Then I pretended I didn't. And I just wanted to say so, and to apologize. I was being difficult. And also, I know I must have seemed highly paranoid in some of the things I've said to you over the past weeks, particularly about my mother and so on. I've been making up narratives. I know that now.

Mrs Rock nodded.

Then she told George that the story of the minotaur was one about facing what mazes you. She made it very clear that she was using the word maze, not amaze. Then, when you'd faced it, she said, the thing to do to get out of the labyrinth was to go back the way you'd come, follow your own thread, the thread you'd left behind you, and that this had a lot to do with knowing where we come from and what our roots are –

I disagree with your interpretation, George said.

Mrs Rock stopped. She looked amazed (or perhaps mazed) that someone had interrupted her.

George shook her head.

It just needs the twist in the plot. It needs the outside help, George said. If a girl hadn't given Theseus the ball of string, chances are he'd never have got out of there. He'd probably still be in there today and that minotaur'd still be demanding and eating the required number of Athenian virgins.

Yes, of course, Mrs Rock said. But it's also possible, Georgia, that it means, metaphorically speaking –

Aw Mrs Rock, to tell you the truth, I'm so, so tired of what stories are meant to mean, George said. My mother, on the morning of the day she died, annoyed me. She was calling me her little prince, because of that new royal baby and me happening to have the same name, both my parents started doing that last summer. All of which meant that I shied away from her when she tried to kiss me on my way out the door to school. Then the next time she came home was two weeks after and it was in the form of bits of rubble in a cardboard box, which my father put in the passenger seat of his work van then drove round town stopping to leave handfuls of her in places she'd really liked. Only outdoor places, though, so as not to be too shocking or too illegal. Though he did put some of her in his pocket and take her to London, where he went looking specifically for cracks and crevices in the outsides *and* the insides of the buildings of her favourite art places and theatre places and work places. Into which he pressed, with his thumb, some of my mother. And there's still quite a lot of her left in the box so that this summer we can take her to Scotland and abroad, to some of the other places she liked. The thing being. What I mean is. It's not very metaphorical, if you'll forgive me, Mrs Rock.

Silence.

(What you might even call a stony silence.)

Had George really said all that out loud?

No.

Phew.

George had said only the first sentence out loud. She hadn't said anything past the words *what stories are meant to mean*.

But think of her mother. Think of her smiling, looking the minotaur in the eye and – winking.

Think of her father taking what was left of the shape her mother had when she was alive and driving round in the rain to find the places she'd want to be.

This thought of her father freed for George a moment of future-tense vision, by chance a summer vision, in which she will come home from school or London one day in a couple of months' time and find him standing on the front lawn with the hose in his hand and what turns out to be a Beethoven symphony playing into his ears through the precious Bose headphones nobody else is allowed to touch, while he conducts a spray of water con brio then andante over the green of the new grass he's had put in.

But back to now, or rather then, and Mrs Rock still a bit in shock at having been interrupted.

Mrs Rock brought her eyebrows down from the top of her head, where they'd gone. She placed a look on her face to show that she was waiting a moment to see if George was going to say anything else.

George placed a look in the same way on her own face to let Mrs Rock know she wasn't going to say anything.

Mrs Rock breathed out slowly. She leaned forward. She told George she was glad George had told her the truth about saying that word and pretending she hadn't. Then she settled back into her chair, because George had stayed silent so far at least, and started on about the Greek notion of the truth-teller.

This, Mrs Rock said, was a very important figure in Greek life and philosophy, usually someone with no power, no social status to speak of, who'd take it upon themselves to stand up to the highest authority when the authority was unjust or wrong, and would express out loud the most uncomfortable truths, even though by doing this they would probably even be risking their life.

Upon himself or herself, George said. He or she. His or her life. And, just to say, I find this second allusion, or example or illustration, much more effective than your minotaur one.

Mrs Rock put her pencil down on the desk with a click. She shook her head. She smiled.

Georgia, she said. As I'm sure you're aware. You can be a little draconian at times.

I'll take that as a compliment, Mrs Rock, George said.

Yes, Georgia, you may. Same time next Tuesday, Mrs Rock said. See you then.

George opens her notebook. It's nearly noon.

This is the point in this story at which, according to its structure so far, a friend enters or a door opens or some kind of plot surfaces (but which kind? the one that means the place where a dead person's buried? the one that means the place where a building's to be built? the one that means a secret stratagem?); this is the place in this book where a spirit of twist in the tale has tended, in the past, to provide a friendly nudge forward to whatever's coming next.

George is ready and waiting.

She plans to count the people and how long and how little time they spend looking or not looking at a random picture in a gallery.

What she doesn't know yet is that in roughly half an hour or so, while she's collating final figures (a hundred and fifty seven people will have passed through the room altogether and out of this number twenty five will have looked or glanced for no longer than a second; one woman will have stopped to look at the carving of the frame but not looked at the picture for longer than three seconds; two girls and a boy in their late teens will have stopped and made amused comments about St Vincent's knot of monk hair, the growth like a third eye at the front of his forehead, and stood there looking at him for thirteen full seconds), this will happen :

[Enter Lisa Goliard]

George will recognize her immediately even from having seen her only once in an airport.

She will walk into this room in this gallery, glance round for a moment, see George, not know George from Adam, then come and stand in front of George between her and the painting of St Vincent Ferrer.

She'll stand right in front of it for several minutes, far longer than anyone except George herself.

Then she'll shoulder her designer bag and she'll leave the room.

George will follow.

Standing close to the woman's back, so long as there are enough people to camouflage her (and there will be), she will say the name like a question (Lisa?) on the stairs, just to make sure it's her. She will see if the woman turns when she hears the name (she will), and will pretend when she does by looking away and making herself as much like an ordinary disaffected teenage girl as possible that it wasn't her who said it.

George will surprise a talent in herself for being surreptitious.

She will track the woman, staying behind her and aping the ordinary disaffected teenage girl all the way across London including down into the Underground and back up into the open air, till that woman gets to a house and goes in and shuts its door.

Then George will stand across the road outside the house for a bit.

She will have no idea what to do next or even where she is in London any more.

She will see a low wall opposite the house. She will go and sit on it.

Okay.

1. Unless the woman is some kind of early renaissance specialist or St Vincent Ferrer expert (unlikely, but possible) there is no way she'd ever know about or think to make the journey specially to see this painting out of all the paintings in the whole of London. This will suggest that for her to have known anything about it, including the basic fact of its existence, she must still have been tailing, one way or another, George's mother – unless she's tracking George right now – at the time they went to Ferrara.

2. George's mother is dead. There was a funeral. Her mother is rubble. So why is this woman still on the trail? Is she tracking George? (Unlikely. Anyway, now George is tracking her.)

3. (and George will feel her own eyes open wider at this one) Perhaps somewhere in all of this if you look there's a proof of love.

This thought will make George furious.

At the same time it will fill her with pride at her mother, right all along. Most of all she will wonder at her mother's sheer talent.

The maze of the minotaur is one thing. The ability to maze the minotaur back is another thing altogether.

Touché.

High five.

Both.

Consider for a moment this moral conundrum. Imagine it. You're an artist.

Sitting on the wall opposite, George will get her phone out. She will take a picture.

Then she will take another picture.

After that she will sit there and keep her eye on that house for a bit.

The next time she comes here she will do the same. In honour of her mother's eyes she will use her own. She will let whoever's watching know she's watching.

But none of the above has happened.

371

Not yet, anyway.

For now, in the present tense, George sits in the gallery and looks at one of the old paintings on the wall.

It's definitely something to do. For the foreseeable.